THE BEST FROM *UNIVERSE*

THE BEST FROM
UNIVERSE

EDITED BY TERRY CARR

DOUBLEDAY & COMPANY, INC.

GARDEN CITY, NEW YORK

1984

Acknowledgments

"Good News from the Vatican" by Robert Silverberg appeared originally in *Universe 1*. Copyright © 1971 by Terry Carr. Reprinted by permission of the author.

"Nor Limestone Islands" by R. A. Lafferty appeared originally in *Universe 1*. Copyright © 1971 by Terry Carr. Reprinted by permission of the author and the author's agent, Virginia Kidd.

"On the Downhill Side" by Harlan Ellison appeared originally in *Universe 2;* subsequently published in the author's collection *Deathbird Stories.* Copyright © 1972 by Harlan Ellison. Reprinted with permission of, and by arrangement with, the author and the author's agent, Richard Curtis.

"Schrödinger's Cat" by Ursula K. Le Guin appeared originally in *Universe 5*. Copyright © 1974 by Ursula K. Le Guin. Reprinted by permission of the author and the author's agent, Virginia Kidd.

"The Death of Doctor Island" by Gene Wolfe appeared originally in *Universe 3*. Copyright © 1973, 1980 by Gene Wolfe. Reprinted by permission of the author and the author's agent, Virginia Kidd.

"The Night Wind" by Edgar Pangborn appeared originally in *Universe 5*. Copyright © 1975 by Terry Carr. Reprinted by permission of Mary C. Pangborn.

"A Rite of Spring" by Fritz Leiber appeared originally in *Universe 7*. Copyright © 1977 by Terry Carr. Reprinted by permission of the author.

"Options" by John Varley appeared originally in *Universe 9*. Copyright © 1979 by Terry Carr. Reprinted by permission of the author and the author's agent, Kirby McCauley.

"The Ugly Chickens" by Howard Waldrop appeared originally in *Universe 10*. Copyright © 1980 by Terry Carr. Reprinted by permission of the author.

Library of Congress Cataloging in Publication Data

Main entry under title:The Best from Universe.

Includes index.
Contents: Good news from the Vatican / Robert Silverberg—Nor Limestone Islands / R. A. Lafferty—On the downhill side / Harlan Ellison—[etc.]
1. Science fiction, American. I. Carr, Terry. PS648.S3B49 1984   813'.0876'08

ISBN 0-385-17512-4
Library of Congress Catalog Card Number 82–45318
Copyright © 1984 by Terry Carr
All Rights Reserved
Printed in the United States of America
First Edition

CONTENTS

INTRODUCTION

The first volume of *Universe* was published early in 1971, about a year after I proposed the series to the management of Ace Books. At that time I was working as a regular editor for the company, producing the Ace Science Fiction Specials series of novels as well as various other sf novels, some nonfiction books, TV and movie tie-ins, and several nongenre or "mainstream" novels. In collaboration with Donald A. Wollheim, Ace's senior editor and vice-president, I was editing the original *World's Best Science Fiction* series, which reprinted the best short fiction of each year; those books sold very well.

A phenomenon of the time was the original-stories anthology series, which had been gathering momentum ever since Damon Knight had produced *Orbit 1* in 1966. (*Orbit* wasn't the first such series, however: Frederik Pohl had edited seven volumes of *Star Science Fiction Stories* in the fifties.) Following Knight's success, a number of other editors had recently launched their own such series: Robert Hoskins edited *Infinity,* Robert Silverberg had *New Dimensions,* Harry Harrison offered *Nova,* and Samuel R. Delany and Marilyn Hacker were producing *Quark/.*

On May 25, 1970, I sent a proposal for *Universe* to Ace's managers, offering to do each book for the very low advance of $2,500—a figure that limited my word rates to authors to a top of three cents a word, not a commanding rate but one that I felt would be reasonably competitive in the sf market then. My proposal was immediately accepted and I was given contracts for the first two books in the series.

(A minor footnote: I had actually proposed such a series to Ace two years before, but at that time—when *Orbit* was the only such series appearing—Ace hadn't considered it a good idea. The original proposal, coincidentally, had gone under the title *Nova.)*

The sales success of the original-stories anthology series was due mostly to the fact that science fiction magazines were rapidly fading from view in the late sixties. Distribution, as ever, was a great problem, especially when paperback publishing was becoming dominant. Regular readers of sf short stories and novelettes found themselves with fewer and fewer magazines to read, so they were joining the already established market for paperbacks, especially those that published new stories.

This movement was increased by the fact that Knight was doing an excellent job in acquiring for *Orbit* many of the best sf stories available; he had a substantial budget with which to attract top writers, and he offered them more freedom in style and content than the magazines did. Silverberg and Delany/Hacker did the same when they started their series, and Harlan Ellison had produced in 1967 a landmark book of original science fiction, *Dangerous Visions*. The original-stories anthologies became known for offering most of the best science fiction; readers bought them quickly and writers tended to send their best stories to these books.

When I got the contracts for *Universe 1* and *2,* I sent out announcements to professional sf writers and their agents, inviting submissions; I also buttonholed people at parties and conventions to ask for stories. They began coming in quickly, and within a few months I'd bought all the contents of the first book, plus several stories to be published in the second.

By the time *Universe 1* was published, I had left my job at Ace Books. While finishing up *Universe 2* from my apartment in Brooklyn, I sold the next three volumes in the series to Random House; then my wife and I moved to California. I was now a free-lance editor and writer, and the sales success of books such as *Universe* became important to whether or not there would be meat on the table. Random House treated me very well, but they weren't able to establish a profitable science fiction program, so I took the series to Doubleday starting with #6. *Universe* has appeared under the Doubleday imprint ever since.

The word rates are a bit higher now, still by no means the highest in the field but enough to attract a good number of established writers and talented newer writers, as you'll see from the index in the back of this book. The quality of the stories has remained gratifyingly high, too: *Universe* has established itself as a series in which science fiction's best writers want their work to appear. In the decade 1971–80 which the present book covers, no other such series has published more Hugo and Nebula awards nominees or winners.

Three of those awards winners are presented here, along with half a dozen others, most of them awards nominees, that I think will stand tall in their company. Originality of imagination, in stories told with craft and humanity, has been my criterion in choosing manuscripts for publication. In this compilation of the very best of all of them from the seventies, I've been given the opportunity to present a book full of wonders.

—Terry Carr

THE BEST FROM *UNIVERSE*

Once when I gave a talk on science fiction to a university audience, someone in the auditorium asked me who I thought was the best writer in science fiction. I knew I couldn't answer that, because there are at least half a dozen candidates for the position (Gene Wolfe, Ursula Le Guin, Gregory Benford, etc.). Instead, I answered, "To my mind, the most *consistently good* writer in science fiction is Robert Silverberg. He almost never writes a bad story, and the vast majority of his stories are very good indeed."

I'd had a number of occasions to find this out myself, and the writing of "Good News from the Vatican" was certainly one of them. At a party at Bob's house New Year's Eve 1970, I told him that I was starting an original-stories anthology series and would like to have a story from him. He nodded and said he thought he could fit one into his writing schedule around the end of January; and sure enough, on February 1, 1971, this story appeared in my mailbox.

I bought it and published it in *Universe 1*. It promptly won the Nebula Award as the best short story of the year. Would that it were always that easy to acquire top stories.

Good News from the Vatican

Robert Silverberg

This is the morning everyone has waited for, when at last the robot cardinal is to be elected Pope. There can no longer be any doubt of the outcome. The conclave has been deadlocked for many days between the obstinate advocates of Cardinal Asciuga of Milan and Cardinal Carciofo of Genoa, and word has gone out that a compromise is in the making. All factions now are agreed on the selection of the robot. This morning I read in *Osservatore Romano* that the Vatican computer itself has taken a hand in the deliberations. The computer has been strongly urging the candidacy of the robot. I suppose we should not be surprised by this loyalty among machines. Nor should we let it distress us. We *absolutely must not* let it distress us.

"Every era gets the Pope it deserves," Bishop FitzPatrick observed somewhat gloomily today at breakfast. "The proper Pope for our times is a robot, certainly. At some future date it may be desirable for the Pope to be a whale, an automobile, a cat, a mountain." Bishop FitzPatrick stands well over two meters in height and his normal facial expression is a morbid, mournful one. Thus it is impossible for us to determine whether any particular pronouncement of his reflects existential despair or placid acceptance. Many years ago he was a star player for the Holy Cross championship basketball team. He has come to Rome to do research for a biography of St. Marcellus the Righteous.

We have been watching the unfolding drama of the papal election from an outdoor cafe several blocks from the Square of St. Peter's. For all of us, this has been an unexpected dividend of our holiday in Rome; the previous Pope was reputed to be in good health and there was no reason to suspect that a successor would have to be chosen for him this summer.

Each morning we drive across by taxi from our hotel near the Via Veneto and take up our regular positions around "our" table. From where we sit, we all have a clear view of the Vatican chimney through which the smoke of the burning ballots rises: black smoke if no Pope has been elected, white if the conclave has been successful. Luigi, the owner and head waiter, automatically brings us our preferred beverages: fernet branca for Bishop FitzPatrick, campari and soda for Rabbi Mueller, Turkish coffee for Miss Harshaw, lemon squash for Kenneth and Beverly, and pernod on the rocks for me. We take turns paying the check, although Kenneth has not paid it even once since our vigil began. Yesterday, when Miss Harshaw paid, she emptied her purse and found herself 350 lire short; she had nothing else except hundred-dollar travelers' checks. The rest of us looked pointedly at Kenneth but he went on calmly sipping his lemon squash. After a brief period of tension Rabbi Mueller produced a 500-lire coin and rather irascibly slapped the heavy silver piece against the table. The rabbi is known for his short temper and vehement style. He is 28 years old, customarily dresses in a fashionable plaid cassock and silvered sunglasses, and frequently boasts that he has never performed a bar mitzvah ceremony for his congregation, which is in Wicomico County, Maryland. He believes that the rite is vulgar and obsolete, and invariably farms out all his bar mitzvahs to a franchised organization of itinerant clergymen who handle such affairs on a commission basis. Rabbi Mueller is an authority on angels.

Our group is divided over the merits of electing a robot as the new Pope. Bishop FitzPatrick, Rabbi Mueller and I are in favor of the idea. Miss Harshaw, Kenneth and Beverly are opposed. It is interesting to note that both of our gentlemen of the cloth, one quite elderly and one fairly young, support this remarkable departure from tradition. Yet the three "swingers" among us do not.

I am not sure why I align myself with the progressives. I am a man of mature years and fairly sedate ways. Nor have I ever concerned myself with the doings of the Church of Rome. I am unfamiliar with Catholic dogma and unaware of recent currents of thought within the Church. Still, I have been hoping for the election of the robot since the start of the conclave.

Why, I wonder? Is it because the image of a metal creature upon the Throne of St. Peter's stimulates my imagination and tickles my sense of the incongruous? That is, is my support of the robot purely an esthetic matter? Or is it, rather, a function of my moral cowardice? Do I secretly think that this gesture will buy the robots off? Am I privately saying, Give them the papacy and maybe they won't want other things for a while? No. I can't believe anything so unworthy of myself. Possibly I am for the robot because I am a person of unusual sensitivity to the needs of others.

"If he's elected," says Rabbi Mueller, "he plans an immediate time-sharing agreement with the Dalai Lama and a reciprocal plug-in with the head programmer of the Greek Orthodox Church, just for starters. I'm told he'll make ecumenical overtures to the Rabbinate as well, which is certainly something for all of us to look forward to."

"I don't doubt that there'll be many corrections in the customs and practices of the hierarchy," Bishop FitzPatrick declares. "For example we can look forward to superior information-gathering techniques as the Vatican computer is given a greater role in the operations of the Curia. Let me illustrate by—"

"What an utterly ghastly notion," Kenneth says. He is a gaudy young man with white hair and pink eyes. Beverly is either his wife or his sister. She rarely speaks. Kenneth makes the sign of the Cross with offensive brusqueness and murmurs, "In the name of the Father, the

Son, and the Holy Automaton." Miss Harshaw giggles but chokes the giggle off when she sees my disapproving face.

Dejectedly, but not responding at all to the interruption, Bishop Fitz-Patrick continues, "Let me illustrate by giving you some figures I obtained yesterday afternoon. I read in the newspaper *Oggi* that during the last five years, according to a spokesman for the *Missiones Catholicae,* the Church has increased its membership in Yugoslavia from 19,381,403 to 23,501,062. But the government census taken last year gives the total population of Yugoslavia at 23,575,194. That leaves only 74,132 for the other religious and irreligious bodies. Aware of the large Moslem population of Yugoslavia, I suspected an inaccuracy in the published statistics and consulted the computer in St. Peter's, which informed me"—the bishop, pausing, produces a lengthy print-out and unfolds it across much of the table—"that the last count of the Faithful in Yugoslavia, made a year and a half ago, places our numbers at 14,206,198. Therefore an overstatement of 9,294,864 has been made. Which is absurd. And perpetuated. Which is damnable."

"What does he look like?" Miss Harshaw asks. "Does anyone have any idea?"

"He's like all the rest," says Kenneth. "A shiny metal box with wheels below and eyes on top."

"You haven't seen him," Bishop FitzPatrick interjects. "I don't think it's proper for you to assume that—"

"They're all alike," Kenneth says. "Once you've seen one, you've seen all of them. Shiny boxes. Wheels. Eyes. And voices coming out of their bellies like mechanized belches. Inside, they're all cogs and gears." Kenneth shudders delicately. "It's too much for me to accept. Let's have another round of drinks, shall we?"

Rabbi Mueller says, "It so happens that I've seen him with my own eyes."

"You *have?*" Beverly exclaims.

Kenneth scowls at her. Luigi, approaching, brings a tray of new drinks for everyone. I hand him a 5000-lire note. Rabbi Mueller removes his sunglasses and breathes on their brilliantly reflective surfaces. He has small, watery gray eyes and a bad squint. He says, "The cardinal was the keynote speaker at the Congress of World Jewry that was held last fall in Beirut. His theme was 'Cybernetic Ecumenicism for Contemporary Man.' I was there. I can tell you that His Eminency is tall and distinguished, with a fine voice and a gentle smile. There's something inherently melancholy about his manner that reminds me greatly of our friend the bishop, here. His movements are graceful and his wit is keen."

"But he's mounted on wheels, isn't he?" Kenneth persists.

"On treads," replies the rabbi, giving Kenneth a fiery, devastating look and resuming his sunglasses. "Treads, like a tractor has. But I don't think that treads are spiritually inferior to feet, or, for that matter, to wheels. If I were a Catholic I'd be proud to have a man like that as my Pope."

"Not a man," Miss Harshaw puts in. A giddy edge enters her voice whenever she addresses Rabbi Mueller. "A robot," she says. "He's not a man, remember?"

"A *robot* like that as my Pope, then," Rabbi Mueller says, shrugging at the correction. He raises his glass. "To the new Pope!"

"To the new Pope!" cries Bishop FitzPatrick.

Luigi comes rushing from his cafe. Kenneth waves him away. "Wait a second," Kenneth says. "The election isn't over yet. How can you be so sure?"

"The *Osservatore Romano*," I say, "indicates in this morning's edition that everything will be decided today. Cardinal Carciofo has agreed to withdraw in his favor, in return for a larger real-time allotment when the new computer hours are decreed at next year's consistory."

"In other words, the fix is in," Kenneth says.

Bishop FitzPatrick sadly shakes his head. "You state things much too harshly, my son. For three weeks now we have been without a Holy Father. It is God's Will that we shall have a Pope; the conclave, unable to choose between the candidacies of Cardinal Carciofo and Cardinal Asciuga, thwarts that Will; if necessary, therefore, we must make certain accommodations with the realities of the times so that His Will shall not be further frustrated. Prolonged politicking within the conclave now becomes sinful. Cardinal Carciofo's sacrifice of his personal ambitions is not as self-seeking an act as you would claim."

Kenneth continues to attack poor Carciofo's motives for withdrawing. Beverly occasionally applauds his cruel sallies. Miss Harshaw several times declares her unwillingness to remain a communicant of a Church whose leader is a machine. I find this dispute distasteful and swing my chair away from the table to have a better view of the Vatican. At this moment the cardinals are meeting in the Sistine Chapel. How I wish I were there! What splendid mysteries are being enacted in that gloomy, magnificent room! Each prince of the Church now sits on a small throne surmounted by a violet-hued canopy. Fat wax tapers glimmer on the desk before each throne. Masters-of-ceremonies move solemnly through the vast chamber, carrying the silver basins in which the blank ballots repose. These basins are placed on the table before the altar. One by one the cardinals advance to the table, take ballots, return to their desks. Now, lifting their quill pens, they begin to write. "I, Cardinal ———, elect to the Supreme Pontificate the Most Reverend Lord my Lord Cardinal ———." What name do they fill in? Is it Carciofo? Is it Asciuga? Is it the name of some obscure and shriveled prelate from Madrid or Heidelberg, some last-minute choice of the anti-robot faction in its desperation? Or are they writing *his* name? The sound of scratching pens is loud in the chapel. The cardinals are completing their ballots, sealing them at the ends, folding them, folding them again and again, carrying them to the altar, dropping them into the great gold chalice. So have they done every morning and every afternoon for days, as the deadlock has prevailed.

"I read in the *Herald Tribune* a couple of days ago," says Miss Harshaw, "that a delegation of 250 young Catholic robots from Iowa is waiting at the Des Moines airport for news of the election. If their man gets in, they've got a chartered flight ready to leave, and they intend to request that they be granted the Holy Father's first public audience."

"There can be no doubt," Bishop FitzPatrick agrees, "that his election will bring a great many people of synthetic origin into the fold of the Church."

"While driving out plenty of flesh-and-blood people!" Miss Harshaw says shrilly.

"I doubt that," says the bishop. "Certainly there will be some feelings of shock, of dismay, of injury, of loss, for some of us at first. But these will pass. The inherent goodness of the new Pope, to which Rabbi Mueller alluded, will prevail. Also I believe that technologically-minded young folk everywhere will be encouraged to join the Church. Irresistible religious impulses will be awakened throughout the world."

"Can you imagine 250 robots clanking into St. Peter's?" Miss Harshaw demands.

I contemplate the distant Vatican. The morning sunlight is brilliant and dazzling, but the assembled cardinals, walled away from the world, cannot enjoy its gay sparkle. They all have voted, now. The three cardinals who were chosen by lot as this morning's scrutators of the vote have risen. One of them lifts the chalice and shakes it, mixing the ballots. Then he places it on the table before the altar; a second scrutator removes the ballots and counts them. He ascertains that the number of ballots is identical to the number of cardinals present. The ballots now have been transferred to a ciborium, which is a goblet ordinarily used to hold the consecrated bread of the Mass. The first scrutator withdraws a ballot, unfolds it, reads its inscription; passes it to the second scrutator, who reads it also; then it is given to the third scrutator, who reads the name aloud. Asciuga? Carciofo? Some other? *His?*

Rabbi Mueller is discussing angels. "Then we have the Angels of the Throne, known in Hebrew as *arelim* or *ophanim.* There are 70 of them, noted primarily for their steadfastness. Among them are the angels Orifiel, Ophaniel, Zabkiel, Jophiel, Ambriel, Tychagar, Barael, Quelamia, Paschar, Boel, and Raum. Some of these are no longer found in Heaven and are numbered among the fallen angels in Hell."

"So much for their steadfastness," says Kenneth.

"Then, too," the rabbi goes on, "there are the Angels of the Presence, who apparently were circumcised at the moment of their creation. These are Michael, Metatron, Suriel, Sandalphon, Uriel, Saraqael, Astanphaeus, Phanuel, Jehoel, Zagzagael, Yefefiah, and Akatriel. But I think my favorite of the whole group is the Angel of Lust, who is mentioned in Talmud *Bereshith Rabba* 85 as follows, that when Judah was about to pass by—"

They have finished counting the votes by this time, surely. An immense throng has assembled in the Square of St. Peter's. The sunlight gleams off hundreds if not thousands of steel-jacketed crania. This must be a wonderful day for the robot population of Rome. But most of those in the piazza are creatures of flesh and blood: old women in black, gaunt young pickpockets, boys with puppies, plump vendors of sausages, and an assortment of poets, philosophers, generals, legislators, tourists and fishermen. How has the tally gone? We will have our answer shortly. If no candidate has had a majority, they will mix the ballots with wet straws before casting them into the chapel stove, and black smoke will billow from the chimney. But if a Pope has been elected, the straw will be dry, the smoke will be white.

The system has agreeable resonances. I like it. It gives me the satisfaction one normally derives from a flawless work of art: the *Tristan* chord, let us say, or the teeth of the frog in Bosch's *Temptation of St. Anthony.* I await the outcome with fierce concentration. I am certain of the result; I can already feel the irresistible religious impulses awakening in me. Although I feel, also, an odd nostalgia for the days of flesh-and-blood popes. Tomorrow's newspapers will have no interviews with the Holy Father's aged mother in Sicily, nor with his proud younger brother in San Francisco. And will this grand ceremony of election ever be held again? Will we need another Pope, when this one whom we will soon have can be repaired so easily?

Ah. The white smoke! The moment of revelation comes!

A figure emerges on the central balcony of the facade of St. Peter's, spreads a web of cloth-of-gold, and disappears. The blaze of light against that fabric stuns the eye. It reminds me perhaps of moonlight coldly kissing the sea at Castellamare, or, perhaps even more, of the noonday glare rebounding from the breast of the Caribbean off the coast of St. John. A second figure, clad in ermine and vermilion, has appeared on the balcony. "The cardinal-archdeacon," Bishop FitzPatrick whispers. People have started to faint. Luigi stands beside me, listening to the proceedings on a tiny radio. Kenneth says, "It's all been fixed." Rabbi Mueller hisses at him to be still. Miss Harshaw begins to sob. Beverly softly recites the Pledge of Allegiance, crossing herself throughout. This is a wonderful moment for me. I think it is the most truly contemporary moment I have ever experienced.

The amplified voice of the cardinal-archdeacon cries, "I announce to you great joy. We have a Pope."

Cheering commences, and grows in intensity as the cardinal-archdeacon tells the world that the newly chosen Pontiff is indeed *that* cardinal, that noble and distinguished person, that melancholy and austere individual, whose elevation to the Holy See we have all awaited so intensely for so long. "He has imposed upon himself," says the cardinal-archdeacon, "the name of—"

Lost in the cheering. I turn to Luigi. "Who? What name?"

"Sisto Settimo," Luigi tells me.

Yes, and there he is, Pope Sixtus the Seventh, as we now must call him. A tiny figure clad in the silver and gold papal robes, arms outstretched to the multitude, and, yes! the sunlight glints on his cheeks, his lofty forehead, there is the brightness of polished steel. Luigi is already on his knees. I kneel beside him. Miss Harshaw, Beverly, Kenneth, even the rabbi all kneel, for beyond doubt this is a miraculous event. The Pope comes forward on his balcony. Now he will deliver the traditional apostolic benediction to the city and to the world. "Our help is in the Name of the Lord," he declares gravely. He activates the levitator-jets beneath his arms; even at this distance I can see the two small puffs of smoke. White smoke, again. He begins to rise into the air. "Who hath made heaven and earth," he says. "May Almighty God, Father, Son, and Holy Ghost, bless you." His voice rolls majestically toward us. His shadow extends across the whole piazza. Higher and higher he goes, until he is lost to sight. Kenneth taps Luigi. "Another round of drinks," he says, and presses a bill of high denomination into the innkeeper's fleshy palm. Bishop FitzPatrick weeps. Rabbi Mueller embraces Miss Harshaw. The new Pontiff, I think, has begun his reign in an auspicious way.

A lot of the stories editors buy come to them through literary agents. Not all agents these days deal with short fiction, since the commissions they'd receive often amount to little more than they'd spend submitting stories to market after market; instead, many of them prefer to represent authors only for novels, leaving the marketing of their shorter stories to the writers themselves.

The most notable exception in the science fiction field is Virginia Kidd, who represents a good number of sf's top authors. Whenever I begin to read for a new volume of *Universe,* I immediately send a note to Virginia asking for stories, and she responds with a thick sheaf of manuscripts. I buy a lot of them: about 20 percent of the stories in the first ten *Universe*s came to me through her.

R. A. Lafferty, the puckish author of such novels as *Past Master* and *Fourth Mansions,* is one of her clients. When I asked Virginia for stories for *Universe 1,* the batch she sent me included two stories by Lafferty. I liked both of them, so I bought both, saving one for *Universe 2* and publishing the one I slightly preferred, "Nor Limestone Islands," in the first number. (A line from this story provided the title for Lafferty's story collection *Does Anyone Else Have Something Further to Add?)*

Lafferty, through Virginia, went on to sell me more stories than anyone else who appeared in *Universe.*

Nor Limestone Islands

R. A. Lafferty

A lapidary is one who cuts, polishes, engraves and sets small stones. He is also a scrivener with a choppy style who sets in little stones or pieces here and there and attempts to make a mosaic out of them.

But what do you call one who cuts and sets very large stones?

Take a small *lapillus* or stone for instance:

"The origin of painting as an art in Greece is connected with definite historical personages; but that of sculpture is lost in the mists of legend. Its authentic history does not begin until about the year B.C. 600. It was regarded as an art imparted to men by the gods; for such is the thought expressed in the assertion that the earliest statues fell from heaven."

Article *Statuaria Ars; Sculpture—*
Harper's Dictionary of Classical Literature
and Antiquities.

We set that little stone in one corner, even though it contains a misunderstanding of what fell from heaven: it wasn't finished statues.

Then we set another small stone:

(We haven't the exact citation of this. It's from Charles Fort or from one of his imitators.) It's of a scientist who refused to believe that several pieces of limestone had fallen from the sky, even though two farmers had seen them fall. They could not have fallen from the sky, the scientist said, because there is no limestone in the sky. (What would that scientist have done if he had been confronted with the question of Whales in the Sky?)

We set that little stone of wisdom into one corner. And we look around for other stones to set.

The limestone salesman was making his pitch to the city commissioners. He had been making a poor pitch and he was a poor salesman. All he had was price (much less than one tenth that of the other bidders) and superior quality. But the limestone salesman did not make a good appearance. He was bare-chested (and colossally deep-chested). He had only a little shoulder jacket above, and a folded drape below. On his feet he had the *crepida* or Hermes-sandals, made of buckskin apparently: a silly affectation. He was darkly burnt in skin and hair, but the roots of his hair and of his skin indicated that he was blond in both. He was golden-bearded, but the beard (and in fact the whole man) was covered with chalk-dust or rock-dust. The man was sweaty, and he smelled. His was a composite smell of limestone and edged bronze and goats and clover and honey and ozone and lentils and sour milk and dung and strong cheese.

"No, I don't believe that we want to deal with you at all," the mayor of the city was saying. "The other firms are all reputable and long established."

"Our firm is long established," the limestone salesman said. "It has been doing business from the same—ah—cart for nine thousand years."

"Balderdash," the streets and sewers commissioner swore. "You won't even give us the address of your firm, and you haven't put in a formal bid."

"The address is Stutzamutza," the limestone salesman said. "That's all the address I can give you. There isn't any other address. And I will put in a formal bid if you will show me how to do it. I offer you three hundred tons of the finest marble-limestone, cut exactly to specification, and set in place, guaranteed to take care of your project, guaranteed to be without flaw, in either pure white or variegated; I offer this delivered and set within one hour, all for the price of three hundred dollars or three hundred bushels of cracked corn."

"Oh take it, take it!" a Miss Phosphor McCabe cried out. "We elect you gentlemen to do our business for us at bargain prices. Do not pass up this fine bargain, I beg you." Phosphor McCabe was a lady photographer who had nine fingers in every pie.

"You be quiet, young lady, or we will have you put out of the hearing room," said the parks and playgrounds commissioner. "You will wait your turn, and you will not interfere in other cases. I shudder to think what your own petition will be today. Was ever a group so put upon by cranks as ourselves?"

"You have a very bad reputation, man," the finance commissioner said to the limestone salesman, "insofar as anyone has heard of you before. There is some mumble that your limestone or marble is not substantial, that it will melt away like hailstones. There is even a rumor that you had something to do with the terrible hailstorm of the night before last."

"Ah, we just had a little party at our place that night," the limestone salesman said. "We had a few dozen bottles of Tontitown wine from some stone that we set over in Arkansas, and we drank it up. We didn't hurt anybody or anything with those hailstones. Hey, some of them were as big as basketballs, weren't they! But we were careful where we let them fall. How often do you see a hailstorm as wild as that that doesn't do any damage at all to anything?"

"We can't afford to look silly," the schools and activities commissioner said. "We have been made to look silly in quite a few cases lately, not all of them our own fault. We can't afford to buy limestone for a project like this from someone like you."

"I wonder if you could get me about a hundred and twenty tons of good quality pink granite?" asked a smiling pinkish man in the hearing room.

"No, that's another island entirely," the limestone salesman said. "I'll tell them if I see them."

"Mr. Chalupa, I don't know what your business is here today," the mayor said severely to the smiling pinkish man, "but you will wait your turn, and you will not mix into this case. Lately it seems that our open hearings are just one nut after another."

"How can you lose?" the limestone salesman asked the commissioners. "I will supply and cut and set the stones. If you are not satisfied, I will leave the stones at no cost, or I will remove them again. And not until you are completely satisfied do you pay me the three hundred dollars or the three hundred bushels of cracked corn."

"I want to go to your country with you," Miss Phosphor McCabe burst out. "I am fascinated by what I have heard of it. I want to do a photographic article about it for the *Heritage Geographical Magazine.* How far away is your country now?"

"All right," the limestone salesman said. "I'll wait for you. We'll go just as soon as I have transacted my business and you have transacted yours. We like everybody and we want everybody to come and visit us, but hardly anybody wants to. Right now, my country is about three miles from here. Last chance, gentlemen: I offer you the best bargain in quality marble-limestone that you'll ever find if you live two hundred years. And I hope you do all live to be two hundred. We like everybody and we'd like to see everybody live two hundred years at least."

"Absolutely not," said the mayor of the city. "We'd be the laughing-stock of the whole state if we did business with someone like you. What kind of a country of yours are you talking about that's only three miles from here? Absolutely not. You are wasting your time and ours, man."

"No, no, it just couldn't be," said the streets and sewers commissioner. "What would the papers print if they heard that we had bought limestone from somebody nearly as disreputable as a saucerian?"

"Rejected, rejected," said the parks and playgrounds commissioner. "We were elected to transact the city's business with economy *and dignity.*"

"Ah well, all right," the limestone salesman said. "You can't sell a stylobate every time you try. Good day, commissioners. No hurry, lady.

I'll wait for you." And the limestone salesman went out, leaving, as it seemed, a cloud of rock-dust in his wake.

"What a day!" the schools and activities commissioner moaned. "What a procession of jokers we have had! Anyhow, that one can't be topped."

"I'm not so sure," the mayor grumbled. "Miss Phosphor McCabe is next."

"Oh, I'll be brief," Phosphor said brightly. "All I want is a permit to build a pagoda on that thirty-acre hill that my grandfather left me. It won't interfere with anything. There won't be any utilities to run to it. And it will be pretty."

"Ah, why do you want to build a pagoda?" the streets and sewers commissioner asked.

"So I can take pictures of it. And just because I want to build a pagoda."

"What kind of a pagoda will it be?" the parks and playgrounds commissioner asked.

"A pink pagoda."

"How big will it be?" the schools and activities commissioner asked.

"Thirty acres big. And four hundred feet high. It will be big and it won't bother anything."

"Why do you want it so big?" the mayor asked.

"So it will be ten times as big as the Black Pagoda in India. It'll be real pretty and an attraction to the area."

"Do you have the money to build this with?" the streets and sewers commissioner asked.

"No, I don't have hardly any money. If I sell my photographic article "With Camera and Canoe on Sky-High Stutzamutza" to the *Heritage Geographical Magazine* I will get some money for it. And I have been snapping unrehearsed camera portraits of all you gentlemen for the last few minutes, and I may be able to sell them to *Comic Weekly* if I can think of cute headings for them. As to the money to build the Pink Pagoda, oh, I'll think of something."

"Miss McCabe, your request is remanded or remaindered or whatever, which is the same thing as being tabled," the mayor said.

"What does that mean?"

"I'm not sure. The legal commissioner is absent today, but he always says something like that when we want to pass the buck for a little while."

"It means come back in one week, Miss McCabe," the streets and sewers commissioner said.

"All right," Miss Phosphor McCabe agreed. "I couldn't possibly start on the Pink Pagoda before a week anyhow."

And now we set this odd-shaped stone over in the other corner:

"The seventeenth century discovery of the Polynesian Islands by common seamen was one of the ancient paradise promises fulfilled. The green islands, the blue sea, the golden beaches and the golden sunlight, the dusky girls! Fruit incomparable, fish incomparable, roast pig and baked bird beyond believing, breadfruit and volcano, absolute and continuing perfection of weather, brown-skin paradise maidens such as are promised in alcoran, song and string-music and surf-music! This was the Promised Paradise of the Islands, and it came true.

"But even this was a weak thing beside the less known, the earlier and continuing discovery of the Floating Islands (or the Travertine Islands) by more intrepid farers. The girls of the Floating Islands are lighter (except for the cool blacks on the Green-stone Dolomites) than the Polynesian maidens; they are more intelligent and much more full of fun; are more handsome and fuller-bodied; are of an artier and more vital culture. They are livelier. Oh how they are livelier! And the regions themselves defy description. For color and zest, there is nothing in Polynesia or Aegea or Antilla to compare at all. And all the Travertine people are so friendly! Perhaps it is well that they are little known and little visited. We may be too weak for their experience."
                    Facts of the Paradise Legend: Harold Bluewater.

Look closely at that little stone ere we leave it. Are you sure that you have correctly noted the shape of it?

Then a still smaller stone to be set in, here where there seems too empty a little gap. It's a mere quotation:

"In Lapidary Inscription a Man is not upon Oath."
                    Doctor Johnson.

Miss Phosphor McCabe did visit the limestone salesman's country, and she did do the photographic article "With Camera and Canoe in Sky-High Stutzamutza." The stunning, eye-blowing, heart-swelling, joy-filled color photography cannot be given here, but these are a few extracts from the sustaining text:

"Stutzamutza is a limestone land of such unbelievable whiteness as to make the eyes ache with delight. It is this super-whiteness as a basis that makes all the other colors stand out with such clarity. There cannot be anywhere a bluer sky than, for most of the hours and days, surrounds Stutzamutza (see plates I and II). There cannot be greener fields, where there are fields, nor more silvery water (plates IV and V). The waterfalls are absolute rainbows, especially Final Falls, when it flows clear off the high land (plate VI). There cannot be more variegated cliffs, blue, black, pink, ochre, red, green, but always with that more-white-than-white basic (plate VII). There cannot be such a sun anywhere else. It shines here as it shines nowhere on the world.

"Due to the high average elevation of Stutzamutza (there will be some boggled eyes when I reveal just what I do mean by the *average* elevation of this place), the people are all wonderfully deep-chested or deep-breasted. They are like something out of fable. The few visitors who come here from lower, from more *mundane* elevations, are uniform in their disbelief. 'Oh, oh,' they will say. 'There can't *be* girls like that.' There are, however (see plate VIII). 'How long has this been going on?' these occasional visitors ask. It has been going on for the nine thousand years of recorded Stutzamutza history; and, beyond that, it has been going on as long as the world has been going on.

"Perhaps due to their deep-breastedness the Stutzamutza people are superb in their singing. They are lusty, they are loud, they are beautiful and enchanting in this. Their instruments, besides the conventional flutes and bagpipes (with their great lung-power, these people do wonderful things with the bagpipes) and lyric harps and tabors, are the thunder-drum (plate IX) and the thirteen-foot-long trumpets (plates X and XI). It is doubted whether any other people anywhere would be able to blow these roaring trumpets.

"Perhaps it is due also to their deep-breastedness that the Stutzamutza people are all so lustily affectionate. There is something both breath-taking and breath-giving in their Olympian carnality. They have a robustness and glory in their man and woman interfluents that leave this underdeveloped little girl more than amazed (plates X to XIX). Moreover, these people are witty and wise, and always pleasant.

"It is said that originally there was not any soil at all on Stutzamutza. The people would trade finest quality limestone, marble, and dolomite for equal amounts of soil, be it the poorest clay or sand. They filled certain crevices with this soil and got vegetation to begin. And, in a few thousand years, they built countless verdant terraces, knolls and valleys. Grapes, olives and clover are now grown in profusion. Wine and oil and honey gladden the deep hearts of the people. The wonderful blue-green clover (see plate XX) is grazed by the bees and the goats. These are two separate species of goats, the meadow and pasture goat kept for its milk and cheese and mohair, and the larger and wilder mountain goat hunted on the white crags and eaten for its flavorsome randy meat. Woven mohair and dressed buckskin are used for the Stutzamutza clothing. The people are not voluminously clothed, in spite of the fact that it becomes quite chilly on the days when the elevation suddenly increases.

"There is very little grain grown on Stutzamutza. Mostly, quarried stones are bartered for grain. Quarrying stone is the main industry, it is really the only one on Stutzamutza. The great quarries in their cutaways sometimes reveal amazing fossil deposits. There is a complete fossilized body of a whale (it is an extinct Zeuglodon or Eocene Whale) (see plate XXI).

" 'If this is whale indeed, then this all must have been under ocean once,' I said to one of my deep-chested friends. 'Oh certainly,' he said, 'nowhere else is limestone formed than in ocean.' 'Then how has it risen so far above it?' I asked. 'That is something for the Geologists and the Hyphologists to figure out,' my friend said.

"The fascinating aspect of the water on Stutzamutza is its changeableness. A lake is sometimes formed in a single day, and it may be emptied out in one day again by mere tipping. The rain is prodigious sometimes, when it is decided to come into that aspect. To shoot the rapids on the sudden swollen rivers is a delight. Sometimes ice will form all over Stutzamutza in a very few minutes. The people delight in this sudden ice, all except the little under-equipped guest. The beauty of it is stupendous; so is its cold. They shear the ice off in great sheets and masses and blocks, and let it fall for fun.

"But all lesser views are forgotten when one sees the waterfalls tumbling in the sunlight. And the most wonderful of all of them is Final Falls. Oh to watch it fall clear off Stutzamutza (see plate XXII), to see it fall into practically endless space, thirty thousand feet, sixty thousand feet, turning into mist, into sleet or snow or rain or hail depending on the sort of day it is, to see the miles-long rainbow of it extending to the vanishing point so far below your feet!

"There is a particularly striking pink marble cliff towards the north end of the land (the *temporary* north end of the land). 'You like it? You can have it,' my friends say. That is what I had been fishing for them to say."

Yes, Miss Phosphor McCabe did the really stunning photographic article for *Heritage Geographical Magazine. Heritage Geographical* did not accept it, however. Miss Phosphor McCabe had arrived at some unacceptable conclusions, the editor said.

"What really happened is that I arrived at an unacceptable place," Miss Phosphor said. "I remained there for six days. I photographed it and I narrated it."

"Ah, we'd never get by with that," the editor said. Part of the trouble was Miss Phosphor McCabe's explanations of just what she did mean by the average elevation of Stutzamutza (it was quite high), and by "days of increasing elevation."

Now here is another stone of silly shape. At first glimpse, it will not seem possible to fit it into the intended gap. But the eye is deceived: this shape will fit into the gap nicely. It is a recollection in age of a thing observed during a long lifetime by a fine weather eye.

"Already as a small boy I was interested in clouds. I believed that certain clouds preserve their identities and appear again and again; and that some clouds are more solid than others.

"Later, when I took meteorology and weather courses at the university, I had a class-mate who held a series of seemingly insane beliefs. At the heart of these was the theory that certain apparent clouds are not vapor masses at all but are floating stone islands in the sky. He believed that there were some thirty of these islands, most of them composed of limestone, but some of them of basalt, or sand-stone, even of shale. He said that one, at least, of them was composed of pot-stone or soapstone.

"This class-mate said that these floating islands were sometimes large, one of them being at least five miles long: that they were intelligently navigated to follow the best camouflage, the limestone islands usually traveling with masses of white fleecy clouds, the basalt islands traveling with dark thunder-heads, and so on. He believed that these islands sometimes came to rest on earth, that each of them had its own several nests in unfrequented regions. And he believed that the floating islands were peopled.

"We had considerable fun with Mad Anthony Tummley our eccentric class-mate. His ideas, we told each other, were quite insane. And, indeed, Anthony himself was finally institutionalized. It was a sad case, but one that could hardly be discussed without laughter.

"But later, after more than fifty years in the weather profession, I have come to the conclusion that Anthony Tummley was right in every respect. Several of us veteran weathermen share this knowledge now, but we have developed a sort of code for the thing, not daring to admit it openly, even to ourselves. 'Whales in the Sky' is the code-name for this study, and we pretend to keep it on a humorous basis.

"Some thirty of these floating stone islands are continuously over our own country (there may be more than a hundred of them in the world). They are tracked on radar; they are sighted again and again in their slightly charged forms (some of them, now and then, seem to sluff off small masses of stone and deposit it somehow on earth); they are known, they are named.

"They are even visited by some persons of odd character: always a peculiar combination of simplicity, acceptance, intelligence and strange rapport. There are persons and families in rural situations who employ these peopled islands to carry messages and goods for them. In rural and swampland Louisiana, there was once some wonder that the people did not more avail themselves of the Intercostal Canal barges to carry their supplies, and their products to market. 'How are the barges better than the stone islands that we have always used?' these people ask. 'They aren't on a much more regular schedule, they aren't much faster, and they won't give you anything like the same amount of service in exchange for a hundredweight of rice. Besides that, the stone-island people are our friends, and some of them have intermarried with us Cajuns.' There are other regions where the same easy cooperation obtains.

"Many of the stone-island people are well known along certain almost regular routes. These people are all of a powerful and rather coarse beauty. They are good-natured and hearty. They actually traffic in stone, trading amazing tonnages of top grade building stone for grain and other simple provisions.

"There is no scientific explanation at all of how these things can be, how the stone islands are able to float in the sky. But that they do so is the open secret of perhaps a million persons.

"Really, I am now too wealthy to be put in a mad-house (though I made my money in a rather mad traffic which would not be generally believed). I am too old to be laughed at openly: I will merely be smiled at as an eccentric. I have now retired from that weather profession which served me as a front for many years (which profession, however, I loved and still love).

"I know what I know. There are more things in the zone fifteen miles above the earth than are dreamt of in your philosophy, Horatio."

Memories of 52 years as a Weather Observer
by Hank Fairday (Privately printed 1970).

Miss Phosphor McCabe did another really stunning photographic article for the *Heritage Geographical Magazine*. It had a catchy title: "All Right, Then You Tell *Me* How I Did It, or The Building of the Pink Pagoda."

"The Pink Pagoda is complete, except for such additions as I shall have made whenever the notion strikes me, and whenever my high-flying friends are in the neighborhood. It is by far the largest structure in the world and also, in my own opinion, the most beautiful. But it is not massive in appearance: it is light and airy. Come see it in the stone, all of you! Come see it in the color photography (plates I to CXXIX) if you are not able to come yourself. This wonderful structure gives the answers to hundreds of questions, if you will just open your eyes and your ears.

"Of ancient megalithic structures it has sometimes been asked how a hundred or more of one hundred ton blocks of stone could have been piled up, and fitted so carefully that even a knife-blade could not be inserted between the blocks. It's easy. You usually don't set a hundred one hundred ton blocks, unless for a certain ornamentation. You set one ten thousand ton block, and the joinings are merely simulated. In the Pink Pagoda I have had set blocks as heavy as three hundred thousand tons of pink limestone (see plate XXI).

"They bring the whole island down in place. They split off what block is wanted at that location (and, believe me, they are some splitters); then they withdraw the island a little bit and leave the block in place.

"Well, how else was it done? How did I get the one hundred and fifty thousand ton main capstone in place four hundred and fifty feet in the air? With ramps? Oh stop it, you'll scare the cuckoos. The stone pillars and turrets all around and below it are like three-dimensional lace-work, and that main capstone had to go on last. It wasn't done by rocking it up on ramps, even if there had been a place for the ramps. It was all done on one Saturday afternoon, and here are the sequence pictures showing just how it was done. It was done by using a floating island, and by detaching pieces of that island as it was floated into place. I tell you that there is no other way that a one hundred and five pound girl can assemble a thirty million ton Pink Pagoda in six hours. She has got to have a floating island, with a north cliff of pink limestone, and she has got to be very good friends with the people on that island.

"Please come and see my Pink Pagoda. All the people and all the officials avert their eyes from it. They say that it is impossible that such a thing could be there, and therefore it cannot be there. But it *is* there. See it yourself (or see plates IV, IX, XXXIII, LXX especially). And it is pretty (see plates XIX, XXIV, V, LIV). But best, come see it as it really

is."

Miss Phosphor McCabe did that rather astonishing photographic article for the *Heritage Geographical Magazine*. *Heritage Geographical* refused to publish it, though, stating that such things were impossible. And they refused to come and see the Pink Pagoda itself, which is a pity, since it is the largest and most beautiful structure on earth.

It stands there yet, on that thirty acre hill right on the north edge of town. And you have not heard the last stone of it yet. The latest, a bad-natured little addition, will not be the last: Miss Phosphor swears that it will not be.

There was a flimsy-winged enemy flew down, shortly after the first completion of the pagoda, and set the latest very small stone (it is called the egg-of-doubt stone) on top of the main capstone. 'Twas a crabbed written little stone, and it read:

> "I will not trow two-headed calves,"
> Say never-seens, and also haves.

> "I'll not believe a hollow earth,"
> Say scepticals of doubtful birth.

> "I'll not concede Atlantis you,
> Nor yet Lemuria or Mu,

> "Nor woodsmen in northwestern lands,
> Nor bandy-legg'd saucerians,

"Nor ancient technologic myth,
Nor charm of timeless megalith.
"I will not credit Whales that fly,
Nor Limestone Islands in the Sky."
Unfolk Ballad

That crabby little ballad-stone on the top almost spoils the Pink Pagoda for me. But it will be removed, Miss Phosphor McCabe says, just as soon as her traveling friends are back in this neighborhood and she can get up there.

That is all that we have to say on the subject of stone setting. Does anyone else have something further to add?

Harlan Ellison is one of my favorite writers, but that doesn't mean I love absolutely everything he writes. He's also a longtime friend; but, again, we've sometimes had our clashes. One such came when I asked him for a story for *Universe 1* and he obligingly sent me a story titled "Corpse." Alas, I didn't care for it, so I rejected it. In reply I got this letter, which I quote now with his permission:

25 February 71

Dear Mr. Carr:

No matter how secure a writer may think himself, with the mute stature of trophies, awards, commendations, praiseworthy reviews and shelves of books bearing his name surrounding him, when he attempts something different with his talent, when he pushes against the self-imposed limitations of what he has done successfully before, he becomes weak and trepidatious, becomes prey to doubts of the validity of the experiment or its success. At that moment he is a novice, submitting his first story. At that moment great care should be exercised with his emotions.

"Corpse" has now been read by Damon, Ben Bova, Gerry Conway, Bob Mills and Prof. Will McNelly. They all tell me it is a new and special thing for me, done well, and quite different in voice from anything I've done before. They tell me it is a good story. Bob Mills has sent it to *Playboy*, with intent, if rejected there, to submit it (in order) to *Harper's, New American Writing* and *Esquire*.

None of this is intended to whip guilt on you. Only to lodge an observation that you messed my mind royally for many days until other precincts were heard from. I don't even quibble with your editorial judgment; there is no fault or complaint to be tendered against you. Only to apprise you of the uncommon potency of your words and your actions.

Or as Cosimo De Medici said, "Nowhere are we commanded to forgive our friends."

Respectfully,
HARLAN ELLISON
(Author of "Corpse," a
good story)

I couldn't believe this letter. I hadn't railed at Harlan about its being a terrible story, I hadn't called him a bad writer, I hadn't screamed or blustered that I never wanted to read a word by him ever again. No such thing; I'd simply declined to buy the story.

So I wrote back to him:

March 2, 1971

Dear Harlan,

Oh, don't be silly. . . . If a non-heated rejection from the first editor you show a story to is enough to put you in a blue funk for days, as you say in your letter and which I really doubt, then you're in the wrong business. And obviously you're *not* in the wrong business or you'd never have accomplished all that you have.

. . . Ah, you're just a temperamental goddam writer, that's what.

Best,
Terry

Harlan was in a better mood by the time he got this letter. He telephoned me and said wotthehell archy, then said he'd write me a different story. "But this time, you tell me what you want, and I'll do my humble best to fulfill your editorial needs. What kind of story do you want?"

I hemmed and hawed, put on the spot, and finally I said I thought it would be interesting, since he'd been writing so many downbeat and angry stories lately, if he'd write one that was warm and happy and upbeat. "You got it, kid," he said; he hung up and went to his typewriter and produced "On the Downhill Side," which I loved and which was nominated for a Nebula (losing to Joanna Russ's "When It Changed," from Harlan's *Again, Dangerous Visions*).

On the Downhill Side

Harlan Ellison

"In love, there is always one who kisses and one who offers the cheek."

—French proverb

I knew she was a virgin because she was able to ruffle the silken mane of my unicorn. Named Lizette, she was a Grecian temple in which no sacrifice had ever been made. Vestal virgin of New Orleans, found walking without shadow in the thankgod coolness of cockroach-crawling Louisiana night. My unicorn whinnied, inclined his head, and she stroked the ivory spiral of his horn.

Much of this took place in what is called the Irish Channel, a strip of street in old New Orleans where the lace curtain micks had settled decades before; now the Irish were gone and the Cubans had taken over the Channel. Now the Cubans were sleeping, recovering from the muggy today that held within its hours the *déjà vu* of muggy yesterday, the *déjà rêvé* of intolerable tomorrow. Now the crippled bricks of side streets off Magazine had given up their nightly ghosts, and one such phantom had come to me, calling my unicorn to her—thus, clearly, a virgin—and I stood waiting.

Had it been Sutton Place, had it been a Manhattan evening, and had we met, she would have kneeled to pet my dog. And I would have waited. Had it been Puerto Vallarta, had it been 20° 36' N, 105° 13' W, and had we met, she would have crouched to run her fingertips over the oil-slick hide of my iguana. And I would have waited. Meeting in streets requires ritual. One must wait and not breathe too loud, if one is to enjoy the congress of the nightly ghosts.

She looked across the fine head of my unicorn and smiled at me. Her eyes were a shade of gray between onyx and miscalculation. "Is it a bit chilly for you?" I asked.

"When I was thirteen," she said, linking my arm, taking a tentative two steps that led me with her, up the street, "or perhaps I was twelve, well no matter, when I was that approximate age, I had a marvelous shawl of Belgian lace. I could look through it and see the mysteries of the sun and the other stars unriddled. I'm sure someone important and very nice has purchased that shawl from an antique dealer, and paid handsomely for it."

It seemed not a terribly responsive reply to a simple question.

"A queen of the Mardi Gras Ball doesn't get chilly," she added, unasked. I walked along beside her, the cool evasiveness of her arm binding us, my mind a welter of answer choices, none satisfactory.

Behind us, my unicorn followed silently. Well, not entirely silently. His platinum hoofs clattered on the bricks. I'm afraid I felt a straight pin of jealousy. Perfection does that to me.

"When were you queen of the Ball?"

The date she gave me was one hundred and thirteen years before.

It must have been brutally cold down there in the stones.

There is a little book they sell, a guide to manners and dining in New Orleans: I've looked: nowhere in the book do they indicate the proper responses to a ghost. But then, it says nothing about the wonderful cemeteries of New Orleans' West Bank, or Metairie. Or the gourmet dining at such locations. One seeks, in vain, through the mutable, mercurial universe, for the compleat guide. To everything. And, failing in the search, one makes do the best one can. And suffers the frustration, suffers the ennui.

Perfection does that to me.

We walked for some time, and grew to know each other, as best we'd allow. These are some of the high points. They lack continuity. I don't apologize, I merely point it out, adding with some truth, I feel, that *most* liaisons lack continuity. We find ourselves in odd places at various times, and for a brief span we link our lives to others—even as Lizette had linked her arm with mine—and then, our time elapsed, we move apart. Through a haze of pain occasionally; usually through a veil of memory that clings, then passes; sometimes as though we have never touched.

"My name is Paul Ordahl," I told her. "And the most awful thing that ever happened to me was my first wife, Bernice. I don't know how else to put it—even if it sounds melodramatic, it's simply what happened—she went insane, and I divorced her, and her mother had her committed to a private mental home."

"When I was eighteen," Lizette said, "my family gave me my coming-out party. We were living in the Garden District, on Prytania Street. The house was a lovely white Plantation—they call them antebellum now—with Grecian pillars. We had a persimmon-green gazebo in the rear gardens, directly beside a weeping willow. It was six-sided. Octagonal. Or is that hexagonal? It was the loveliest party. And while it was going on, I sneaked away with a boy . . . I don't remember his name . . . and we went into the gazebo, and I let him touch my breasts. I don't remember his name."

We were on Decatur Street, walking toward the French Quarter; the Mississippi was on our right, dark but making its presence known.

"Her mother was the one had her committed, you see. I only heard from them twice after the divorce. It had been four stinking years and I really didn't want any more of it. Once, after I'd started making some money, the mother called and said Bernice had to be put in the state asylum. There wasn't enough money to pay for the private home any more. I sent a little; not much. I suppose I could have sent more, but I was remarried, there was a child from her previous marriage. I didn't want to send any more. I told the mother not to call me again. There was only once after that . . . it was the most terrible thing that ever happened to me."

We walked around Jackson Square, looking in at the very black grass, reading the plaques bolted to the spear-topped fence, plaques telling how New Orleans had once belonged to the French. We sat on one of the benches in the street. The street had been closed to traffic, and we sat on one of the benches.

"Our name was Charbonnet. Can you say that?"

I said it, with a good accent.

"I married a very wealthy man. He was in real estate. At one time he owned the entire block where the *Vieux Carré* now stands, on Bourbon Street. He admired me greatly. He came and sought my hand, and my *maman* had to strike the bargain because my father was too weak to do it; he drank. I can admit that now. But it didn't matter, I'd already found out how my suitor was set financially. He wasn't common, but he wasn't quality, either. But he was wealthy and I married him. He gave me presents. I did what I had to do. But I refused to let him make love to me after he became friends with that awful Jew who built the Metairie Cemetery over the race track because they wouldn't let him race his Jew horses. My husband's name was Dunbar. Claude Dunbar, you may have heard the name? Our parties were *de rigueur.*"

"Would you like some coffee and *beignets* at Du Monde?"

She stared at me for a moment, as though she wanted me to say something more, then she nodded and smiled.

We walked around the Square. My unicorn was waiting at the curb. I scratched his rainbow flank and he struck a spark off the cobblestones with his right front hoof. "I know," I said to him, "we'll soon start the downhill side. But not just yet. Be patient. I won't forget you."

Lizette and I went inside the Café Du Monde and I ordered two coffees with warm milk and two orders of *beignets* from a waiter who was originally from New Jersey but had lived most of his life only a few miles from College Station, Texas.

There was a coolness coming off the levee.

"I was in New York," I said. "I was receiving an award at an architects' convention—did I mention I was an architect—yes, that's what I was at the time, an architect—and I did a television interview. The mother saw me on the program, and checked the newspapers to find out what hotel we were using for the convention, and she got my room number and called me. I had been out quite late after the banquet where I'd gotten my award, quite late. I was sitting on the side of the bed, taking off my shoes, my tuxedo tie hanging from my unbuttoned collar, getting ready to just throw clothes on the floor and sink away, when the phone rang. It was the mother. She was a terrible person, one of the worst I ever knew, a shrike, a terrible, just a terrible person. She started telling me about Bernice in the asylum. How they had her in this little room and how she stared out the window most of the time. She'd reverted to childhood, and most of the time she couldn't even recognize the mother; but when she did, she'd say something like, 'Don't let them hurt me, Mommy, don't let them hurt me.' So I asked her what she wanted me to do, did she want money for Bernice or what . . . Did she want me to go see her since I was in New York . . . and she said God no. And then she did an awful thing to me. She said the last time she'd been to see Bernice, my ex-wife had turned around and put her finger to her lips and said, 'Shhh, we have to be very quiet. Paul is working.' And I swear, a snake uncoiled in my stomach. It was the most terrible thing I'd ever heard. No matter how secure you are that you honest to God had *not* sent someone to a madhouse, there's always that little core of doubt, and saying what she'd said just burned out my head. I couldn't even think about it, couldn't even really *hear* it, or it would have collapsed me. So down came these iron walls and I just kept on talking, and after a while she hung up.

"It wasn't till two years later that I allowed myself to think about it, and then I cried; it had been a long time since I'd cried. Oh, not because I believed that nonsense about a man isn't supposed to cry, but just because I guess there hadn't been anything that important to cry *about*. But when I let myself hear what she'd said, I started crying, and just went on and on till I finally went in and looked into the bathroom mirror and I asked myself face to face if I'd done that, if I'd ever made her be quiet so I could work on blueprints or drawings. . . .

"And after a while I saw myself shaking my head no, and it was easier. That was perhaps three years before I died."

She licked the powdered sugar from the *beignets* off her fingers, and launched into a long story about a lover she had taken. She didn't remember his name.

It was sometime after midnight. I'd thought midnight would signal the start of the downhill side, but the hour had passed, and we were still together, and she didn't seem ready to vanish. We left the Café Du Monde and walked into the Quarter.

I despise Bourbon Street. The strip joints, with the pasties over nipples, the smell of need, the dwarfed souls of men attuned only to flesh. The noise.

We walked through it like art connoisseurs at a showing of motel room paintings. She continued to talk about her life, about the men she had known, about the way they had loved her, the ways in which she had spurned them, and about the trivia of her past existence. I continued to talk about my loves, about all the women I had held dear in my heart for however long each had been linked with me. We talked across each other, our conversation at right angles, only meeting in the intersections of silence at story's end.

She wanted a julep and I took her to the Royal Orleans Hotel and we sat in silence as she drank. I watched her, studying that phantom face, seeking for even the smallest flicker of light off the ice in her eyes, hoping for an indication that glacial melting could be forthcoming. But there was nothing, and I burned to say correct words that might cause heat. She drank and reminisced about evenings with young men in similar hotels, a hundred years before.

We went to a night club where a Flamenco dancer and his two-woman troupe performed on a stage of unpolished woods, their star-shining black shoes setting up resonances in me that I chose to ignore.

Then I realized there were only three couples in the club, and that the extremely pretty Flamenco dancer was playing to Lizette. He gripped the lapels of his bolero jacket and clattered his heels against the stage like a man driving nails. She watched him, and her tongue made a wholly obvious flirtatious trip around the rim of her liquor glass. There was a two-drink minimum, and as I have never liked the taste of alcohol, she was more than willing to prevent waste by drinking mine as well as her own. Whether she was getting drunk or simply indulging herself, I do not know. It didn't matter. I became blind with jealousy, and dragons took possession of my eyes.

When the dancer was finished, when his half hour show was concluded, he came to our table. His suit was skin tight and the color of Arctic lakes. His hair was curly and moist from his exertions, and his prettiness infuriated me. There was a scene. He asked her name, I interposed a comment, he tried to be polite, sensing my ugly mood, she overrode my comment, he tried again in Castilian, *th*-ing his *esses,* she answered, I rose and shoved him, there was a scuffle. We were asked to leave.

Once outside, she walked away from me.

My unicorn was at the curb, eating from a porcelain *Sèvres* soup plate filled with *flan.* I watched her walk unsteadily up the street toward Jackson Square. I scratched my unicorn's neck and he stopped eating the egg custard. He looked at me for a long moment. Ice crystals were sparkling in his mane.

We were on the downhill side.

"Soon, old friend," I said.

He dipped his elegant head toward the plate. "I see you've been to the Las Americas. When you return the plate, give my best to *Señor* Pena."

I followed her up the street. She was walking rapidly toward the Square. I called to her, but she wouldn't stop. She began dragging her left hand along the steel bars of the fence enclosing the Square. Her fingertips thudded softly from bar to bar, and once I heard the chitinous *clak* of a manicured nail.

"Lizette!"

She walked faster dragging her hand across the dark metal bars.

"Lizette! Damn it!"

I was reluctant to run after her; it was somehow terribly demeaning. But she was getting farther and farther away. There were bums in the Square, sitting slouched on the benches, their arms out along the backs. Itinerants, kids with beards and knapsacks. I was suddenly frightened for her. Impossible. She had been dead for a hundred years. There was no reason for it . . . I was afraid for her!

I started running, the sound of my footsteps echoing up and around the Square. I caught her at the corner and dragged her around. She tried to slap me, and I caught her hand. She kept trying to hit me, to scratch my face with the manicured nails. I held her and swung her away from me, swung her around, and around, dizzingly, trying to keep her off balance. She swung wildly, crying out and saying things inarticulately. Finally, she stumbled and I pulled her in to me and held her tight against my body.

"Stop it! Stop, Lizette! I . . . *Stop it!*" She went limp against me and I felt her crying against my chest. I took her into the shadows and my unicorn came down Decatur Street and stood under a streetlamp, waiting.

The chimera winds rose. I heard them, and knew we were well on the downhill side, that time was growing short. I held her close and smelled the woodsmoke scent of her hair. "Listen to me," I said, softly, close to her. "Listen to me, Lizette. Our time's almost gone. This is our last chance. You've lived in stone for a hundred years; I've heard you cry. I've come there, to that place, night after night, and I've heard you cry. You've paid enough, God knows. So have I. We can *do* it. We've got one more chance, and we can make it, if you'll try. That's all I ask. Try."

She pushed away from me, tossing her head so the auburn hair swirled away from her face. Her eyes were dry. Ghosts can do that. Cry without making tears. Tears are denied us. Other things; I won't talk of them here.

"I lied to you," she said.

I touched the side of her face. The high cheekbone just at the hairline. "I know. My unicorn would never have let you touch him if you weren't pure. I'm not, but he has no choice with me. He was assigned to me. He's my familiar and he puts up with me. We're friends."

"No. Other lies. My life was a lie. I've told them all to you. We can't make it. You have to let me go."

I didn't know exactly where, but I knew how it would happen. I argued with her, trying to convince her there was a way for us. But she couldn't believe it, hadn't the strength or the will or the faith. Finally, I let her go.

She put her arms around my neck, and drew my face down to hers, and she held me that way for a few moments. Then the winds rose, and there were sounds in the night, the sounds of calling, and she left me there, in the shadows.

I sat down on the curb and thought about the years since I'd died. Years without much music. Light leached out. Wandering. Nothing to pace me but memories and the unicorn. How sad I was for *him;* assigned to me till I got my chance. And now it had come and I'd taken my best go, and failed.

Lizette and I were the two sides of the same coin; devalued and impossible to spend. Legal tender of nations long since vanished, no longer even names on the cracked papyrus of cartographers' maps. We had been snatched away from final rest, had been set adrift to roam for our crimes, and only once between death and eternity would we receive a chance. This night . . . this nothing-special night . . . this was our chance.

My unicorn came to me, then, and brushed his muzzle against my shoulder. I reached up and scratched around the base of his spiral horn, his favorite place. He gave a long, silvery sigh, and in that sound I heard the sentence I was serving on him, as well as myself. We had been linked, too. Assigned to one another by the one who had ordained this night's chance. But if I lost out, so did my unicorn; he who had wandered with me through all the soundless, lightless years.

I stood up. I was by no means ready to do battle, but at least I could stay in for the full ride . . . all the way on the downhill side. "Do you know where they are?"

My unicorn started off down the street.

I followed, hopelessness warring with frustration. Dusk to dawn is the full ride, the final chance. After midnight is the downhill side. Time was short, and when time ran out there would be nothing for Lizette or me or my unicorn *but* time. Forever.

When we passed the Royal Orleans Hotel I knew where we were going. The sound of the Quarter had already faded. It was getting on toward dawn. The human lice had finally crawled into their flesh-mounds to sleep off the night of revelry. Though I had never experienced directly the New Orleans in which Lizette had grown up, I longed for the power to blot out the cancerous blight that Bourbon Street and the Quarter had become, with its tourist filth and screaming neon, to restore it to the colorful yet healthy state in which it had thrived a hundred years before. But I was only a ghost, not one of the gods with such powers, and at that moment I was almost at the end of the line held by one of those gods.

My unicorn turned down dark streets, heading always in the same general direction, and when I saw the first black shapes of the tombstones against the night sky, the *lightening* night sky, I knew I'd been correct in my assumption of destination.

The Saint Louis Cemetery.

Oh, how I sorrow for anyone who has never seen the world-famous Saint Louis Cemetery in New Orleans. It is the perfect graveyard, the complete graveyard, the finest graveyard in the universe. (There is a perfection in some designs that informs the function totally. There are Danish chairs that could be nothing *but* chairs, are so totally and completely *chair* that if the world as we know it ended, and a billion years from now the New Orleans horsy cockroaches became the dominant species, and they dug down through the alluvial layers, and found one of those chairs, even if they themselves did not use chairs, were not constructed physically for the use of chairs, had never seen a chair, *still* they would know it for what it had been made to be: a chair. Because it would be the essence of *chairness.* And from it, they could reconstruct the human race in replica. *That* is the kind of graveyard one means when one refers to the world-famous Saint Louis Cemetery.)

The Saint Louis Cemetery is ancient. It sighs with shadows and the comfortable bones and their afterimages of deaths that became great merely because those who died went to be interred in the Saint Louis Cemetery. The water table lies just eighteen inches below New Orleans —there are no graves in the earth for that reason. Bodies are entombed aboveground in crypts, in sepulchers, vaults, mausoleums. The gravestones are all different, no two alike, each one a testament to the stonecutter's art. Only secondarily testaments to those who lie beneath the markers.

We had reached the moment of final nightness. That ultimate moment before day began. Dawn had yet to fill the eastern sky, yet there was a warming of tone to the night; it was the last of the downhill side of my chance. Of Lizette's chance.

We approached the cemetery, my unicorn and I. From deep in the center of the skyline of stones beyond the fence I could see the ice-chill glow of a pulsing blue light. The light one finds in a refrigerator, cold and flat and brittle.

I mounted my unicorn, leaned close along his neck, clinging to his mane with both hands, knees tight to his silken sides, now rippling with light and color, and I gave a little hiss of approval, a little sound of go.

My unicorn sailed over the fence, into the world-famous Saint Louis Cemetery.

I dismounted and thanked him. We began threading our way between the tombstones, the sepulchers, the crypts.

The blue glow grew more distinct. And now I could hear the chimera winds rising, whirling, coming in off alien seas. The pulsing of the light, the wail of the winds, the night dying. My unicorn stayed close. Even we of the spirit world know when to be afraid.

After all, I was only operating off a chance; I was under no god's protection. Naked, even in death.

There is no fog in New Orleans.

Mist began to form around us.

Except sometimes in the winter, there is no fog in New Orleans.

I remembered the daybreak of the night I'd died. There had been mist. I had been a suicide.

My third wife had left me. She had gone away during the night, while I'd been at a business meeting with a client; I had been engaged to design a church in Baton Rouge. All that day I'd steamed the old wallpaper off the apartment we'd rented. It was to have been our first home together, paid for by the commission. I'd done the steaming myself, with a tall ladder and a steam condenser and two flat pans with steam holes. Up near the ceiling the heat had been so awful I'd almost fainted. She'd brought me lemonade, freshly squeezed. Then I'd showered and changed and gone to my meeting. When I'd returned, she was gone. No note.

Lizette and I were two sides of the same coin, cast off after death for the opposite extremes of the same crime. She had never loved. I had loved too much. Overindulgence in something as delicate as love is to be found monstrously offensive in the eyes of the God of Love. And some of us—who have never understood the salvation in the Golden Mean—some of us are cast adrift with but one chance. It can happen.

Mist formed around us, and my unicorn crept close to me, somehow smaller, almost timid. We were moving into realms he did not understand, where his limited magics were useless. These were realms of potency so utterly beyond even the limbo creatures—such as my unicorn—so completely alien to even the intermediary zone wanderers—Lizette and myself—that we were as helpless and without understanding as those who live. We had only one advantage over living, breathing, as yet undead humans: we *knew* for certain that the realms on the other side existed.

Above, beyond, deeper: where the gods live. Where the one who had given me my chance, had given Lizette *her* chance, where He lived. Undoubtedly watching.

The mist swirled up around us, as chill and final as the dust of pharaoh's tombs.

We moved through it, toward the pulsing heart of blue light. And as we came into the penultimate circle, we stopped. We were in the outer ring of potency, and we saw the claiming things that had come for Lizette. She lay out on an altar of crystal, naked and trembling. They stood around her, enormously tall and transparent. Man shapes without faces. Within their transparent forms a strange, silvery fog swirled, like smoke from holy censers. Where eyes should have been on a man or a ghost, there were only dull flickering firefly glowings, inside, hanging in the smoke, moving, changing shape and position. No eyes at all. And tall, very tall, towering over Lizette and the altar.

For me, overcommitted to love, when dawn came without salvation, there was only an eternity of wandering, with my unicorn as sole companion. Ghost forevermore. Incense chimera viewed as dust-devil on the horizon, chilling as I passed in city streets, forever gone, invisible, lost, empty, helpless, wandering.

But for her, empty vessel, the fate was something else entirely. The God of Love had allowed her the time of wandering, trapped by day in stones, freed at night to wander. He had allowed her the final chance. And having failed to take it, her fate was with these claiming creatures, gods themselves . . . of another order . . . higher or lower I had no idea. But terrible.

"*Lagniappe!*" I screamed the word. The old Creole word they use in New Orleans when they want a little extra; a bonus of *croissants,* a few additional carrots dumped into the shopping bag, a larger portion of clams or crabs or shrimp. "*Lagniappe!* Lizette, take a little more! Try for the extra! Try . . . demand it . . . there's time . . . you have it coming to you . . . you've paid . . . I've paid . . . it's ours . . . *try!*"

She sat up, her naked body lit by lambent fires of chill blue cold from the other side. She sat up and looked across the inner circle to me, and I stood there with my arms out, trying desperately to break through the outer circle to her. But it was solid and I could not pass. Only virgins could pass.

And they would not let her go. They had been promised a feed, and they were there to claim. I began to cry, as I had cried when I finally heard what the mother had said, when I finally came home to the empty apartment and knew I had spent my life loving too much, demanding too much, myself a feeder at a board that *could* be depleted and emptied and serve up no more. She wanted to come to me, I could *see* she wanted to come to me. But they would have their meal.

Then I felt the muzzle of my unicorn at my neck, and in a step he had moved through the barrier that was impenetrable to me, and he moved across the circle and stood waiting. Lizette leaped from the altar and ran to me.

It all happened at the same time. I felt Lizette's body anchor in to mine, and *we* saw my unicorn standing over there on the other side, and for a moment *we* could not summon up the necessary reactions, the correct sounds. We knew for the first time in either our lives or our deaths what it was to be paralyzed. Then reactions began washing over me, we, us in wave after wave: cascading joy that Lizette had come to . . . us; utter love for this Paul ghost creature; realization that instinctively part of us was falling into the same pattern again; fear that part would love too much at this mystic juncture; resolve to temper our love; and then anguish at the sight of our unicorn standing there, waiting to be claimed. . . .

We called to him . . . using his secret name, one we had never spoken aloud. We could barely speak. Weight pulled at his throat, our throats. "Old friend . . ." We took a step toward him but could not pass the barrier. Lizette clung to me, Paul held me tight as I trembled with terror and the cold of that inner circle still frosting my flesh.

The great transparent claimers stood silently, watching, waiting, as if content to allow us our moments of final decision. But their impatience could be felt in the air, a soft purring, like the death rattle always in the throat of a cat. "Come back! Not for me . . . don't do it for me . . . it's not fair!"

Paul's unicorn turned his head and looked at us.

My friend of starless nights, when we had gone sailing together through the darkness. My friend who had walked with me on endless tours of empty places. My friend of gentle nature and constant companionship. Until Lizette, my friend, my only friend, my familiar assigned to an onerous task, who had come to love me and to whom I had belonged, even as he had belonged to me.

I could not bear the hurt that grew in my chest, in my stomach; my head was on fire, my eyes burned with tears first for Paul, and now for the sweetest creature a god had ever sent to temper a man's anguish . . . and for myself. I could not bear the thought of never knowing—as Paul had known it—the silent company of that gentle, magical beast.

But he turned back, and moved to them, and they took that as final decision, and the great transparent claimers moved in around him, and their quickglass hands reached down to touch him, and for an instant they seemed to hesitate, and I called out, "Don't be afraid . . ." and my unicorn turned his head to look across the mist of potency for the last time, and I saw he *was* afraid, but not as much as he would have been if I had not been there.

Then the first of them touched his smooth, silvery flank and he gave a trembling sigh of pain. A ripple ran down his hide. Not the quick flesh movement of ridding himself of a fly, but a completely alien, unnatural tremor, containing in its swiftness all the agony and loss of eternities. A sigh went out from Paul's unicorn, though he had not uttered it.

We could feel the pain, the loneliness. My unicorn with no time left to him. Ending. All was now a final ending; he had stayed with me, walked with me, and had grown to care for me, until that time when he would be released from his duty by that special God; but now freedom was to be denied him; an ending.

The great transparent claimers all touched him, their ice fingers caressing his warm hide as we watched, helpless, Lizette's face buried in Paul's chest. Colors surged across my unicorn's body, as if by becoming more intense the chill touch of the claimers could be beaten off. Pulsing waves of rainbow color that lived in his hide for moments, then dimmed, brightened again and were bled off. Then the colors leaked away one by one, chroma weakening: purple-blue, manganese violet, discord, cobalt blue, doubt, affection, chrome green, chrome yellow, raw sienna, contemplation, alizarin crimson, irony, silver, severity, compassion, cadmium red, white.

They emptied him . . . he did not fight them . . . going colder and colder . . . flickers of yellow, a whisper of blue, pale as white . . . the tremors blending into one constant shudder . . . the wonderful golden eyes rolled in torment, went flat, brightness dulled, flat metal . . . the platinum hoofs caked with rust . . . and he stood, did not try to escape, gave himself for us . . . and he was emptied. Of everything.

Then, like the claimers, we could see through him. Vapors swirled within the transparent husk, a fogged glass, shimmering . . . then nothing. And then they absorbed even the husk.

The chill blue light faded, and the claimers grew indistinct in our sight. The smoke within them seemed thicker, moved more slowly, horribly, as though they had fed and were sluggish and would go away, back across the line to that dark place where they waited, always waited, till their hunger was aroused again. And my unicorn was gone. I was alone with Lizette. I was alone with Paul. The mist died away, and the claimers were gone, and once more it was merely a cemetery as the first rays of the morning sun came easing through the tumble and disarray of headstones.

We stood together as one, her naked body white and virginal in my weary arms; and as the light of the sun struck us we began to fade, to merge, to mingle our bodies and our wandering spirits one into the other, forming one spirit that would neither love too much, nor too little, having taken our chance on the downhill side.

We faded and were lifted invisibly on the scented breath of that good God who had owned us, and were taken away from there. To be born again as one spirit, in some other human form, man or woman we did not know which. Nor would we remember. Nor did it matter.

This time, love would not destroy us. This time out, we would have luck.

The luck of silken mane and rainbow colors and platinum hoofs and spiral horn.

This is another story bought through the Virginia Kidd Literary Agency—the first story bought for *Universe 5*. It was the only story by Le Guin in *Universe,* but not because I don't like her work. I had published *The Left Hand of Darkness* when I worked for Ace Books in 1969 and it immediately became a bestseller; after that, Le Guin stories were at a premium, and hard to get. This one shows why: based on the famous physics problem, it's a thoughtful and very funny story of the world falling into uncertainty.

Schrödinger's Cat

Ursula K. Le Guin

As things appear to be coming to some sort of climax, I have withdrawn to this place. It is cooler here, and nothing moves fast.

On the way here I met a married couple who were coming apart. She had pretty well gone to pieces, but he seemed, at first glance, quite hearty. While he was telling me that he had no hormones of any kind, she pulled herself together, and by supporting her head in the crook of her right knee and hopping on the toes of the right foot, approached us shouting, "Well, what's *wrong* with a person trying to express themselves?" The left leg, the arms and the trunk, which had remained lying in the heap, twitched and jerked in sympathy.

"Great legs," the husband pointed out, looking at the slim ankle. "My wife has great legs."

A cat has arrived, interrupting my narrative. It is a striped yellow tom with white chest and paws. He has long whiskers and yellow eyes. I never noticed before that cats had whiskers above their eyes; is that normal? There is no way to tell. As he has gone to sleep on my knee, I shall proceed.

Where?

Nowhere, evidently. Yet the impulse to narrate remains. Many things are not worth doing, but almost anything is worth telling. In any case, I have a severe congenital case of Ethica laboris puritanica, or Adam's Disease. It is incurable except by total decephalization. I even like to dream when asleep, and to try and recall my dreams: it assures me that I haven't wasted seven or eight hours just lying there. Now here I am, lying, here. Hard at it.

Well, the couple I was telling you about finally broke up. The pieces of him trotted around bouncing and cheeping, like little chicks, but she was finally reduced to nothing but a mass of nerves: rather like fine chicken-wire, in fact, but hopelessly tangled.

So I came on, placing one foot carefully in front of the other, and grieving. This grief is with me still. I fear it is part of me, like foot or loin or eye, or may even be myself: for I seem to have no other self, nothing further, nothing that lies outside the borders of grief.

Yet I don't know what I grieve for: my wife? my husband? my children, or myself? I can't remember. Most dreams are forgotten, try as one will to remember. Yet later music strikes the note and the harmonic rings along the mandolin-strings of the mind, and we find tears in our eyes. Some note keeps playing that makes me want to cry; but what for? I am not certain.

The yellow cat, who may have belonged to the couple that broke up, is dreaming. His paws twitch now and then, and once he makes a small, suppressed remark with his mouth shut. I wonder what a cat dreams of, and to whom he was speaking just then. Cats seldom waste words. They are quiet beasts. They keep their counsel, they reflect. They reflect all day, and at night their eyes reflect. Overbred Siamese cats may be as noisy as little dogs, and then people say, "They're talking," but the noise is further from speech than is the deep silence of the hound or the tabby. All this cat can say is meow, but maybe in his silences he will suggest to me what it is that I have lost, what I am grieving for. I have a feeling that he knows. That's why he came here. Cats look out for Number One.

It was getting awfully hot. I mean, you could touch less and less. The stove-burners, for instance; now, I know that stove-burners always used to get hot, that was their final cause, they existed in order to get hot. But they began to get hot without having been turned on. Electric units or gas rings, there they'd be when you came into the kitchen for breakfast, all four of them glaring away, the air above them shaking like clear jelly with the heat waves. It did no good to turn them off, because they weren't on in the first place. Besides, the knobs and dials were also hot, uncomfortable to the touch.

Some people tried hard to cool them off. The favorite technique was to turn them on. It worked sometimes, but you could not count on it. Others investigated the phenomenon, tried to get at the root of it, the cause. They were probably the most frightened ones, but man is most human at his most frightened. In the face of the hot stove-burners they acted with exemplary coolness. They studied, they observed. They were like the fellow in Michelangelo's "Last Judgment" who has clapped his hands over his face in horror as the devils drag him down to Hell—but only over one eye. The other eye is busy looking. It's all he can do, but he does it. He observes. Indeed, one wonders if Hell would exist if he did not look at it. However, neither he nor the people I am talking about had enough time left to do much about it. And then finally of course there were the people who did not try to do or think anything about it at all.

When hot water came out of the cold-water taps one morning, however, even people who had blamed it all on the Democrats began to feel a more profound unease. Before long, forks and pencils and wrenches were too hot to handle without gloves; and cars were really terrible. It was like opening the door of an oven going full blast, to open the door of your car. And by then, other people almost scorched your fingers off. A kiss was like a branding iron. Your child's hair flowed along your hand like fire.

Here, as I said, it is cooler; and, as a matter of fact, this animal is cool. A real cool cat. No wonder it's pleasant to pet his fur. Also he moves slowly, at least for the most part, which is all the slowness one can reasonably expect of a cat. He hasn't that frenetic quality most creatures acquired—all they did was ZAP and gone. They lacked presence. I suppose birds always tended to be that way, but even the hummingbird used to halt for a second in the very center of his metabolic frenzy, and hang, still as a hub, present, above the fuchsias—then gone again, but you knew something was there besides the blurring brightness. But it got so that even robins and pigeons, the heavy impudent birds, were a blur; and as for swallows, they cracked the sound barrier. You knew of swallows only by the small, curved sonic booms that looped about the eaves of old houses in the evening.

Worms shot like subway trains through the dirt of gardens, among the writhing roots of roses.

You could scarcely lay a hand on children, by then: too fast to catch, too hot to hold. They grew up before your eyes.

But then, maybe that's always been true.

I was interrupted by the cat, who woke and said meow once, then jumped down from my lap and leaned against my legs diligently. This is a cat who knows how to get fed. He also knows how to jump. There was a lazy fluidity to his leap, as if gravity affected him less than it does other creatures. As a matter of fact there were some localized cases, just before I left, of the failure of gravity; but this quality in the cat's leap was something quite else. I am not yet in such a state of confusion that I can be alarmed by grace. Indeed, I found it reassuring. While I was opening a can of sardines, a person arrived.

Hearing the knock, I thought it might be the mailman. I miss mail very much, so I hurried to the door and said, "Is it the mail?" A voice replied, "Yah!" I opened the door. He came in, almost pushing me aside in his haste. He dumped down an enormous knapsack he had been carrying, straightened up, massaged his shoulders, and said, "Wow!"

"How did you get here?"

He stared at me and repeated, "How?"

At this, my thoughts concerning human and animal speech recurred to me, and I decided that this was probably not a man, but a small dog. (Large dogs seldom go yah, wow, how, unless it is appropriate to do so.) "Come on, fella," I coaxed him. "Come, come on, that's a boy, good doggie!" I opened a can of pork and beans for him at once, for he looked half-starved. He ate voraciously, gulping and lapping. When it was gone he said "Wow!" several times. I was just about to scratch him behind the ears when he stiffened, his hackles bristling, and growled deep in his throat. He had noticed the cat.

The cat had noticed him some time before, without interest, and was now sitting on a copy of *The Well-Tempered Clavichord* washing sardine oil off its whiskers.

"Wow!" the dog, whom I had thought of calling Rover, barked. "Wow! Do you know what that is? *That's Schrödinger's cat!*"

"No, it's not; not any more; it's my cat," I said, unreasonably offended.

"Oh, well, Schrödinger's dead, of course, but it's his cat. I've seen hundreds of pictures of it. Erwin Schrödinger, the great physicist, you know. Oh, wow! To think of finding it here!"

The cat looked coldly at him for a moment, and began to wash its left shoulder with negligent energy. An almost religious expression had come into Rover's face. "It was meant," he said in a low, impressive tone. "Yah. It was *meant.* It can't be a mere coincidence. It's too improbable. Me, with the box; you, with the cat; to meet—here—now." He looked up at me, his eyes shining with happy fervor. "Isn't it wonderful?" he said. "I'll get the box set up right away." And he started to tear open his huge knapsack.

While the cat washed its front paws, Rover unpacked. While the cat washed its tail and belly, regions hard to reach gracefully, Rover put together what he had unpacked, a complex task. When he and the cat finished their operations simultaneously and looked at me, I was impressed. They had come out even, to the very second. Indeed it seemed that something more than chance was involved. I hoped it was not myself.

"What's that?" I asked, pointing to a protuberance on the outside of the box. I did not ask what the box was, as it was quite clearly a box.

"The gun," Rover said with excited pride.

"The gun?"

"To shoot the cat."

"To shoot the cat?"

"Or to *not shoot* the cat. Depending on the photon."

"The photon?"

"Yeah! It's Schrödinger's great *Gedankenexperiment.* You see, there's a little emitter here. At Zero Time, five seconds after the lid of a box is closed, it will emit one photon. The photon will strike a half-silvered mirror. The quantum mechanical probability of the photon passing through the mirror is exactly one-half, isn't it? So! If the photon passes through, the trigger will be activated and the gun will fire. If the photon is deflected, the trigger will not be activated and the gun will not fire. Now, you put the cat in. The cat is in the box. You close the lid. You go away! You stay away! What happens?" Rover's eyes were bright.

"The cat gets hungry?"

"The cat gets shot—or not shot," he said, seizing my arm, though not, fortunately, in his teeth. "But the gun is silent, perfectly silent. The box is soundproof. There is no way to know whether or not the cat has been shot until you lift the lid of the box. There is NO way! Do you see how central this is to the whole of quantum theory? Before Zero Time the whole system, on the quantum level or on our level, is nice and simple. But after Zero Time the whole system can be represented only by a linear combination of two waves. We cannot predict the behavior of the photon, and thus, once it has behaved, we cannot predict the state of the system it has determined. We cannot predict it! God plays dice with the world! So it is beautifully demonstrated that if you desire certainty, any certainty, you must create it yourself!"

"How?"

"By lifting the lid of the box, of course," Rover said, looking at me with sudden disappointment, perhaps a touch of suspicion, like a Baptist who finds he has been talking church matters not to another Baptist as he thought, but to a Methodist, or even, God forbid, an Episcopalian. "To find out whether the cat is dead or not."

"Do you mean," I said carefully, "that until you lift the lid of the box, the cat has neither been shot nor not been shot?"

"Yah!" Rover said, radiant with relief, welcoming me back to the fold. "Or maybe, you know, both."

"But why does opening the box and looking reduce the system back to one probability, either live cat or dead cat? Why don't we get included in the system when we lift the lid of the box?"

There was a pause. "How?" Rover barked distrustfully.

"Well, we would involve ourselves in the system, you see, the superposition of two waves. There's no reason why it should only exist *inside* an open box, is there? So when we came to look, there we would be, you and I, both looking at a live cat, and both looking at a dead cat. You see?"

A dark cloud lowered on Rover's eyes and brow. He barked twice in a subdued, harsh voice, and walked away. With his back turned to me he said in a firm, sad tone, "You must not complicate the issue. It is complicated enough."

"Are you sure?"

He nodded. Turning, he spoke pleadingly. "Listen. It's all we have—the box. Truly it is. The box. And the cat. And they're here. The box, the cat, at last. Put the cat in the box. Will you? Will you let me put the cat in the box?"

"No," I said, shocked.

"Please. Please. Just for a minute. Just for half a minute! Please let me put the cat in the box!"

"Why?"

"I can't stand this terrible uncertainty," he said, and burst into tears.

I stood some while indecisive. Though I felt sorry for the poor son of a bitch, I was about to tell him, gently, No, when a curious thing happened. The cat walked over to the box, sniffed around it, lifted his tail and sprayed a corner to mark his territory, and then lightly, with that marvelous fluid ease, leapt into it. His yellow tail just flicked the edge of the lid as he jumped, and it closed, falling into place with a soft, decisive click.

"The cat is in the box," I said.

"The cat is in the box," Rover repeated in a whisper, falling to his knees. "Oh, wow. Oh, wow. Oh, wow."

There was silence then: deep silence. We both gazed, I afoot, Rover kneeling, at the box. No sound. Nothing happened. Nothing would happen. Nothing would ever happen, until we lifted the lid of the box.

"Like Pandora," I said in a weak whisper. I could not quite recall Pandora's legend. She had let all the plagues and evils out of the box, of course, but there had been something else, too. After all the devils were let loose, something quite different, quite unexpected, had been left. What had it been? Hope? A dead cat? I could not remember.

Impatience welled up in me. I turned on Rover, glaring. He returned the look with expressive brown eyes. You can't tell me dogs haven't got souls.

"Just exactly what are you trying to prove?" I demanded.

"That the cat will be dead, or not dead," he murmured submissively. "Certainty. All I want is certainty. To know for *sure* that God *does* play dice with the world."

I looked at him for a while with fascinated incredulity. "Whether he does, or doesn't," I said, "do you think he's going to leave you a note about it in the box?" I went to the box, and with a rather dramatic gesture, flung the lid back. Rover staggered up from his knees, gasping, to look. The cat was, of course, not there.

Rover neither barked, nor fainted, nor cursed, nor wept. He really took it very well.

"Where is the cat?" he asked at last.

"Where is the box?"

"Here."

"Where's here?"

"Here is now."

"We used to think so," I said, "but really we should use larger boxes."

He gazed about him in mute bewilderment, and did not flinch even when the roof of the house was lifted off just like the lid of a box, letting in the unconscionable, inordinate light of the stars. He had just time to breathe, "Oh, wow!"

I have identified the note that keeps sounding. I checked it on the mandolin before the glue melted. It is the note A, the one that drove Robert Schumann mad. It is a beautiful, clear tone, much clearer now that the stars are visible. I shall miss the cat. I wonder if he found what it was we lost?

This story has a curious history. In 1970 Gene Wolfe published a short story titled "The Island of Doctor Death and Other Stories" in Damon Knight's *Orbit;* it was an excellent story and was nominated for the 1970 Nebula Award. At that year's Nebula Banquet, Isaac Asimov announced Wolfe's story as the winner—but when Wolfe was halfway to the dais to accept the award, Asimov suddenly said, "Oh no! I'm sorry —the winner is No Award!"

Wolfe retreated to his seat, probably no more embarrassed than everyone else in the room, especially Asimov, who later said that he'd seen "No Award" listed as the verdict on the list but had thought it must be some kind of joke, so he'd announced the title right under it. (No Award is always a possible choice on the Nebula ballot, in case the voters feel that no story was sufficiently outstanding to deserve a Nebula, but in the seventeen-year history of the Nebulas this was the only time No Award "won." Indeed, several voters that year later said they'd marked No Award thinking it simply indicated an abstention, so Wolfe's story, which received more votes than any other nominee, really should have won the award.)

Shortly after that Nebula Banquet, Wolfe says, "I went down to Madison to see Joe Hensley, and Joe said that everybody felt so sorry for me that if I wrote a story called 'The Death of Doctor Island' it would probably win. He thought of this—I feel sure—as a nonsense title, and so, at the time, did I. But it stuck in my mind: if you just called one of the characters 'Dr. Island,' that would only be a kind of swindle; the only way to make the title legitimate would be to make the name meaningful. So how about a whole island that *was* a doctor? It also seemed to me that if I was going to invert the title I would have to invert the tale too. In 'Doctor Death' Dr. Death himself is a heroic villain in the tradition of Long John Silver; he is kind, in an attractively sinister way. Dr. Island, then, would be a smarmy hypocrite, and genuinely deadly. In 'Doctor Death' Tackie's world is split—reality and fantasy. So I split Nicholas himself by dividing the hemispheres of his brain. And so on . . . Naturally the parallels are not perfect everywhere—I was trying to tell a good story, not to produce a literary curiosity."

Since Damon Knight had published the first story, Wolfe sent "The

Death of Doctor Island" to him. "I can truthfully say that I have never
sent Damon anything with more confidence—it was a real shock when
he turned it down."

Which was how I got the story for *Universe*. I loved it, and after a few
revisions in the ending I bought it. It won the Nebula Award, de-
servedly, for this is a fascinating tale of people in an artificial environment orbiting Jupiter. Wolfe later wrote a third story in the "series,"
"The Doctor of Death Island"; these three formed the basis for his
collection *The Island of Doctor Death and Other Stories and Other Stories.*

The Death of Doctor Island

Gene Wolfe

> I have desired to go
>> Where springs not fail,
> To fields where flies no sharp and sided hail
>> And a few lilies blow.
>
> And I have asked to be
>> Where no storms come,
> Where the green swell is in the havens dumb,
>> And out of the swing of the sea.
>> —Gerard Manley Hopkins

A grain of sand, teetering on the brink of the pit, trembled and fell in;
the ant lion at the bottom angrily flung it out again. For a moment there
was quiet. Then the entire pit, and a square meter of sand around it,
shifted drunkenly while two coconut palms bent to watch. The sand
rose, pivoting at one edge, and the scarred head of a boy appeared—a
stubble of brown hair threatened to erase the marks of the sutures; with

dilated eyes hypnotically dark he paused, his neck just where the ant lion's had been; then, as though goaded from below, he vaulted up and onto the beach, turned, and kicked sand into the dark hatchway from which he had emerged. It slammed shut. The boy was about fourteen.

For a time he squatted, pushing the sand aside and trying to find the door. A few centimeters down, his hands met a gritty, solid material which, though neither concrete nor sandstone, shared the qualities of both—a sand-filled organic plastic. On it he scraped his fingers raw, but he could not locate the edges of the hatch.

Then he stood and looked about him, his head moving continually as the heads of certain reptiles do—back and forth, with no pauses at the terminations of the movements. He did this constantly, ceaselessly—always—and for that reason it will not often be described again, just as it will not be mentioned that he breathed. He did; and as he did, his head, like a rearing snake's, turned from side to side. The boy was thin, and naked as a frog.

Ahead of him the sand sloped gently down toward sapphire water; there were coconuts on the beach, and sea shells, and a scuttling crab that played with the finger-high edge of each dying wave. Behind him there were only palms and sand for a long distance, the palms growing ever closer together as they moved away from the water until the forest of their columniated trunks seemed architectural; like some palace maze becoming as it progressed more and more draped with creepers and lianas with green, scarlet and yellow leaves, the palms interspersed with bamboo and deciduous trees dotted with flaming orchids until almost at the limit of his sight the whole ended in a spangled wall whose predominant color was black-green.

The boy walked toward the beach, then down the beach until he stood in knee-deep water as warm as blood. He dipped his fingers and tasted it—it was fresh, with no hint of the disinfectants to which he was accustomed. He waded out again and sat on the sand about five meters up from the high-water mark, and after ten minutes, during which he heard no sound but the wind and the murmuring of the surf, he threw back his head and began to scream. His screaming was high-pitched, and each breath ended in a gibbering, ululant note, after which came the hollow, iron gasp of the next indrawn breath. On one occasion he had screamed in this way, without cessation, for fourteen hours and twenty-two minutes, at the end of which a nursing nun with an exemplary record stretching back seventeen years had administered an injection without the permission of the attending physician.

After a time the boy paused—not because he was tired, but in order to listen better. There was, still, only the sound of the wind in the palm fronds and the murmuring surf, yet he felt that he had heard a voice. The boy could be quiet as well as noisy, and he was quiet now, his left hand sifting white sand as clean as salt between its fingers while his right tossed tiny pebbles like beachglass beads into the surf.

"Hear me," said the surf. *"Hear me. Hear me."*

"I hear you," the boy said.

"Good," said the surf, and it faintly echoed itself: *"Good, good, good."*

The boy shrugged.

"What shall I call you?" asked surf.

"My name is Nicholas Kenneth de Vore."

"Nick, *Nick . . . Nick?"*

The boy stood, and turning his back on the sea, walked inland. When he was out of sight of the water he found a coconut palm growing sloped and angled, leaning and weaving among its companions like the plume of an ascending jet blown by the wind. After feeling its rough exterior with both hands, the boy began to climb; he was inexpert and climbed slowly and a little clumsily, but his body was light and he was strong. In time he reached the top, and disturbed the little brown plush monkeys there, who fled chattering into other palms, leaving him to nestle alone among the stems of the fronds and the green coconuts. "I am here also," said a voice from the palm.

"Ah," said the boy, who was watching the tossing, sapphire sky far over his head.

"I will call you Nicholas."

The boy said, "I can see the sea."

"Do you know my name?"

The boy did not reply. Under him the long, long stem of the twisted palm swayed faintly.

"My friends all call me Dr. Island."

"I will not call you that," the boy said.

"You mean that you are not my friend."

A gull screamed.

"But you see, I take you for my friend. You may say that I am not yours, but I say that you are mine. I like you, Nicholas, and I will treat you as a friend."

"Are you a machine or a person or a committee?" the boy asked.

"I am all those things and more. I am the spirit of this island, the tutelary genius."

"Bullshit."

"Now that we have met, would you rather I leave you alone?"

Again the boy did not reply.

"You may wish to be alone with your thoughts. I would like to say that we have made much more progress today than I anticipated. I feel that we will get along together very well."

After fifteen minutes or more, the boy asked, "Where does the light come from?" There was no answer. The boy waited for a time, then climbed back down the trunk, dropping the last five meters and rolling as he hit in the soft sand.

He walked to the beach again and stood staring out at the water. Far off he could see it curving up and up, the distant combers breaking in white foam until the sea became white-flecked sky. To his left and his right the beach curved away, bending almost infinitesimally until it disappeared. He began to walk, then saw, almost at the point where perception was lost, a human figure. He broke into a run; a moment later, he halted and turned around. Far ahead another walker, almost invisible, strode the beach; Nicholas ignored him; he found a coconut and tried to open it, then threw it aside and walked on. From time to time fish jumped, and occasionally he saw a wheeling sea bird dive. The light grew dimmer. He was aware that he had not eaten for some time, but he was not in the strict sense hungry—or rather, he enjoyed his hunger now in the same way that he might, at another time, have gashed his arm to watch himself bleed. Once he said, "Dr. Island!" loudly as he passed a coconut palm, and then later began to chant "Dr. Island, Dr. Island, Dr. Island" as he walked until the words had lost all meaning. He swam in the sea as he had been taught to swim in the great quartanary treatment tanks on Callisto to improve his coordination, and spluttered and snorted until he learned to deal with the waves. When it was so dark he could see only the white sand and the white foam of the breakers, he drank from the sea and fell asleep on the beach, the right side of his taut, ugly face relaxing first, so that it seemed asleep even while the left eye was open and staring; his head rolling from side to side; the left corner of his mouth preserving, like a death mask, his characteristic expression—angry, remote, tinged with that inhuman quality which is found nowhere but in certain human faces.

When he woke it was not yet light, but the night was fading to a gentle gray. Headless, the palms stood like tall ghosts up and down the beach, their tops lost in fog and the lingering dark. He was cold. His hands rubbed his sides; he danced on the sand and sprinted down the edge of the lapping water in an effort to get warm; ahead of him a pinpoint of red light became a fire, and he slowed.

A man who looked about twenty-five crouched over the fire. Tangled black hair hung over this man's shoulders, and he had a sparse beard; otherwise he was as naked as Nicholas himself. His eyes were dark, and large and empty, like the ends of broken pipes; he poked at his fire, and the smell of roasting fish came with the smoke. For a time Nicholas stood at a distance, watching.

Saliva ran from a corner of the man's mouth, and he wiped it away with one hand, leaving a smear of ash on his face. Nicholas edged closer until he stood on the opposite side of the fire. The fish had been wrapped in broad leaves and mud, and lay in the center of the coals. "I'm Nicholas," Nicholas said. "Who are you?" The young man did not look at him, had never looked at him.

"Hey, I'd like a piece of your fish. Not much. All right?"

The young man raised his head, looking not at Nicholas but at some point far beyond him; he dropped his eyes again. Nicholas smiled. The smile emphasized the disjointed quality of his expression, his mouth's uneven curve.

"Just a little piece? Is it about done?" Nicholas crouched, imitating the young man, and as though this were a signal, the young man sprang for him across the fire. Nicholas jumped backward, but the jump was too late—the young man's body struck his and sent him sprawling on the sand; fingers clawed for his throat. Screaming, Nicholas rolled free, into the water; the young man splashed after him; Nicholas dove.

He swam underwater, his belly almost grazing the wave-rippled sand until he found deeper water; then he surfaced, gasping for breath, and saw the young man, who saw him as well. He dove again, this time surfacing far off, in deep water. Treading water, he could see the fire on the beach, and the young man when he returned to it, stamping out of the sea in the early light. Nicholas then swam until he was five hundred meters or more down the beach, then waded in to shore and began walking back toward the fire.

The young man saw him when he was still some distance off, but he continued to sit, eating pink-tinted tidbits from his fish, watching

Nicholas. "What's the matter?" Nicholas said while he was still a safe distance away. "Are you mad at me?"

From the forest, birds warned, "Be careful, Nicholas."

"I won't hurt you," the young man said. He stood up, wiping his oily hands on his chest, and gestured toward the fish at his feet. "You want some?"

Nicholas nodded, smiling his crippled smile.

"Come then."

Nicholas waited, hoping the young man would move away from the fish, but he did not; neither did he smile in return.

"Nicholas," the little waves at his feet whispered, "this is Ignacio."

"Listen," Nicholas said, "is it really all right for me to have some?"

Ignacio nodded, unsmiling.

Cautiously Nicholas came forward; as he was bending to pick up the fish, Ignacio's strong hands took him; he tried to wrench free but was thrown down, Ignacio on top of him. "Please!" he yelled. "Please!" Tears started into his eyes. He tried to yell again, but he had no breath; the tongue was being forced, thicker than his wrist, from his throat.

Then Ignacio let go and struck him in the face with his clenched fist. Nicholas had been slapped and pummeled before, had been beaten, had fought, sometimes savagely, with other boys; but he had never been struck by a man as men fight. Ignacio hit him again and his lips gushed blood.

He lay a long time on the sand beside the dying fire. Consciousness returned slowly; he blinked, drifted back into the dark, blinked again. His mouth was full of blood, and when at last he spit it out onto the sand, it seemed a soft flesh, dark and polymerized in strange shapes; his left cheek was hugely swollen, and he could scarcely see out of his left eye. After a time he crawled to the water; a long time after that, he left it and walked shakily back to the ashes of the fire. Ignacio was gone, and there was nothing left of the fish but bones.

"Ignacio is gone," Dr. Island said with lips of waves.

Nicholas sat on the sand, cross-legged.

"You handled him very well."

"You saw us fight?"

"I saw you; I see everything, Nicholas."

"This is the worst place," Nicholas said; he was talking to his lap.

"What do you mean by that?"

"I've been in bad places before—places where they hit you or squirted big hoses of ice water that knocked you down. But not where they would let someone else—"

"Another patient?" asked a wheeling gull.

"—do it."

"You were lucky, Nicholas. Ignacio is homicidal."

"You could have stopped him."

"No, I could not. All this world is my eye, Nicholas, my ear and my tongue; but I have no hands."

"I thought you did all this."

"Men did all this."

"I mean, I thought you kept it going."

"It keeps itself going, and you—all the people here—direct it."

Nicholas looked at the water. "What makes the waves?"

"The wind and the tide."

"Are we on Earth?"

"Would you feel more comfortable on Earth?"

"I've never been there; I'd like to know."

"I am more like Earth than Earth now is, Nicholas. If you were to take the best of all the best beaches of Earth, and clear them of all the poisons and all the dirt of the last three centuries, you would have me."

"But this isn't Earth?"

There was no answer. Nicholas walked around the ashes of the fire until he found Ignacio's footprints. He was no tracker, but the depressions in the soft beach sand required none; he followed them, his head swaying from side to side as he walked, like the sensor of a mine detector.

For several kilometers Ignacio's trail kept to the beach; then, abruptly, the footprints swerved, wandered among the coconut palms, and at last were lost on the firmer soil inland. Nicholas lifted his head and shouted, "Ignacio? Ignacio!" After a moment he heard a stick snap, and the sound of someone pushing aside leafy branches. He waited.

"Mum?"

A girl was coming toward him, stepping out of the thicker growth of the interior. She was pretty, though too thin, and appeared to be about nineteen; her hair was blond where it had been most exposed to sunlight, darker elsewhere. "You've scratched yourself," Nicholas said. "You're bleeding."

"I thought you were my mother," the girl said. She was a head taller than Nicholas. "Been fighting, haven't you. Have you come to get me?"

Nicholas had been in similar conversations before and normally would have preferred to ignore the remark, but he was lonely now. He said, "Do you want to go home?"

"Well, I think I should, you know."

"But do you want to?"

"My mum always says if you've got something on the stove you don't want to burn—she's quite a good cook. She really is. Do you like cabbage with bacon?"

"Have you got anything to eat?"

"Not now. I had a thing a while ago."

"What kind of thing?"

"A bird." The girl made a vague little gesture, not looking at Nicholas. "I'm a memory that has swallowed a bird."

"Do you want to walk down by the water?" They were moving in the direction of the beach already.

"I was just going to get a drink. You're a nice tot."

Nicholas did not like being called a "tot." He said, "I set fire to places."

"You won't set fire to this place; it's been nice the last couple of days, but when everyone is sad, it rains."

Nicholas was silent for a time. When they reached the sea, the girl dropped to her knees and bent forward to drink, her long hair falling over her face until the ends trailed in the water, her nipples, then half of each breast, in the water. "Not there," Nicholas said. "It's sandy, because it washes the beach so close. Come on out here." He waded out into the sea until the lapping waves nearly reached his armpits, then bent his head and drank.

"I never thought of that," the girl said. "Mum says I'm stupid. So does Dad. Do you think I'm stupid?"

Nicholas shook his head.

"What's your name?"

"Nicholas Kenneth de Vore. What's yours?"

"Diane. I'm going to call you Nicky. Do you mind?"

"I'll hurt you while you sleep," Nicholas said.

"You wouldn't."

"Yes I would. At St. John's where I used to be, it was zero G most of the time, and a girl there called me something I didn't like, and I got loose one night and came into her cubical while she was asleep and nulled her restraints, and then she floated around until she banged into something, and that woke her up and she tried to grab, and then that made her bounce all around inside and she broke two fingers and her nose and got blood all over. The attendants came, and one told me— they didn't know then I did it—when he came out his white suit was, like, polka-dot red all over because wherever the blood drops had touched him they soaked right in."

The girl smiled at him, dimpling her thin face. "How did they find out it was you?"

"I told someone and he told them."

"I bet you told them yourself."

"I bet I didn't!" Angry, he waded away, but when he had stalked a short way up the beach he sat down on the sand, his back toward her.

"I didn't mean to make you mad, Mr. de Vore."

"I'm not mad!"

She was not sure for a moment what he meant. She sat down beside and a trifle behind him, and began idly piling sand in her lap.

Dr. Island said, "I see you've met."

Nicholas turned, looking for the voice. "I thought you saw everything."

"Only the important things, and I have been busy on another part of myself. I am happy to see that you two know one another; do you find you interact well?"

Neither of them answered.

"You should be interacting with Ignacio; he needs you."

"We can't find him," Nicholas said.

"Down the beach to your left until you see the big stone, then turn inland. About five hundred meters."

Nicholas stood up, and turning to his right, began to walk away. Diane followed him, trotting until she caught up.

"I don't like," Nicholas said, jerking a shoulder to indicate something behind him.

"Ignacio?"

"The doctor."

"Why do you move your head like that?"

"Didn't they tell you?"

"No one told me anything about you."

"They opened it up"—Nicholas touched his scars—"and took this knife and cut all the way through my corpus . . . corpus . . ."

"Corpus callosum," muttered a dry palm frond.

"—corpus callosum," finished Nicholas. "See, your brain is like a walnut inside. There are the two halves, and then right down in the middle a kind of thick connection of meat from one to the other. Well, they cut that."

"You're having a bit of fun with me, aren't you?"

"No, he isn't," a monkey who had come to the water line to look for shellfish told her. "His cerebrum has been surgically divided; it's in his file." It was a young monkey, with a trusting face full of small, ugly beauties.

Nicholas snapped, "It's in my head."

Diane said, "I'd think it would kill you, or make you an idiot or something."

"They say each half of me is about as smart as both of us were together. Anyway, this half is . . . the half . . . the *me* that talks."

"There are two of you now?"

"If you cut a worm in half and both parts are still alive, that's two, isn't it? What else would you call us? We can't ever come together again."

"But I'm talking to just one of you?"

"We both can hear you."

"Which one answers?"

Nicholas touched the right side of his chest with his right hand. "Me; I do. They told me it was the left side of my brain, that one has the speech centers, but it doesn't feel that way; the nerves cross over coming out, and it's just the right side of me, I talk. Both my ears hear for both of us, but out of each eye we only see half and half—I mean, I only see what's on the right of what I'm looking at, and the other side, I guess, only sees the left, so that's why I keep moving my head. I guess it's like being a little bit blind; you get used to it."

The girl was still thinking of his divided body. She said, "If you're only half, I don't see how you can walk."

"I can move the left side a little bit, and we're not mad at each other. We're not supposed to be able to come together at all, but we do: down through the legs and at the ends of the fingers and then back up. Only I can't talk with my other side because he can't, but he understands."

"Why did they do it?"

Behind them the monkey, who had been following them, said, "He had uncontrollable seizures."

"Did you?" the girl asked. She was watching a sea bird swooping low over the water and did not seem to care.

Nicholas picked up a shell and shied it at the monkey, who skipped out of the way. After half a minute's silence he said, "I had visions."

"Ooh, did you?"

"They didn't like that. They said I would fall down and jerk around horrible, and sometimes I guess I would hurt myself when I fell, and sometimes I'd bite my tongue and it would bleed. But that wasn't what it felt like to me; I wouldn't know about any of those things until afterward. To me it was like I had gone way far ahead, and I had to come back. I didn't want to."

The wind swayed Diane's hair, and she pushed it back from her face. "Did you see things that were going to happen?" she asked.

"Sometimes."

"Really? Did you?"

"Sometimes."

"Tell me about it. When you saw what was going to happen."

"I saw myself dead. I was all black and shrunk up like the dead stuff they cut off in the 'pontic gardens; and I was floating and turning, like in water but it wasn't water—just floating and turning out in space, in nothing. And there were lights on both sides of me, so both sides were bright but black, and I could see my teeth because the stuff"—he pulled at his cheeks—"had fallen off there, and they were really white."

"That hasn't happened yet."

"Not here."

"Tell me something you saw that happened."

"You mean, like somebody's sister was going to get married, don't you? That's what the girls where I was mostly wanted to know. Or were they going to go home; mostly it wasn't like that."

"But sometimes it was?"

"I guess."

"Tell me one."

Nicholas shook his head. "You wouldn't like it, and anyway it wasn't like that. Mostly it was lights like I never saw anyplace else, and voices like I never heard any other time, telling me things there aren't any words for; stuff like that, only now I can't ever go back. Listen, I wanted to ask you about Ignacio."

"He isn't anybody," the girl said.

"What do you mean, he isn't anybody? Is there anybody here besides you and me and Ignacio and Dr. Island?"

"Not that we can see or touch."

The monkey called, "There are other patients, but for the present, Nicholas, for your own well-being as well as theirs, it is best for you to remain by yourselves." It was a long sentence for a monkey.

"What's that about?"

"If I tell you, will you tell me about something you saw that really happened?"

"All right."

"Tell me first."

"There was this girl where I was—her name was Maya. They had, you know, boys' and girls' dorms, but you saw everybody in the rec room and the dining hall and so on, and she was in my psychodrama group." Her hair had been black, and shiny as the lacquered furniture in Dr. Hong's rooms, her skin white like the mother-of-pearl, her eyes long and narrow (making him think of cats' eyes) and darkly blue. She was fifteen, or so Nicholas believed—maybe sixteen. *"I'm going home,"* she told him. It was psychodrama, and he was her brother, younger than she, and she was already at home; but when she said this the floating ring of light that gave them the necessary separation from the small doctor-and-patient audience, ceased, by instant agreement, to be Maya's mother's living room and became a visiting lounge. Nicholas/Jerry said: "Hey, that's great! Hey, I got a new bike—when you come home you want to ride it?"

Maureen/Maya's mother said, "Maya, don't. You'll run into something and break your teeth, and you know how much they cost."

"You don't want me to have any fun."

"We do, dear, but *nice* fun. A girl has to be so much more careful— oh, Maya, I wish I could make you understand, really, how careful a girl has to be."

Nobody said anything, so Nicholas/Jerry filled in with, "It has a three-bladed prop, and I'm gong to tape streamers to them with little weights at the ends, an' when I go down old thirty-seven B passageway, look out, here comes that old coleslaw grater!"

"Like this," Maya said, and held her legs together and extended her arms, to make a three-bladed bike prop or a crucifix. She had thrown herself into a spin as she made the movement, and revolved slowly, stage center—red shorts, white blouse, red shorts, white blouse, red shorts, no shoes.

Diane asked, "And you saw that she was never going home, she was going to hospital instead, she was going to cut her wrist there, she was going to die?"

Nicholas nodded.

"Did you tell her?"

"Yes," Nicholas said. "No."

"Make up your mind. Didn't you tell her? Now, don't get mad."

"Is it telling, when the one you tell doesn't understand?"

Diane thought about that for a few steps while Nicholas dashed water on the hot bruises Ignacio had left upon his face. "If it was plain and clear and she ought to have understood—that's the trouble I have with my family."

"What is?"

"They won't say things—do you know what I mean? I just say look, just tell me, just tell me what I'm supposed to do, tell me what it is you want, but it's different all the time. My mother says, 'Diane, you ought to meet some boys, you can't go out with him, your father and I have never met him, we don't even know his family at all, Douglas, there's something I think you ought to know about Diane, she gets confused sometimes, we've had her to doctors, she's been in a hospital, try—' "

"Not to get her excited," Nicholas finished for her.

"Were you listening? I mean, are you from the Trojan Planets? Do you know my mother?"

"I only live in these places," Nicholas said, "that's for a long time. But you talk like other people."

"I feel better now that I'm with you; you're really nice. I wish you were older."

"I'm not sure I'm going to get much older."

"It's going to rain—feel it?"

Nicholas shook his head.

"Look." Diane jumped, bunnyrabbit-clumsy, three meters into the air. "See how high I can jump? That means people are sad and it's going to rain. I told you."

"No, you didn't."

"Yes, I did, Nicholas."

He waved the argument away, struck by a sudden thought. "You ever been to Callisto?"

The girl shook her head, and Nicholas said, "I have; that's where they did the operation. It's so big the gravity's mostly from natural mass, and it's all domed in, with a whole lot of air in it."

"So?"

"And when I was there it rained. There was a big trouble at one of the generating piles, and they shut it down and it got colder and colder until everybody in the hospital wore their blankets, just like Amerinds in books, and they locked the switches off on the heaters in the bathrooms, and the nurses and the comscreen told you all the time it wasn't dangerous, they were just rationing power to keep from blacking out the important stuff that was still running. And then it rained, just like on Earth. They said it got so cold the water condensed in the air, and it was like the whole hospital was right under a shower bath. Everybody on the top floor had to come down because it rained right on their beds, and for two nights I had a man in my room with me that had his arm cut off in a machine. But we couldn't jump any higher, and it got kind of dark."

"It doesn't always get dark here," Diane said. "Sometimes the rain sparkles. I think Dr. Island must do it to cheer everyone up."

"No," the waves explained, "or at least not in the way you mean, Diane."

Nicholas was hungry and started to ask them for something to eat, then turned his hunger in against itself, spat on the sand, and was still.

"It rains here when most of you are sad," the waves were saying, "because rain is a sad thing, to the human psyche. It is that, that sadness, perhaps because it recalls to unhappy people their own tears, that palliates melancholy."

Diane said, "Well, I know sometimes I feel better when it rains."

"That should help you to understand yourself. Most people are soothed when their environment is in harmony with their emotions, and anxious when it is not. An angry person becomes less angry in a red room, and unhappy people are only exasperated by sunshine and bird-song. Do you remember:

> "And, missing thee, I walk unseen
> On the dry smooth-shaven green
> To behold the wandering moon,
> Riding near her highest noon,
> Like one that had been led astray
> Through the heaven's wide pathless way?"

The girl shook her head.

Nicholas said, "No. Did somebody write that?" and then "You said you couldn't do anything."

The waves replied, "I can't—except talk to you."

"You make it rain."

"Your heart beats; I sense its pumping even as I speak—do you control the beating of your heart?"

"I can stop my breath."

"Can you stop your heart? Honestly, Nicholas?"

"I guess not."

"No more can I control the weather of my world, stop anyone from doing what he wishes, or feed you if you are hungry; with no need of volition on my part your emotions are monitored and averaged, and our weather responds. Calm and sunshine for tranquillity, rain for melancholy, storms for rage, and so on. This is what mankind has always wanted."

Diane asked, "What is?"

"That the environment should respond to human thought. That is the core of magic and the oldest dream of mankind; and here, on me, it is fact."

"So that we'll be well?"

Nicholas said angrily, "You're not sick!"

Dr. Island said, "So that some of you, at least, can return to society."

Nicholas threw a sea shell into the water as though to strike the mouth that spoke. "Why are we talking to this thing?"

"Wait, tot, I think it's interesting."

"Lies and lies."

Dr. Island said, "How do I lie, Nicholas?"

"You said it was magic—"

"No, I said that when humankind has dreamed of magic, the wish behind that dream has been the omnipotence of thought. Have you never wanted to be a magician, Nicholas, making palaces spring up overnight, or riding an enchanted horse of ebony to battle with the demons of the air?"

"I am a magician—I have preternatural powers, and before they cut us in two—"

Diane interrupted him. "You said you averaged emotions. When you made it rain."

"Yes."

"Doesn't that mean that if one person was really, terribly sad, he'd move the average so much he could make it rain all by himself? Or whatever? That doesn't seem fair."

The waves might have smiled. "That has never happened. But if it did, Diane, if one person felt such deep emotion, think how great her need would be. Don't you think we should answer it?"

Diane looked at Nicholas, but he was walking again, his head swinging, ignoring her as well as the voice of the waves. "Wait," she called. "You said I wasn't sick; I am, you know."

"No, you're not."

She hurried after him. "Everyone says so, and sometimes I'm so confused, and other times I'm boiling inside, just boiling. Mum says if you've got something on the stove you don't want to have burn, you just have to keep one finger on the handle of the pan and it won't, but I can't, I can't always find the handle or remember."

Without looking back the boy said, "Your mother is probably sick; maybe your father too, I don't know. But you're not. If they'd just let you alone you'd be all right. Why shouldn't you get upset, having to live with two crazy people?"

"Nicholas!" She grabbed his thin shoulders. "That's not true!"

"Yes, it is."

"I am sick. Everyone says so."

"I don't; so 'everyone' just means the ones that do—isn't that right? And if you don't either, that will be two; it can't be everyone then."

The girl called, "Doctor? Dr. Island?"

Nicholas said, "You aren't going to believe that, are you?"

"Dr. Island, is it true?"

"Is what true, Diane?"

"What he said. Am I sick?"

"Sickness—even physical illness—is relative, Diane; and complete health is an idealization, an abstraction, even if the other end of the scale is not."

"You know what I mean."

"You are not physically ill." A long, blue comber curled into a line of hissing spray reaching infinitely along the sea to their left and right. "As you said yourself a moment ago, you are sometimes confused, and sometimes disturbed."

"He said if it weren't for other people, if it weren't for my mother and father, I wouldn't have to be here."

"Diane . . ."

"Well, is that true or isn't it?"

"Most emotional illness would not exist, Diane, if it were possible in every case to separate oneself—in thought as well as circumstance—if only for a time."

"Separate oneself?"

"Did you ever think of going away, at least for a time?"

The girl nodded, then as though she were not certain Dr. Island could see her, said, "Often, I suppose; leaving the school and getting my own compartment somewhere—going to Achilles. Sometimes I wanted to so badly."

"Why didn't you?"

"They would have worried. And anyway, they would have found me, and made me come home."

"Would it have done any good if I—or a human doctor—had told them not to?"

When the girl said nothing Nicholas snapped, "You could have locked them up."

"They were functioning, Nicholas. They bought and sold; they worked, and paid their taxes—"

Diane said softly, "It wouldn't have done any good anyway, Nicholas; they are inside me."

"Diane was no longer functioning: she was failing every subject at the university she attended, and her presence in her classes, when she came, disturbed the instructors and the other students. You were not functioning either, and people of your own age were afraid of you."

"That's what counts with you, then. Functioning."

"If I were different from the world, would that help you when you got back into the world?"

"You are different." Nicholas kicked the sand. "Nobody ever saw a place like this."

"You mean that reality to you is metal corridors, rooms without windows, noise."

"Yes."

"That is the unreality, Nicholas. Most people have never had to endure such things. Even now, this—my beach, my sea, my trees—is more in harmony with most human lives than your metal corridors; and here, I am your social environment—what individuals call 'they.' You see, sometimes if we take people who are troubled back to something like me, to an idealized natural setting, it helps them."

"Come on," Nicholas told the girl. He took her arm, acutely conscious of being so much shorter than she.

"A question," murmured the waves. "If Diane's parents had been taken here instead of Diane, do you think it would have helped them?"

Nicholas did not reply.

"We have treatments for disturbed persons, Nicholas. But, at least for the time being, we have no treatment for disturbing persons." Diane and the boy had turned away, and the waves' hissing and slapping ceased to be speech. Gulls wheeled overhead, and once a red-and-yellow parrot fluttered from one palm to another. A monkey running on all fours like a little dog approached them, and Nicholas chased it, but it escaped.

"I'm going to take one of those things apart someday," he said, "and pull the wires out."

"Are we going to walk all the way round?" Diane asked. She might have been talking to herself.

"Can you do that?"

"Oh, you can't walk all around Dr. Island; it would be too long, and you can't get there anyway. But we could walk until we get back to where we started—we're probably more than halfway now."

"Are there other islands you can't see from here?"

The girl shook her head. "I don't think so; there's just this one big island in this satellite, and all the rest is water."

"Then if there's only the one island, we're going to have to walk all around it to get back to where we started. What are you laughing at?"

"Look down the beach, as far as you can. Never mind how it slips off to the side—pretend it's straight."

"I don't see anything."

"Don't you? Watch." Diane leaped into the air, six meters or more this time, and waved her arms.

"It looks like there's somebody ahead of us, way down the beach."

"Uh-huh. Now look behind."

"Okay, there's somebody there too. Come to think of it, I saw someone on the beach when I first got here. It seemed funny to see so far, but I guess I thought they were other patients. Now I see two people."

"They're us. That was probably yourself you saw the other time, too. There are just so many of us to each strip of beach, and Dr. Island only wants certain ones to mix. So the space bends around. When we get to one end of our strip and try to step over, we'll be at the other end."

"How did you find out?"

"Dr. Island told me about it when I first came here." The girl was silent for a moment, and her smile vanished. "Listen, Nicholas, do you want to see something really funny?"

Nicholas asked, "What?" As he spoke, a drop of rain struck his face.

"You'll see. Come on, though. We have to go into the middle instead of following the beach, and it will give us a chance to get under the trees and out of the rain."

When they had left the sand and the sound of the surf, and were walking on solid ground under green-leaved trees, Nicholas said, "Maybe we can find some fruit." They were so light now that he had to be careful not to bound into the air with each step. The rain fell slowly around them, in crystal spheres.

"Maybe," the girl said doubtfully. "Wait, let's stop here." She sat down where a huge tree sent twenty-meter wooden arches over dark, mossy ground. "Want to climb up there and see if you can find us something?"

"All right," Nicholas agreed. He jumped, and easily caught hold of a branch far above the girl's head. In a moment he was climbing in a green world, with the rain pattering all around him; he followed narrowing limbs into leafy wildernesses where the cool water ran from every twig he touched, and twice found the empty nests of birds, and once a slender snake, green as any leaf with a head as long as his thumb; but there was no fruit. "Nothing," he said, when he dropped down beside the girl once more.

"That's all right, we'll find something."

He said, "I hope so," and noticed that she was looking at him oddly, then realized that his left hand had lifted itself to touch her right breast. It dropped as he looked, and he felt his face grow hot. He said, "I'm sorry."

"That's all right."

"We like you. He—over there—he can't talk, you see. I guess I can't talk either."

"I think it's just you—in two pieces. I don't care."

"Thanks." He had picked up a leaf, dead and damp, and was tearing it to shreds; first his right hand tearing while the left held the leaf, then turnabout. "Where does the rain come from?" The dirty flakes clung to the fingers of both.

"Hmm?"

"Where does the rain come from? I mean, it isn't because it's colder here now, like on Callisto; it's because the gravity's turned down some way, isn't it?"

"From the sea. Don't you know how this place is built?"

Nicholas shook his head.

"Didn't they show it to you from the ship when you came? It's beautiful. They showed it to me—I just sat there and looked at it, and I wouldn't talk to them, and the nurse thought I wasn't paying any attention, but I heard everything. I just didn't want to talk to her. It wasn't any use."

"I know how you felt."

"But they didn't show it to you?"

"No, on my ship they kept me locked up because I burned some stuff. They thought I couldn't start a fire without an igniter, but if you have electricity in the wall sockets it's easy. They had a thing on me—you know?" He clasped his arms to his body to show how he had been restrained. "I bit one of them, too—I guess I didn't tell you that yet: I bite people. They locked me up, and for a long time I had nothing to do, and then I could feel us dock with something, and they came and got me and pulled me down a regular companionway for a long time, and it just seemed like a regular place. Then they stuck me full of Tranquil-C —I guess they didn't know it doesn't hardly work on me at all—with a pneumogun, and lifted a kind of door thing and shoved me up."

"Didn't they make you undress?"

"I already was. When they put the ties on me I did things in my clothes and they had to take them off me. It made them mad." He grinned unevenly. "Does Tranquil-C work on you? Or any of that other stuff?"

"I suppose they would, but then I never do the sort of thing you do anyway."

"Maybe you ought to."

"Sometimes they used to give me medication that was supposed to cheer me up; then I couldn't sleep, and I walked and walked, you know, and ran into things and made a lot of trouble for everyone; but what good does it do?"

Nicholas shrugged. "Not doing it doesn't do any good either—I mean, we're both here. My way, I know I've made them jump; they shoot that stuff in me and I'm not mad any more, but I know what it is and I just think what I would do if I *were* mad, and I do it, and when it wears off I'm glad I did."

"I think you're still angry somewhere, deep down."

Nicholas was already thinking of something else. "This island says Ignacio kills people." He paused. "What does it look like?"

"Ignacio?"

"No, I've seen him. Dr. Island."

"Oh, you mean when I was in the ship. The satellite's round of course, and all clear except where Dr. Island is, so that's a dark spot. The rest of it's temperglass, and from space you can't even see the water."

"That *is* the sea up there, isn't it?" Nicholas asked, trying to look up at it through the tree leaves and the rain. "I thought it was when I first came."

"Sure. It's like a glass ball, and we're inside, and the water's inside too, and just goes all around up the curve."

"That's why I could see so far out on the beach, isn't it? Instead of dropping down from you like on Callisto it bends up so you can see it."

The girl nodded. "And the water lets the light through, but filters out the ultraviolet. Besides, it gives us thermal mass, so we don't heat up too much when we're between the sun and the Bright Spot."

"Is that what keeps us warm? The Bright Spot?"

Diane nodded again. "We go around in ten hours, you see, and that holds us over it all the time."

"Why can't I see it, then? It ought to look like Sol does from the Belt, only bigger; but there's just a shimmer in the sky, even when it's not raining."

"The waves diffract the light and break up the image. You'd see the Focus, though, if the air weren't so clear. Do you know what the Focus is?"

Nicholas shook his head.

"We'll get to it pretty soon, after this rain stops. Then I'll tell you."

"I still don't understand about the rain."

Unexpectedly Diane giggled. "I just thought—do you know what I was supposed to be? While I was going to school?"

"Quiet," Nicholas said.

"No, silly. I mean what I was being trained to do, if I graduated and all that. I was going to be a teacher, with all those cameras on me and tots from everywhere watching and popping questions on the two-way. Jolly time. Now I'm doing it here, only there's no one but you."

"You mind?"

"No, I suppose I enjoy it." There was a black-and-blue mark on Diane's thigh, and she rubbed it pensively with one hand as she spoke. "Anyway, there are three ways to make gravity. Do you know them? Answer, clerk."

"Sure; acceleration, mass, and synthesis."

"That's right; motion and mass are both bendings of space, of course, which is why Zeno's paradox doesn't work out that way, and why masses move toward each other—what we call falling—or at least try to; and if they're held apart it produces the tension we perceive as a force and call weight and all that rot. So naturally if you bend the space direct, you synthesize a gravity effect, and that's what holds all that water up against the translucent shell—there's nothing like enough mass to do it by itself."

"You mean"—Nicholas held out his hand to catch a slow-moving globe of rain—"that this is water from the sea?"

"Right-o, up on top. Do you see, the temperature differences in the air make the winds, and the winds make the waves and surf you saw when we were walking along the shore. When the waves break they throw up these little drops, and if you watch you'll see that even when it's clear they go up a long way sometimes. Then if the gravity is less they can get away altogether, and if we were on the outside they'd fly off into space; but we aren't, we're inside, so all they can do is go across the center, more or less, until they hit the water again, or Dr. Island."

"Dr. Island said they had storms sometimes, when people got mad."

"Yes. Lots of wind, and so there's lots of rain too. Only the rain then is because the wind tears the tops off the waves, and you don't get light like you do in a normal rain."

"What makes so much wind?"

"I don't know. It happens somehow."

They sat in silence, Nicholas listening to the dripping of the leaves. He remembered then that they had spun the hospital module, finally, to get the little spheres of clotting blood out of the air; Maya's blood was building up on the grills of the purification intake ducts, spotting them black, and someone had been afraid they would decay there and smell. He had not been there when they did it, but he could imagine the droplets settling, like this, in the slow spin. The old psychodrama group had already been broken up, and when he saw Maureen or any of the others in the rec room they talked about Good Old Days. It had not seemed like Good Old Days then except that Maya had been there.

Diane said, "It's going to stop."

"It looks just as bad to me."

"No, it's going to stop—see, they're falling a little faster now, and I feel heavier."

Nicholas stood up. "You rested enough yet? You want to go on?"

"We'll get wet."

He shrugged.

"I don't want to get my hair wet, Nicholas. It'll be over in a minute."

He sat down again. "How long have you been here?"

"I'm not sure."

"Don't you count the days?"

"I lose track a lot."

"Longer than a week?"

"Nicholas, don't ask me, all right?"

"Isn't there anybody on this piece of Dr. Island except you and me and Ignacio?"

"I don't think there was anyone but Ignacio before you came."

"Who is he?"

She looked at him.

"Well, who is he? You know me—us—Nicholas Kenneth de Vore; and you're Diane who?"

"Phillips."

"And you're from the Trojan Planets, and I was from the Outer Belt, I guess, to start with. What about Ignacio? You talk to him sometimes, don't you? Who is he?"

"I don't know. He's important."

For an instant, Nicholas froze. "What does that mean?"

"Important." The girl was feeling her knees, running her hands back and forth across them.

"Maybe everybody's important."

"I know you're just a tot, Nicholas, but don't be so stupid. Come on, you wanted to go, let's go now. It's pretty well stopped." She stood, stretching her thin body, her arms over her head. "My knees are rough —you made me think of that. When I came here they were still so smooth, I think. I used to put a certain lotion on them. Because my dad would feel them, and my hands and elbows too, and he'd say if they weren't smooth nobody'd ever want me; Mum wouldn't say anything, but she'd be cross after, and they used to come and visit, and so I kept a bottle in my room and I used to put it on. Once I drank some."

Nicholas was silent.

"Aren't you going to ask me if I died?" She stepped ahead of him, pulling aside the dripping branches. "See here, I'm sorry I said you were stupid."

"I'm just thinking," Nicholas said. "I'm not mad at you. Do you really know anything about him?"

"No, but look at it." She gestured. "Look around you; someone *built* all this."

"You mean it cost a lot."

"It's automated, of course, but still . . . well, the other places where you were before—how much space was there for each patient? Take the total volume and divide it by the number of people there."

"Okay, this is a whole lot bigger, but maybe they think we're worth it."

"Nicholas . . ." She paused. "Nicholas, Ignacio is homicidal. Didn't Dr. Island tell you?"

"Yes."

"And you're fourteen and not very big for it, and I'm a girl. Who are they worried about?"

The look on Nicholas's face startled her.

After an hour or more of walking they came to it. It was a band of withered vegetation, brown and black and tumbling, and as straight as if it had been drawn with a ruler. "I was afraid it wasn't going to be here," Diane said. "It moves around whenever there's a storm. It might not have been in our sector any more at all."

Nicholas asked, "What is it?"

"The Focus. It's been all over, but mostly the plants grow back quickly when it's gone."

"It smells funny—like the kitchen in a place where they wanted me to work in the kitchen once."

"Vegetables rotting, that's what that is. What did you do?"

"Nothing—put detergent in the stuff they were cooking. What makes this?"

"The Bright Spot. See, when it's just about overhead the curve of the sky and the water up there make a lens. It isn't a very good lens—a lot of the light scatters. But enough is focused to do this. It wouldn't fry us if it came past right now, if that's what you're wondering, because it's not that hot. I've stood right in it, but you want to get out in a minute."

"I thought it was going to be about seeing ourselves down the beach."

Diane seated herself on the trunk of a fallen tree. "It was, really. The last time I was here it was further from the water, and I suppose it had been there a long time, because it had cleared out a lot of the dead stuff. The sides of the sector are nearer here, you see; the whole sector narrows down like a piece of pie. So you could look down the Focus either way and see yourself nearer than you could on the beach. It was almost as if you were in a big, big room, with a looking-glass on each wall, or as if you could stand behind yourself. I thought you might like it."

"I'm going to try it here," Nicholas announced, and he clambered up one of the dead trees while the girl waited below, but the dry limbs creaked and snapped beneath his feet, and he could not get high enough to see himself in either direction. When he dropped to the ground beside her again, he said, "There's nothing to eat here either, is there?"

"I haven't found anything."

"They—I mean, Dr. Island wouldn't just let us starve, would he?"

"I don't think he could do anything; that's the way this place is built. Sometimes you find things, and I've tried to catch fish, but I never could. A couple of times Ignacio gave me part of what he had, though; he's good at it. I bet you think I'm skinny, don't you? But I was a lot fatter when I came here."

"What are we going to do now?"

"Keep walking, I suppose, Nicholas. Maybe go back to the water."

"Do you think we'll find anything?"

From a decaying log, insect stridulations called, "Wait."

Nicholas asked, "Do *you* know where anything is?"

"Something for you to eat? Not at present. But I can show you something much more interesting, not far from here, than this clutter of dying trees. Would you like to see it?"

Diane said, "Don't go, Nicholas."

"What is it?"

"Diane, who calls this 'the Focus,' calls what I wish to show you 'the Point.' "

Nicholas asked Diane, "Why shouldn't I go?"

"I'm not going. I went there once anyway."

"I took her," Dr. Island said. "And I'll take you. I wouldn't take you if I didn't think it might help you."

"I don't think Diane liked it."

"Diane may not wish to be helped—help may be painful, and often people do not. But it is my business to help them if I can, whether or not they wish it."

"Suppose I don't want to go?"

"Then I cannot compel you; you know that. But you will be the only patient in this sector who has not seen it, Nicholas, as well as the youngest; both Diane and Ignacio have, and Ignacio goes there often."

"Is it dangerous?"

"No. Are you afraid?"

Nicholas looked questioningly at Diane. "What is it? What will I see?"

She had walked away while he was talking to Dr. Island, and was now sitting cross-legged on the ground about five meters from where Nicholas stood, staring at her hands. Nicholas repeated, "What will I see, Diane?" He did not think she would answer.

She said, "A glass. A mirror."

"Just a mirror?"

"You know how I told you to climb the tree here? The Point is where the edges come together. You can see yourself—like on the beach—but closer."

Nicholas was disappointed. "I've seen myself in mirrors lots of times."

Dr. Island, whose voice was now in the sighing of the dead leaves, whispered, "Did you have a mirror in your room, Nicholas, before you came here?"

"A steel one."

"So that you could not break it?"

"I guess so. I threw things at it sometimes, but it just got puckers in it." Remembering dimpled reflections, Nicholas laughed.

"You can't break this one either."

"It doesn't sound like it's worth going to see."

"I think it is."

"Diane, do you still think I shouldn't go?"

There was no reply. The girl sat staring at the ground in front of her. Nicholas walked over to look at her and found a tear had washed a damp trail down each thin cheek, but she did not move when he touched her. "She's catatonic, isn't she," he said.

A green limb just outside the Focus nodded. "Catatonic schizophrenia."

"I had a doctor once that said those names—like that. They didn't mean anything." (The doctor had been a therapy robot, but a human doctor gave more status. Robots' patients sat in doorless booths—two and a half hours a day for Nicholas: an hour and a half in the morning, an hour in the afternoon—and talked to something that appeared to be a small, friendly food freezer. Some people sat every day in silence, while others talked continually, and for such patients as these the attendants seldom troubled to turn the machines on.)

"He meant cause and treatment. He was correct."

Nicholas stood looking down at the girl's streaked, brown-blond head. "What *is* the cause? I mean for her."

"I don't know."

"And what's the treatment?"

"You are seeing it."

"Will it help her?"

"Probably not."

"Listen, she can hear you, don't you know that? She hears everything we say."

"If my answer disturbs you, Nicholas, I can change it. It will help her if she wants to be helped; if she insists on clasping her illness to her it will not."

"We ought to go away from here," Nicholas said uneasily.

"To your left you will see a little path, a very faint one. Between the twisted tree and the bush with the yellow flowers."

Nicholas nodded and began to walk, looking back at Diane several times. The flowers were butterflies, who fled in a cloud of color when he approached them, and he wondered if Dr. Island had known. When he had gone a hundred paces and was well away from the brown and rotting vegetation, he said, "She was sitting in the Focus."

"Yes."

"Is she still there?"

"Yes."

"What will happen when the Bright Spot comes?"

"Diane will become uncomfortable and move, if she is still there."

"Once in one of the places I was in there was a man who was like that, and they said he wouldn't get anything to eat if he didn't get up and get it, they weren't going to feed him with the nose tube any more; and they didn't, and he died. We told them about it and they wouldn't do anything and he starved to death right there, and when he was dead they rolled him off onto a stretcher and changed the bed and put somebody else there."

"I know, Nicholas. You told the doctors at St. John's about all that, and it is in your file; but think: well men have starved themselves—yes, to death—to protest what they felt were political injustices. Is it so surprising that your friend killed himself in the same way to protest what he felt as a psychic injustice?"

"He wasn't my friend. Listen, did you really mean it when you said the treatment she was getting here would help Diane if she wanted to be helped?"

"No."

Nicholas halted in mid-stride. "You didn't mean it? You don't think it's true?"

"No. I doubt that anything will help her."

"I don't think you ought to lie to us."

"Why not? If by chance you become well you will be released, and if you are released you will have to deal with your society, which will lie to you frequently. Here, where there are so few individuals, I must take the place of society. I have explained that."

"Is that what you are?"

"Society's surrogate? Of course. Who do you imagine built me? What else could I be?"

"The doctor."

"You have had many doctors, and so has she. Not one of them has benefited you much."

"I'm not sure you even want to help us."

"Do you wish to see what Diane calls 'the Point'?"

"I guess so."

"Then you must walk. You will not see it standing here."

Nicholas walked, thrusting aside leafy branches and dangling creepers wet with rain. The jungle smelled of the life of green things; there were ants on the tree trunks, and dragonflies with hot, red bodies and wings as long as his hands. "Do you want to help us?" he asked after a time.

"My feelings toward you are ambivalent. But when you wish to be helped, I wish to help you."

The ground sloped gently upward, and as it rose became somewhat more clear, the big trees a trifle farther apart, the underbrush spent in grass and fern. Occasionally there were stone outcrops to be climbed, and clearings open to the tumbling sky. Nicholas asked, "Who made this trail?"

"Ignacio. He comes here often."

"He's not afraid, then? Diane's afraid."

"Ignacio is afraid too, but he comes."

"Diane says Ignacio is important."

"Yes."

"What do you mean by that? Is he important? More important than we are?"

"Do you remember that I told you I was the surrogate of society? What do you think society wants, Nicholas?"

"Everybody to do what it says."

"You mean conformity. Yes, there must be conformity, but something else too—consciousness."

"I don't want to hear about it."

"Without consciousness, which you may call sensitivity if you are careful not to allow yourself to be confused by the term, there is no progress. A century ago, Nicholas, mankind was suffocating on Earth;

now it is suffocating again. About half of the people who have contributed substantially to the advance of humanity have shown signs of emotional disturbance."

"I told you, I don't want to hear about it. I asked you an easy question—is Ignacio more important than Diane and me—and you won't tell me. I've heard all this you're saying. I've heard it fifty, maybe a hundred times from everybody, and it's lies; it's the regular thing, and you've got it written down on a card somewhere to read out when anybody asks. Those people you talk about that went crazy, they went crazy because while they were 'advancing humanity,' or whatever you call it, people kicked them out of their rooms because they couldn't pay, and while they were getting thrown out you were making other people rich that had never done anything in their whole lives except think about how to get that way."

"Sometimes it is hard, Nicholas, to determine before the fact—or even at the time—just who should be honored."

"How do you know if you've never tried?"

"You asked if Ignacio was more important than Diane or yourself. I can only say that Ignacio seems to me to hold a brighter promise of a full recovery coupled with a substantial contribution to human progress."

"If he's so good, why did he crack up?"

"Many do, Nicholas. Even among the inner planets space is not a kind environment for mankind; and our space, trans-Martian space, is worse. Any young person here, anyone like yourself or Diane who would seem to have a better-than-average chance of adapting to the conditions we face, is precious."

"Or Ignacio."

"Yes, or Ignacio. Ignacio has a tested IQ of two hundred and ten, Nicholas. Diane's is one hundred and twenty. Your own is ninety-five."

"They never took mine."

"It's on your records, Nicholas."

"They tried to and I threw down the helmet and it broke; Sister Carmela—she was the nurse—just wrote down something on the paper and sent me back."

"I see. I will ask for a complete investigation of this, Nicholas."

"Sure."

"Don't you believe me?"

"I don't think you believed me."

"Nicholas, Nicholas . . ." The long tongues of grass now beginning to appear beneath the immense trees sighed. "Can't you see that a certain measure of trust between the two of us is essential?"

"Did you believe me?"

"Why do you ask? Suppose I were to say I did; would you believe that?"

"When you told me I had been reclassified."

"You would have to be retested, for which there are no facilities here."

"If you believed me, why did you say retested? I told you I haven't ever been tested at all—but anyway you could cross out the ninety-five."

"It is impossible for me to plan your therapy without some estimate of your intelligence, Nicholas, and I have nothing with which to replace it."

The ground was sloping up more sharply now, and in a clearing the boy halted and turned to look back at the leafy film, like algae over a pool, beneath which he had climbed, and at the sea beyond. To his right and left his view was still hemmed with foliage, and ahead of him a meadow on edge (like the square of sand through which he had come, though he did not think of that), dotted still with trees, stretched steeply toward an invisible summit. It seemed to him that under his feet the mountainside swayed ever so slightly. Abruptly he demanded of the wind, "Where's Ignacio?"

"Not here. Much closer to the beach."

"And Diane?"

"Where you left her. Do you enjoy the panorama?"

"It's pretty, but it feels like we're rocking."

"We are. I am moored to the temperglass exterior of our satellite by two hundred cables, but the tide and the currents none the less impart a slight motion to my body. Naturally this movement is magnified as you go higher."

"I thought you were fastened right onto the hull; if there's water under you, how do people get in and out?"

"I am linked to the main air lock by a communication tube. To you when you came, it probably seemed an ordinary companionway."

Nicholas nodded and turned his back on leaves and sea and began to climb again.

"You are in a beautiful spot, Nicholas; do you open your heart to beauty?" After waiting for an answer that did not come, the wind sang:

"The mountain wooded to the peak, the lawns
And winding glades high up like ways to Heaven,
The slender coco's drooping crown of plumes,
The lightning flash of insect and of bird,
The lustre of the long convolvuluses
That coil'd around the stately stems, and ran
Ev'n to the limit of the land, the glows
And glories of the broad belt of the world,
All these he saw."

"Does this mean nothing to you, Nicholas?"

"You read a lot, don't you?"

"Often, when it is dark, everyone else is asleep and there is very little else for me to do."

"You talk like a woman; are you a woman?"

"How could I be a woman?"

"You know what I mean. Except, when you were talking mostly to Diane, you sounded more like a man."

"You haven't yet said you think me beautiful."

"You're an Easter egg."

"What do you mean by that, Nicholas?"

"Never mind." He saw the egg as it had hung in the air before him, shining with gold and covered with flowers.

"Eggs are dyed with pretty colors for Easter, and my colors are beautiful—is that what you mean, Nicholas?"

His mother had brought the egg on visiting day, but she could never have made it. Nicholas knew who must have made it. The gold was that very pure gold used for shielding delicate instruments; the clear flakes of crystallized carbon that dotted the egg's surface with tiny stars could only have come from a laboratory high-pressure furnace. How angry he must have been when she told him she was going to give it to him.

"It's pretty, isn't it, Nicky?"

It hung in the weightlessness between them, turning very slowly with the memory of her scented gloves.

"The flowers are meadowsweet, fraxinella, lily of the valley, and moss rose—though I wouldn't expect you to recognize them, darling." His mother had never been below the orbit of Mars, but she pretended to have spent her girlhood on Earth; each reference to the lie filled Nicholas with inexpressible fury and shame. The egg was about twenty centimeters long and it revolved, end over end, in some small fraction more than eight of the pulsebeats he felt in his cheeks. Visiting time had twenty-three minutes to go.

"Aren't you going to look at it?"

"I can see it from here." He tried to make her understand. "I can see every part of it. The little red things are aluminum oxide crystals, right?"

"I mean, look *inside*, Nicky."

He saw then that there was a lens at one end, disguised as a dewdrop in the throat of an asphodel. Gently he took the egg in his hands, closed one eye, and looked. The light of the interior was not, as he had half expected, gold tinted, but brilliantly white, deriving from some concealed source. A world surely meant for Earth shone within, as though seen from below the orbit of the moon—indigo sea and emerald land. Rivers brown and clear as tea ran down long plains.

His mother said, "Isn't it pretty?"

Night hung at the corners in funereal purple, and sent long shadows like cold and lovely arms to caress the day; and while he watched and it fell, long-necked birds of so dark a pink that they were nearly red trailed stilt legs across the sky, their wings making crosses.

"They are called flamingos," Dr. Island said, following the direction of his eyes. "Isn't it a pretty word? For a pretty bird, but I don't think we'd like them as much if we called them sparrows, would we?"

His mother said, "I'm going to take it home and keep it for you. It's too nice to leave with a little boy, but if you ever come home again it will be waiting for you. On your dresser, beside your hairbrushes."

Nicholas said, "Words just mix you up."

"You shouldn't despise them, Nicholas. Besides having great beauty of their own, they are useful in reducing tension. You might benefit from that."

"You mean you talk yourself out of it."

"I mean that a person's ability to verbalize his feelings, if only to himself, may prevent them from destroying him. Evolution teaches us, Nicholas, that the original purpose of language was to ritualize men's threats and curses, his spells to compel the gods; communication came later. Words can be a safety valve."

Nicholas said, "I want to be a bomb; a bomb doesn't need a safety valve." To his mother, "Is that South America, Mama?"

"No, dear, India. The Malabar Coast on your left, the Coromandel Coast on your right, and Ceylon below." Words.

"A bomb destroys itself, Nicholas."

"A bomb doesn't care."

He was climbing resolutely now, his toes grabbing at tree roots and the soft, mossy soil; his physician was no longer the wind but a small brown monkey that followed a stone's throw behind him. "I hear someone coming," he said.

"Yes."

"Is it Ignacio?"

"No, it is Nicholas. You are close now."

"Close to the Point?"

"Yes."

He stopped and looked around him. The sounds he had heard, the naked feet padding on soft ground, stopped as well. Nothing seemed strange; the land still rose, and there were large trees, widely spaced, with moss growing in their deepest shade, grass where there was more light. "The three big trees," Nicholas said, "they're just alike. Is that how you know where we are?"

"Yes."

In his mind he called the one before him "Ceylon"; the others were "Coromandel" and "Malabar." He walked toward Ceylon, studying its massive, twisted limbs; a boy naked as himself walked out of the forest to his left, toward Malabar—this boy was not looking at Nicholas, who shouted and ran toward him.

The boy disappeared. Only Malabar, solid and real, stood before Nicholas; he ran to it, touched its rough bark with his hand, and then saw beyond it a fourth tree, similar too to the Ceylon tree, around which a boy peered with averted head. Nicholas watched him for a moment, then said, "I see."

"Do you?" the monkey chattered.

"It's like a mirror, only backwards. The light from the front of me goes out and hits the edge, and comes in the other side, only I can't see it because I'm not looking that way. What I see is the light from my back, sort of, because it comes back this way. When I ran, did I get turned around?"

"Yes, you ran out the left side of the segment, and of course returned immediately from the right."

"I'm not scared. It's kind of fun." He picked up a stick and threw it as hard as he could toward the Malabar tree. It vanished, whizzed over his head, vanished again, slapped the back of his legs. "Did this scare Diane?"

There was no answer. He strode farther, palely naked boys walking to his left and right, but always looking away from him, gradually coming closer.

"Don't go farther," Dr. Island said behind him. "It can be dangerous if you try to pass through the Point itself."

"I see it," Nicholas said. He saw three more trees, growing very close together, just ahead of him; their branches seemed strangely intertwined as they danced together in the wind, and beyond them there was nothing at all.

"You can't actually go through the Point," Dr. Island Monkey said. "The tree covers it."

"Then why did you warn me about it?" Limping and scarred, the boys to his right and left were no more than two meters away now; he had discovered that if he looked straight ahead he could sometimes glimpse their bruised profiles.

"That's far enough, Nicholas."

"I want to touch the tree."

He took another step, and another, then turned. The Malabar boy turned too, presenting his narrow back, on which the ribs and spine seemed welts. Nicholas reached out both arms and laid his hands on the thin shoulders, and as he did, felt other hands—the cool, unfeeling hands of a stranger, dry hands too small—touch his own shoulders and creep upward toward his neck.

"Nicholas!"

He jumped sidewise away from the tree and looked at his hands, his head swaying. "It wasn't me."

"Yes, it was, Nicholas," the monkey said.

"It was one of them."

"You are all of them."

In one quick motion Nicholas snatched up an arm-long section of fallen limb and hurled it at the monkey. It struck the little creature, knocking it down, but the monkey sprang up and fled on three legs. Nicholas sprinted after it.

He had nearly caught it when it darted to one side; as quickly, he turned toward the other, springing for the monkey he saw running toward him there. In an instant it was in his grip, feebly trying to bite. He slammed its head against the ground, then catching it by the ankles swung it against the Ceylon tree until at the third impact he heard the skull crack, and stopped.

He had expected wires, but there were none. Blood oozed from the battered little face, and the furry body was warm and limp in his hands.

Leaves above his head said, "You haven't killed me, Nicholas. You never will."

"How does it work?" He was still searching for wires, tiny circuit cards holding micro-logic. He looked about for a sharp stone with which to open the monkey's body, but could find none.

"It is just a monkey," the leaves said. "If you had asked, I would have told you."

"How did you make him talk?" He dropped the monkey, stared at it for a moment, then kicked it. His fingers were bloody, and he wiped them on the leaves of the tree.

"Only my mind speaks to yours, Nicholas."

"Oh," he said. And then, "I've heard of that. I didn't think it would be like this. I thought it would be in my head."

"Your record shows no auditory hallucinations, but haven't you ever known someone who had them?"

"I knew a girl once . . ." He paused.

"Yes?"

"She twisted noises—you know?"

"Yes."

"Like, it would just be a service cart out in the corridor, but she'd hear the fan, and think . . ."

"What?"

"Oh, different things. That it was somebody talking, calling her."

"Hear them?"

"What?" He sat up in his bunk. "Maya?"

"They're coming after me."

"Maya?"

Dr. Island, through the leaves, said, "When I talk to you, Nicholas, your mind makes any sound you hear the vehicle for my thoughts' content. You may hear me softly in the patter of rain, or joyfully in the singing of a bird—but if I wished I could amplify what I say until every idea and suggestion I wished to give would be driven like a nail into your consciousness. Then you would do whatever I wished you to."

"I don't believe it," Nicholas said. "If you can do that, why don't you tell Diane not to be catatonic?"

"First, because she might retreat more deeply into her disease in an effort to escape me; and second, because ending her catatonia in that way would not remove its cause."

"And thirdly?"

"I did not say 'thirdly,' Nicholas."

"I thought I heard it—when two leaves touched."

"Thirdly, Nicholas, because both you and she have been chosen for your effect on someone else; if I were to change her—or you—so abruptly, that effect would be lost." Dr. Island was a monkey again now, a new monkey that chattered from the protection of a tree twenty meters away. Nicholas threw a stick at him.

"The monkeys are only little animals, Nicholas; they like to follow people, and they chatter."

"I bet Ignacio kills them."

"No, he likes them; he only kills fish to eat."

Nicholas was suddenly aware of his hunger. He began to walk.

He found Ignacio on the beach, praying. For an hour or more, Nicholas hid behind the trunk of a palm watching him, but for a long time he could not decide to whom Ignacio prayed. He was kneeling just where the lacy edges of the breakers died, looking out toward the water; and from time to time he bowed, touching his forehead to the damp sand; then Nicholas could hear his voice, faintly, over the crashing and hissing of the waves. In general, Nicholas approved of prayer, having observed that those who prayed were usually more interesting companions than those who did not; but he had also noticed that though it made no difference what name the devotee gave the object of his devotions, it was important to discover how the god was conceived. Ignacio did not seem to be praying to Dr. Island—he would, Nicholas thought, have been facing the other way for that—and for a time he wondered if he were not praying to the waves. From his position behind him he followed Ignacio's line of vision out and out, wave upon wave into the bright, confused sky, up and up until at last it curved completely around and came to rest on Ignacio's back again; and then it occurred to him that Ignacio might be praying to himself. He left the palm trunk then and walked about halfway to the place where Ignacio knelt, and sat down. Above the sounds of the sea and the murmuring of Ignacio's voice hung a silence so immense and fragile that it seemed that at any moment the entire crystal satellite might ring like a gong.

After a time Nicholas felt his left side trembling. With his right hand he began to stroke it, running his fingers down his left arm, and from his left shoulder to the thigh. It worried him that his left side should be so frightened, and he wondered if perhaps that other half of his brain, from which he was forever severed, could hear what Ignacio was saying to the waves. He began to pray himself, so that the other (and perhaps

Ignacio too) could hear, saying not quite beneath his breath, "Don't worry, don't be afraid, he's not going to hurt us, he's nice, and if he does we'll get him; we're only going to get something to eat, maybe he'll show us how to catch fish, I think he'll be nice this time." But he knew, or at least felt he knew, that Ignacio would not be nice this time.

Eventually Ignacio stood up; he did not turn to face Nicholas, but waded out to sea; then, as though he had known Nicholas was behind him all the time (though Nicholas was not sure he had been heard— perhaps, so he thought, Dr. Island had told Ignacio), he gestured to indicate that Nicholas should follow him.

The water was colder than he remembered, the sand coarse and gritty between his toes. He thought of what Dr. Island had told him—about floating—and that a part of her must be this sand, under the water, reaching out (how far?) into the sea; when she ended there would be nothing but the clear temperglass of the satellite itself, far down.

"Come," Ignacio said. "Can you swim?" Just as though he had forgotten the night before. Nicholas said yes, he could, wondering if Ignacio would look around at him when he spoke. He did not.

"And do you know why you are here?"

"You told me to come."

"Ignacio means *here*. Does this not remind you of any place you have seen before, little one?"

Nicholas thought of the crystal grong and the Easter egg, then of the micro-thin globes of perfumed vapor that, at home, were sometimes sent floating down the corridors at Christmas to explode in clean dust and a cold smell of pine forests when the children struck them with their hopping-canes; but he said nothing.

Ignacio continued, "Let Ignacio tell you a story. Once there was a man—a boy, actually—on the Earth, who—"

Nicholas wondered why it was always men (most often doctors and clinical psychologists, in his experience) who wanted to tell you stories. Jesus, he recalled, was always telling everyone stories, and the Virgin Mary almost never, though a woman he had once known who thought she was the Virgin Mary had always been talking about her son. He thought Ignacio looked a little like Jesus. He tried to remember if his mother had ever told him stories when he was at home, and decided that she had not; she just turned on the comscreen to the cartoons.

"—wanted to—"

"—tell a story," Nicholas finished for him.

"How did you know?" Angry and surprised.

"It was you, wasn't it? And you want to tell one now."

"What you said was not what Ignacio would have said. He was going to tell you about a fish."

"Where is it?" Nicholas asked, thinking of the fish Ignacio had been eating the night before, and imagining another such fish, caught while he had been coming back, perhaps, from the Point, and now concealed somewhere waiting the fire. "Is it a big one?"

"It is gone now," Ignacio said, "but it was only as long as a man's hand. I caught it in the big river."

Huckleberry—"I know, the Mississippi; it was a catfish. Or a sunfish."—*Finn.*

"Possibly that is what you call them; for a time he was as the sun to a certain one." The light from nowhere danced on the water. "In any event he was kept on that table in the salon in the house where life was lived. In a tank, but not the old kind in which one sees the glass, with metal at the corner. But the new kind in which the glass is so strong, but very thin, and curved so that it does not reflect, and there are no corners, and a clever device holds the water clear." He dipped up a handful of sparkling water, still not meeting Nicholas's eyes. "As clear even as this, and there were no ripples, and so you could not see it at all. My fish floated in the center of my table above a few stones."

Nicholas asked, "Did you float on the river on a raft?"

"No, we had a little boat. Ignacio caught this fish in a net, of which he almost bit through the strands before he could be landed; he possessed wonderful teeth. There was no one in the house but him and the other, and the robots; but each morning someone would go to the pool in the patio and catch a goldfish for him. Ignacio would see this goldfish there when he came down for his breakfast, and would think, 'Brave goldfish, you have been cast to the monster, will you be the one to destroy him? Destroy him and you shall have his diamond house forever.' And then the fish, who had a little spot of red beneath his wonderful teeth, a spot like a cherry, would rush upon that young goldfish, and for an instant the water would be all clouded with blood."

"And then what?" Nicholas asked.

"And then the clever machine would make the water clear once more, and the fish would be floating above the stones as before, the fish with the wonderful teeth, and Ignacio would touch the little switch on the table, and ask for more bread, and more fruit."

"Are you hungry now?"

"No, I am tired and lazy now; if I pursue you I will not catch you, and if I catch you—through your own slowness and clumsiness—I will not kill you, and if I kill you I will not eat you."

Nicholas had begun to back away, and at the last words, realizing that they were a signal, he turned and began to run, splashing through the shallow water. Ignacio ran after him, much helped by his longer legs, his hair flying behind his dark young face, his square teeth—each white as a bone and as big as Nicholas's thumbnail—showing like spectators who lined the railings of his lips.

"Don't run, Nicholas," Dr. Island said with the voice of a wave. "It only makes him angry that you run." Nicholas did not answer, but cut to his left, up the beach and among the trunks of the palms, sprinting all the way because he had no way of knowing Ignacio was not right behind him, about to grab him by the neck. When he stopped it was in the thick jungle, among the boles of the hardwoods, where he leaned, out of breath, the thumping of his own heart the only sound in an atmosphere silent and unwaked as Earth's long, prehuman day. For a time he listened for any sound Ignacio might make searching for him; there was none. He drew a deep breath then and said, "Well, that's over," expecting Dr. Island to answer from somewhere; there was only the green hush.

The light was still bright and strong and nearly shadowless, but some interior sense told him the day was nearly over, and he noticed that such faint shades as he could see stretched long, horizontal distortions of their objects. He felt no hunger, but he had fasted before and knew on which side of hunger he stood; he was not as strong as he had been only a day past, and by this time next day he would probably be unable to outrun Ignacio. He should, he now realized, have eaten the monkey he had killed; but his stomach revolted at the thought of the raw flesh, and he did not know how he might build a fire, although Ignacio seemed to have done so the night before. Raw fish, even if he were able to catch a fish, would be as bad, or worse, than raw monkey; he remembered his effort to open a coconut—he had failed, but it was surely not impossible. His mind was hazy as to what a coconut might contain, but there had to be an edible core, because they were eaten in books. He decided to make a wide sweep through the jungle that would bring him back to the beach well away from Ignacio; he had several times seen coconuts lying in the sand under the trees.

He moved quietly, still a little afraid, trying to think of ways to open the coconut when he found it. He imagined himself standing before a large and raggedly faceted stone, holding the coconut in both hands. He

raised it and smashed it down, but when it struck it was no longer a
coconut but Maya's head; he heard her nose cartilage break with a
distinct, rubbery snap. Her eyes, as blue as the sky above Madhya
Pradesh, the sparkling blue sky of the egg, looked up at him, but he
could no longer look into them, they retreated from his own, and it
came to him quite suddenly that Lucifer, in falling, must have fallen up,
into the fires and the coldness of space, never again to see the warm
blues and browns and greens of Earth: *I was watching Satan fall as
lightning from heaven.* He had heard that on tape somewhere, but he
could not remember where. He had read that on Earth lightning did not
come down from the clouds, but leaped up from the planetary surface
toward them, never to return.

"Nicholas."

He listened, but did not hear his name again. Faintly water was bab-
bling; had Dr. Island used that sound to speak to him? He walked
toward it and found a little rill that threaded a way among the trees,
and followed it. In a hundred steps it grew broader, slowed, and ended
in a long blind pool under a dome of leaves. Diane was sitting on moss
on the side opposite him; she looked up as she saw him, and smiled.

"Hello," he said.

"Hello, Nicholas. I thought I heard you. I wasn't mistaken after all,
was I?"

"I didn't think I said anything." He tested the dark water with his
foot and found that it was very cold.

"You gave a little gasp, I fancy. I heard it, and I said to myself, *that's
Nicholas,* and I called you. Then I thought I might be wrong, or that it
might be Ignacio."

"Ignacio was chasing me. Maybe he still is, but I think he's probably
given up by now."

The girl nodded, looking into the dark waters of the pool, but did not
seem to have heard him. He began to work his way around to her,
climbing across the snakelike roots of the crowding trees. "Why does
Ignacio want to kill me, Diane?"

"Sometimes he wants to kill me too," the girl said.

"But why?"

"I think he's a bit frightened of us. Have you ever talked to him,
Nicholas?"

"Today I did a little. He told me a story about a pet fish he used to
have."

"Ignacio grew up all alone; did he tell you that? On Earth. On a plantation in Brazil, way up the Amazon—Dr. Island told me."

"I thought it was crowded on Earth."

"The cities are crowded, and the countryside closest to the cities. But there are places where it's emptier than it used to be. Where Ignacio was, there would have been Red Indian hunters two or three hundred years ago; when he was there, there wasn't anyone, just the machines. Now he doesn't want to be looked at, doesn't want anyone around him."

Nicholas said slowly, "Dr. Island said lots of people wouldn't be sick if only there weren't other people around all the time. Remember that?"

"Only there are other people around all the time; that's how the world is."

"Not in Brazil, maybe," Nicholas said. He was trying to remember something about Brazil, but the only thing he could think of was a parrot singing in a straw hat from the comview cartoons; and then a turtle and a hedgehog that turned into armadillos for the love of God, Montressor. He said, "Why didn't he stay there?"

"Did I tell you about the bird, Nicholas?" She had been not-listening again.

"What bird?"

"I have a bird. Inside." She patted the flat stomach below her small breasts, and for a moment Nicholas thought she had really found food. "She sits in here. She has tangled a nest in my entrails, where she sits and tears at my breath with her beak. I look healthy to you, don't I? But inside I'm hollow and rotten and turning brown, dirt and old feathers, oozing away. Her beak will break through soon."

"Okay." Nicholas turned to go.

"I've been drinking water here, trying to drown her. I think I've swallowed so much I couldn't stand up now if I tried, but she isn't even wet, and do you know something, Nicholas? I've found out I'm not really me, I'm her."

Turning back Nicholas asked, "When was the last time you had anything to eat?"

"I don't know. Two, three days ago. Ignacio gave me something."

"I'm going to try to open a coconut. If I can I'll bring you back some."

When he reached the beach, Nicholas turned and walked slowly back in the direction of the dead fire, this time along the rim of dampened sand between the sea and the palms. He was thinking about machines.

There were hundreds of thousands, perhaps millions, of machines out beyond the belt, but few or none of the sophisticated servant robots of Earth—those were luxuries. Would Ignacio, in Brazil (whatever that was like), have had such luxuries? Nicholas thought not; those robots were almost like people, and living with them would be like living with people. Nicholas wished that he could speak Brazilian.

There had been the therapy robots at St. John's; Nicholas had not liked them, and he did not think Ignacio would have liked them either. If he had liked his therapy robot he probably would not have had to be sent here. He thought of the chipped and rusted old machine that had cleaned the corridors—Maya had called it Corradora, but no one else ever called it anything but *Hey!* It could not (or at least did not) speak, and Nicholas doubted that it had emotions, except possibly a sort of love of cleanness that did not extend to its own person. "You will understand," someone was saying inside his head, "that motives of all sorts can be divided into two sorts." A doctor? A therapy robot? It did not matter. "Extrinsic and intrinsic. An extrinsic motive has always some further end in view, and that end we call an intrinsic motive. Thus when we have reduced motivation to intrinsic motivation we have reduced it to its simplest parts. Take that machine over there."

What machine?

"Freud would have said that it was fixated at the latter anal stage, perhaps due to the care its builders exercised in seeing that the dirt it collects is not released again. Because of its fixation it is, as you see, obsessed with cleanliness and order; compulsive sweeping and scrubbing palliate its anxieties. It is a strength of Freud's theory, and not a weakness, that it serves to explain many of the activities of machines as well as the acts of persons."

Hello there, Corradora.

And hello, Ignacio.

My head, moving from side to side, must remind you of a radar scanner. My steps are measured, slow, and precise. I emit a scarcely audible humming as I walk, and my eyes are fixed, as I swing my head, not on you, Ignacio, but on the waves at the edge of sight, where they curve up into the sky. I stop ten meters short of you, and I stand.

You go, I follow, ten meters behind. What do I want? Nothing.

Yes, I will pick up the sticks, and I will follow—five meters behind.

"Break them, and put them on the fire. Not all of them, just a few."

Yes.

"Ignacio keeps the fire here burning all the time. Sometimes he takes the coals of fire from it to start others, but here, under the big palm log, he has a fire always. The rain does not strike it here. Always the fire. Do you know how he made it the first time? Reply to him!"

"No."

"No, *Patrão!*"

" 'No, *Patrão.*' "

"Ignacio stole it from the gods, from Poseidon. Now Poseidon is dead, lying at the bottom of the water. Which is the top. Would you like to see him?"

"If you wish it, *Patrão.*"

"It will soon be dark, and that is the time to fish; do you have a spear?"

"No, *Patrão.*"

"Then Ignacio will get you one."

Ignacio took a handful of the sticks and thrust the ends into the fire, blowing on them. After a moment Nicholas leaned over and blew too, until all the sticks were blazing.

"Now we must find you some bamboo, and there is some back here. Follow me."

The light, still nearly shadowless, was dimming now, so that it seemed to Nicholas that they walked on insubstantial soil, though he could feel it beneath his feet. Ignacio stalked ahead, holding up the burning sticks until the fire seemed about to die, then pointing the ends down, allowing it to lick upward toward his hand and come to life again. There was a gentle wind blowing out toward the sea, carrying away the sound of the surf and bringing a damp coolness; and when they had been walking for several minutes, Nicholas heard in it a faint, dry, almost rhythmic rattle.

Ignacio looked back at him and said, "The music. The big stems talking; hear it?"

They found a cane a little thinner than Nicholas's wrist and piled the burning sticks around its base, then added more. When it fell, Ignacio burned through the upper end too, making a pole about as long as Nicholas was tall, and with the edge of a sea shell scraped the larger end to a point. "Now you are a fisherman," he said. Nicholas said, "Yes, *Patrão,*" still careful not to meet his eyes.

"You are hungry?"

"Yes, *Patrão*."

"Then let me tell you something. Whatever you get is Ignacio's, you understand? And what he catches, that is his too. But when he has eaten what he wants, what is left is yours. Come on now, and Ignacio will teach you to fish or drown you."

Ignacio's own spear was buried in the sand not far from the fire; it was much bigger than the one he had made for Nicholas. With it held across his chest he went down to the water, wading until it was waist high, then swimming, not looking to see if Nicholas was following. Nicholas found that he could swim with the spear by putting all his effort into the motion of his legs, holding the spear in his left hand and stroking only occasionally with his right. "You breathe," he said softly, "and watch the spear," and after that he had only to allow his head to lift from time to time.

He had thought Ignacio would begin to look for fish as soon as they were well out from the beach, but the Brazilian continued to swim, slowly but steadily, until it seemed to Nicholas that they must be a kilometer or more from land. Suddenly, as though the lights in a room had responded to a switch, the dark sea around them became an opalescent blue. Ignacio stopped, treading water and using his spear to buoy himself.

"Here," he said. "Get them between yourself and the light."

Open-eyed, he bent his face to the water, raised it again to breathe deeply, and dove. Nicholas followed his example, floating belly-down with open eyes.

All the world of dancing glitter and dark island vanished as though he had plunged his face into a dream. Far, far below him Jupiter displayed its broad, striped disk, marred with the spreading Bright Spot where man-made silicone enzymes had stripped the hydrogen from methane for kindled fusion: a cancer and a burning infant sun. Between that sun and his eyes lay invisible a hundred thousand kilometers of space, and the temperglass shell of the satellite; hundreds of meters of illuminated water, and in it the spread body of Ignacio, dark against the light, still kicking downward, his spear a pencil line of blackness in his hand.

Involuntarily Nicholas's head came up, returning to the universe of sparkling waves, aware now that what he had called "night" was only the shadow cast by Dr. Island when Jupiter and the Bright Spot slid beneath her. That shadow line, indetectable in air, now lay sharp across the water behind him. He took breath and plunged.

Almost at once a fish darted somewhere below, and his left arm thrust the spear forward, but it was far out of reach. He swam after it, then saw another, larger, fish farther down and dove for that, passing Ignacio surfacing for air. The fish was too deep, and he had used up his oxygen; his lungs aching for air, he swam up, wanting to let go of his spear, then realizing at the last moment that he could, that it would only bob to the surface if he released it. His head broke water and he gasped, his heart thumping; water struck his face and he knew again, suddenly, as though they had ceased to exist while he was gone, the pulsebeat pounding of the waves.

Ignacio was waiting for him. He shouted, "This time you will come with Ignacio, and he will show you the dead sea god. Then we will fish."

Unable to speak, Nicholas nodded. He was allowed three more breaths; then Ignacio dove and Nicholas had to follow, kicking down until the pressure sang in his ears. Then through blue water he saw, looming at the edge of the light, a huge mass of metal anchored to the temperglass hull of the satellite itself; above it, hanging lifelessly like the stem of a great vine severed from the root, a cable twice as thick as a man's body; and on the bottom, sprawled beside the mighty anchor, a legged god that might have been a dead insect save that it was at least six meters long. Ignacio turned and looked back at Nicholas to see if he understood; he did not, but he nodded, and with the strength draining from his arms, surfaced again.

After Ignacio brought up the first fish, they took turns on the surface guarding their catch, and while the Bright Spot crept beneath the shelving rim of Dr. Island, they speared two more, one of them quite large. Then when Nicholas was so exhausted he could scarcely lift his arms, they made their way back to shore, and Ignacio showed him how to gut the fish with a thorn and the edge of a shell, and reclose them and pack them in mud and leaves to be roasted by the fire. After Ignacio had begun to eat the largest fish, Nicholas timidly drew out the smallest, and ate for the first time since coming to Dr. Island. Only when he had finished did he remember Diane.

He did not dare to take the last fish to her, but he looked covertly at Ignacio, and began edging away from the fire. The Brazilian seemed not to have noticed him. When he was well into the shadows he stood, backed a few steps, then—slowly, as his instincts warned him—walked away, not beginning to trot until the distance between them was nearly a hundred meters.

He found Diane sitting apathetic and silent at the margin of the cold pool, and had some difficulty persuading her to stand. At last he lifted her, his hands under her arms pressing against her thin ribs. Once on her feet she stood steadily enough, and followed him when he took her by the hand. He talked to her, knowing that although she gave no sign of hearing she heard him, and that the right words might wake her to response. "We went fishing—Ignacio showed me how. And he's got a fire, Diane, he got it from a kind of robot that was supposed to be fixing one of the cables that holds Dr. Island, I don't know how. Anyway, listen, we caught three big fish, and I ate one and Ignacio ate a great big one, and I don't think he'd mind if you had the other one, only say, 'Yes Patrão,' and 'No, Patrão,' to him—he likes that, and he's only used to machines. You don't have to smile at him or anything—just look at the fire, that's what I do, just look at the fire."

To Ignacio, perhaps wisely, he at first said nothing at all, leading Diane to the place where he had been sitting himself a few minutes before and placing some scraps from his fish in her lap. When she did not eat he found a sliver of the tender, roasted flesh and thrust it into her mouth. Ignacio said, "Ignacio believed that one dead," and Nicholas answered, "No, Patrão."

"There is another fish. Give it to her."

Nicholas did, raking the gob of baked mud from the coals to crack with the heel of his hand, and peeling the broken and steaming fillets from the skin and bones to give to her when they had cooled enough to eat; after the fish had lain in her mouth for perhaps half a minute she began to chew and swallow, and after the third mouthful she fed herself, though without looking at either of them.

"Ignacio believed that one dead," Ignacio said again.

"No, Patrão," Nicholas answered, and then added, "Like you can see, she's alive."

"She is a pretty creature, with the firelight on her face—no?"

"Yes, Patrão, very pretty."

"But too thin." Ignacio moved around the fire until he was sitting almost beside Diane, then reached for the fish Nicholas had given her. Her hands closed on it, though she still did not look at him.

"You see, she knows us after all," Ignacio said. "We are not ghosts."

Nicholas whispered urgently, "Let him have it."

Slowly Diane's fingers relaxed, but Ignacio did not take the fish. "I was only joking, little one," he said. "And I think not such a good joke after all." Then when she did not reply, he turned away from her, his eyes reaching out across the dark, tossing water for something Nicholas could not see.

"She likes you, *Patrão,*" Nicholas said. The words were like swallowing filth, but he thought of the bird ready to tear through Diane's skin, and Maya's blood soaking in little round dots into the white cloth, and continued. "She is only shy. It is better that way."

"You. What do you know?"

At least Ignacio was no longer looking at the sea. Nicholas said, "Isn't it true, *Patrão?*"

"Yes, it is true."

Diane was picking at the fish again, conveying tiny flakes to her mouth with delicate fingers; distinctly but almost absently she said, "Go, Nicholas."

He looked at Ignacio, but the Brazilian's eyes did not turn toward the girl, nor did he speak.

"Nicholas, go away. Please."

In a voice he hoped was pitched too low for Ignacio to hear, Nicholas said, "I'll see you in the morning. All right?"

Her head moved a fraction of a centimeter.

Once he was out of sight of the fire, one part of the beach was as good to sleep on as another; he wished he had taken a piece of wood from the fire to start one of his own and tried to cover his legs with sand to keep off the cool wind, but the sand fell away whenever he moved, and his legs and his left hand moved without volition on his part.

The surf, lapping at the rippled shore, said, "That was well done, Nicholas."

"I can feel you move," Nicholas said. "I don't think I ever could before except when I was high up."

"I doubt that you can now; my roll is less than one one-hundredth of a degree."

"Yes, I can. You wanted me to do that, didn't you? About Ignacio."

"Do you know what the Harlow effect is, Nicholas?"

Nicholas shook his head.

"About a hundred years ago Dr. Harlow experimented with monkeys who had been raised in complete isolation—no mothers, no other monkeys at all."

"Lucky monkeys."

"When the monkeys were mature he put them into cages with normal ones; they fought with any that came near them, and sometimes they killed them."

"Psychologists always put things in cages; did he ever think of turning them loose in the jungle instead?"

"No, Nicholas, though we have . . . Aren't you going to say anything?"

"I guess not."

"Dr. Harlow tried, you see, to get the isolate monkeys to breed—sex is the primary social function—but they wouldn't. Whenever another monkey of either sex approached they displayed aggressiveness, which the other monkeys returned. He cured them finally by introducing immature monkeys—monkey children—in place of the mature, socialized ones. These needed the isolate adults so badly that they kept on making approaches no matter how often or how violently they were rejected, and in the end they were accepted, and the isolates socialized. It's interesting to note that the founder of Christianity seems to have had an intuitive grasp of the principle—but it was almost two thousand years before it was demonstrated scientifically."

"I don't think it worked here," Nicholas said. "It was more complicated than that."

"Human beings are complicated monkeys, Nicholas."

"That's about the first time I ever heard you make a joke. You like not being human, don't you?"

"Of course. Wouldn't you?"

"I always thought I would, but now I'm not sure. You said that to help me, didn't you? I don't like that."

A wave higher than the others splashed chill foam over Nicholas's legs, and for a moment he wondered if this were Dr. Island's reply. Half a minute later another wave wet him, and another, and he moved farther up the beach to avoid them. The wind was stronger, but he slept despite it, and was awakened only for a moment by a flash of light from the direction from which he had come; he tried to guess what might have caused it, thought of Diane and Ignacio throwing the burning sticks into the air to see the arcs of fire, smiled—too sleepy now to be angry—and slept again.

Morning came cold and sullen; Nicholas ran up and down the beach, rubbing himself with his hands. A thin rain, or spume (it was hard to tell which), was blowing in the wind, clouding the light to gray radiance. He wondered if Diane and Ignacio would mind if he came back now and decided to wait, then thought of fishing so that he would have something to bring when he came; but the sea was very cold and the waves so high they tumbled him, wrenching his bamboo spear from his hand. Ignacio found him dripping with water, sitting with his back to a palm trunk and staring out toward the lifting curve of the sea.

"Hello, you," Ignacio said.

"Good morning, *Patrão.*"

Ignacio sat down. "What is your name? You told me, I think, when we first met, but I have forgotten. I am sorry."

"Nicholas."

"Yes."

"*Patrão,* I am very cold. Would it be possible for us to go to your fire?"

"My name is Ignacio; call me that."

Nicholas nodded, frightened.

"But we cannot go to my fire, because the fire is out."

"Can't you make another one, *Patrão?*"

"You do not trust me, do you? I do not blame you. No, I cannot make another—you may use what I had, if you wish, and make one after I have gone. I came only to say goodbye."

"You're leaving?"

The wind in the palm fronds said, "Ignacio is much better now. He will be going to another place, Nicholas."

"A hospital?"

"Yes, a hospital, but I don't think he will have to stay there long."

"But . . ." Nicholas tried to think of something appropriate. At St. John's and the other places where he had been confined, when people left, they simply left, and usually were hardly spoken of once it was learned that they were going and thus were already tainted by whatever it was that froze the smiles and dried the tears of those outside. At last he said, "Thanks for teaching me how to fish."

"That was all right," Ignacio said. He stood up and put a hand on Nicholas's shoulder, then turned away. Four meters to his left the damp sand was beginning to lift and crack. While Nicholas watched, it opened on a brightly lit companionway walled with white. Ignacio pushed his curly black hair back from his eyes and went down, and the sand closed with a thump.

"He won't be coming back, will he?" Nicholas said.

"No."

"He said I could use his stuff to start another fire, but I don't even know what it is."

Dr. Island did not answer. Nicholas got up and began to walk back to where the fire had been, thinking about Diane and wondering if she was hungry; he was hungry himself.

He found her beside the dead fire. Her chest had been burned away, and lying close by, near the hole in the sand where Ignacio must have kept it hidden, was a bulky nuclear welder. The power pack was too heavy for Nicholas to lift, but he picked up the welding gun on its short cord and touched the trigger, producing a two-meter plasma discharge which he played along the sand until Diane's body was ash. By the time he had finished the wind was whipping the palms and sending stinging rain into his eyes, but he collected a supply of wood and built another fire, bigger and bigger until it roared like a forge in the wind. "He killed her!" he shouted to the waves.

"YES." Dr. Island's voice was big and wild.

"You said he was better."

"HE IS," howled the wind. "YOU KILLED THE MONKEY THAT WANTED TO PLAY WITH YOU, NICHOLAS—AS I BELIEVED IGNACIO WOULD EVENTUALLY KILL YOU, WHO ARE SO EASILY HATED, SO DIFFERENT FROM WHAT IT IS THOUGHT A BOY SHOULD BE. BUT KILLING THE MONKEY HELPED YOU, REMEMBER? MADE YOU BETTER. IGNACIO WAS FRIGHTENED BY WOMEN; NOW HE KNOWS THAT THEY ARE REALLY VERY WEAK, AND HE HAS ACTED UPON CERTAIN FANTASIES AND FINDS THEM BITTER."

"You're rocking," Nicholas said. "Am I doing that?"

"YOUR THOUGHT."

A palm snapped in the storm; instead of falling, it flew crashing among the others, its fronded head catching the wind like a sail. "I'm killing you," Nicholas said. "Destroying you." The left side of his face was so contorted with grief and rage that he could scarcely speak.

Dr. Island heaved beneath his feet. "NO."

"One of your cables is already broken—I saw that. Maybe more than one. You'll pull loose. I'm turning this world, isn't that right? The attitude rockets are tuned to my emotions, and they're spinning us around, and the slippage is the wind and the high sea, and when you come loose nothing will balance any more."

"NO."

"What's the stress on your cables? Don't you know?"

"THEY ARE VERY STRONG."

"What kind of talk is that? You ought to say something like: 'The D-twelve cable tension is twenty-billion kilograms' force. WARNING! WARNING! Expected time to failure is ninety-seven seconds! WARNING!' *Don't you even know how a machine is supposed to talk?*" Nicholas was screaming now, and every wave reached farther up the beach than the last, so that the bases of the most seaward palms were awash.

"GET BACK, NICHOLAS. FIND HIGHER GROUND. GO INTO THE JUNGLE." It was the crashing waves themselves that spoke.

"I won't."

A long serpent of water reached for the fire, which hissed and sputtered.

"GET BACK!"

"I won't!"

A second wave came, striking Nicholas calf-high and nearly extinguishing the fire.

"ALL THIS WILL BE UNDER WATER SOON. GET BACK!"

Nicholas picked up some of the still-burning sticks and tried to carry them, but the wind blew them out as soon as he lifted them from the fire. He tugged at the welder, but it was too heavy for him to lift.

"GET BACK!"

He went into the jungle, where the trees lashed themselves to leafy rubbish in the wind and broken branches flew through the air like debris from an explosion; for a while he heard Diane's voice crying in the wind; it became Maya's, then his mother's or Sister Carmela's, and a hundred others; in time the wind grew less, and he could no longer feel the ground rocking. He felt tired. He said, "I didn't kill you after all, did I?" but there was no answer. On the beach, when he returned to it, he found the welder half buried in sand. No trace of Diane's ashes, nor of his fire. He gathered more wood and built another, lighting it with the welder.

"Now," he said. He scooped aside the sand around the welder until he reached the rough understone beneath it, and turned the flame of the welder on that; it blackened and bubbled.

"No," Dr. Island said.

"Yes." He was bending intently over the flame, both hands locked on the welder's trigger.

"Nicholas, stop that." When he did not reply, "Look behind you." There was a splashing louder than the crashing of the waves, and a groaning of metal. He whirled and saw the great, beetle-like robot Ignacio had shown him on the sea floor. Tiny shellfish clung to its metal skin, and water, faintly green, still poured from its body. Before he could turn the welding gun toward it, it shot forward hands like clamps and wrenched it from him. All up and down the beach similar machines were smoothing the sand and repairing the damage of the storm.

"That thing was dead," Nicholas said. "Ignacio killed it."

It picked up the power pack, shook it clean of sand, and turning, stalked back toward the sea.

"That is what Ignacio believed, and it was better that he believed so."

"And you said you couldn't do anything, you had no hands."

"I also told you that I would treat you as society will when you are released, that that was my nature. After that, did you still believe all I told you? Nicholas, you are upset now because Diane is dead—"

"You could have protected her!"

"—but by dying she made someone else—someone very important—well. Her prognosis was bad; she really wanted only death, and this was the death I chose for her. You could call it the death of Dr. Island, a death that would help someone else. Now you are alone, but soon there will be more patients in this segment, and you will help them, too—if you can—and perhaps they will help you. Do you understand?"

"No," Nicholas said. He flung himself down on the sand. The wind had dropped, but it was raining hard. He thought of the vision he had once had, and of describing it to Diane the day before. "This isn't ending the way I thought," he whispered. It was only a squeak of sound far down in his throat. "Nothing ever turns out right."

The waves, the wind, the rustling palm fronds and the pattering rain, the monkeys who had come down to the beach to search for food washed ashore, answered, "Go away—go back—don't move."

Nicholas pressed his scarred head against his knees, rocking back and forth.

"Don't move."

For a long time he sat still while the rain lashed his shoulders and the dripping monkeys frolicked and fought around him. When at last he lifted his face, there was in it some element of personality which had been only potentially present before, and with this an emptiness and an expression of surprise. His lips moved, and the sounds were the sounds made by a deaf-mute who tries to speak.

"Nicholas is gone," the waves said. "Nicholas, who was the right side of your body, the left half of your brain, I have forced into catatonia; for the remainder of your life he will be to you only what you once were to him—or less. Do you understand?"

The boy nodded.

"We will call you Kenneth, silent one. And if Nicholas tries to come again, Kenneth, you must drive him back—or return to what you have been."

The boy nodded a second time, and a moment afterward began to collect sticks for the dying fire. As though to themselves the waves chanted:

> "Seas are wild tonight . . .
> Stretching over Sado island
> Silent clouds of stars."

There was no reply.

Edgar Pangborn, who wrote *A Mirror for Observers, West of the Sun, Davy,* and several other science fiction novels, was a fine writer and a fine man. We met in 1971 when my wife and I visited him and his sister Mary in Woodstock, New York, and talked late into the night while listening to Beethoven quartets, stayed the night, and had breakfast to the strains of Gilbert and Sullivan. Thereafter we moved to California, but kept up a delightful correspondence till his death in 1976.

During those years he contributed four stories to *Universe;* three of these were set in the post-holocaust world of *Davy.* "The Night Wind" was his best, I think: a richly detailed, human, and very moving story about a world afraid of mutations, and one young outcast suffering the pain of being *different.* He said of it, "In some respects I think it goes beyond anything else I've been able to do," and he was right.

The Night Wind

Edgar Pangborn

At Mam Miriam's house beyond Trempa, Ottoba 20, 402

I will do it somewhere down this road, not yet but after dark; it will be when the night wind is blowing.

Always I have welcomed the sound of the night wind moving, as the leaves are passing on their secrets and sometimes falling, but falling lightly, easily, because their time to fall is come. Dressed in high colors, they fall to the day winds too this time of year, this autumn season. The smell of earth mold is spice on the tongue. I catch scent of apples ripening, windfalls rich-rotten pleasuring the yellow hornets. Rams and he-goats are mounting and crazy for it—O this time of year! They fall to the day winds echoing the sunlight, the good bright leaves, and that's no bad way to fall.

I know the dark of autumn too. The night wind hurts. Even now writing of it, only to think of it. Ottoba was in me when I said to my heart: I will do it somewhere down this road, I will end it, my life, for they believe it should never have begun. (I think there may be good spirits down that road. Perhaps the people I met were spirits, or they were human beings and spirits too, or we all are.) And I remembered how Father Horan also believes I ought never to have been born. I saw that in him; he believes it as the town folk do, and what we believe is most of what we are.

For three days I felt their sidelong stares, their anger that I would dare to pass near their houses. They called in their children to safety from me, who never hurt anyone. Passing one of those gray-eyed houses, I heard a woman say, "He ought to be stoned, that Benvenuto." I will not write her name.

Another said, "Only a mue would do what he did."

They call me that; they place me among the sad distorted things— armless or mindless or eyeless, somehow inhuman and corrupted—that so many mothers bear, or have borne, folk say, since the end of Old Time. How could a mue be called beautiful?

When I confessed to Father Horan, he shoved his hands behind his back, afraid he might touch me. "Poor Benvenuto!" But he said it acidly, staring down as if he had tasted poison in his food.

So I will end it (I told the hidden self that is me)—I will end it now in my fifteenth year before the Eternal Corruption that Father Horan spoke of can altogether destroy my soul; and so the hidden self that is me, if that is my soul, may win God's forgiveness for being born a monster.

But why did Father Horan love me once, taking something like a father's place, or seem to love me? Why did he teach me the reading of words and writing too, first showing me how the great words flow in the Book of Abraham, and on to the spelling book and so to all the mystery? Why did he let me see the other books, some of them, the books of Old Time forbidden to common people, even the poets? He would run his fingers through my hair, saying I must never cut it, or rest his arm on my shoulder; and I felt a need, I thought it was loneliness or love, in the curving of his fingers. Why did he say I might rise in the Holy

Amran Church, becoming greater than himself, a bishop—Bishop Benvenuto!—an archbishop!

If I am a monster now, was I not a monster then?

I could ask him no such questions when he was angry. I ran out of the church though I heard him calling after me, commanding me to return in God's name. I will not return.

I ran through the graveyard, past the dead hollow oak where I saw and heard bees swarming in the hot autumn light, and I think he stood among the headstones lamenting for me, but I would not look back, no, I plowed through a thicket and ran down a long golden aisle of maple trees and into Wayland's field (where it happened)—Wayland's field all standing alive with the bound shocks of corn, and into the woods again on the far side, only to be away from him.

It was there in Wayland's field that I first thought, I will do this to myself, I will end it, maybe in that wood I know of; but I was afraid of my knife. How can I cut and tear the body someone called beautiful? And so I looked at the thought of hiding in a shock of corn, the same one where I found Eden idle that day, and staying in it till I starved. But they say starving is a terrible death, and I might not have the courage or the patience to wait for it. I thought too, They will look for me when they know I'm gone, because they want to punish me, stone me, even my mother will want to punish me, and they would think of the cornfield where it happened and come searching like the flail of God.

How bright they stand, the bound stalks in the sun, like little wigwams for the field spirits, like people too, like old women with rustling skirts of yellow-gray; their hair is blowing! Now I know I will remember this when I go on—for I am going on without death, never doubt it, I promise you I shall not die by my own hand.

I saw two hawks circling and circling in the upper wind above Wayland's field. I thought up to them: You are like me, but you have all the world's air to fly away in.

The hawks are bound to the earth as I am, they must hunt food in the grass and branches, men shoot arrows from the earth to tear their hearts. Still they enter regions unknown to us, and maybe they and the wild geese have found an easy way to heaven.

Into the woods again on the far side of Wayland's field I hurried, and down and up the ravine that borders it, shadowed ground with alder and gray birch and a cool place of ferns I know of where sunlight comes late in the morning and mild. The brook in the ravine bottom was running scant from the dry weather, leaves collecting on the bodies of smooth shining stones. I did not go downstream to the pool but climbed the other side of the ravine and took the path—hardly that, merely a known place where my feet have passed before—to the break in the trees that lets you out on this road, and I thought: Here I will do it, somewhere farther on in the shadows.

It is wider than a wood-road and better kept, for wagons use it now and then, and it is supposed to wind through back ways southeast as far as Nupal, ten miles they say or even more—I never believed much of what I hear about Nupal. The trading of our village has always been with Maplestock, and surely nobody goes to Nupal except those tinkers and gyppos and ramblers with their freaky wagons, squirrel-eyed children, scrawny dogs. A sad place it must be, Nupal, more than seven hundred crammed into the one village, as I hear it. I don't understand how human beings can live like that—the houses may not be standing as horridly close together as folk tell. Maybe I'll see the place in passing. I've noticed a dozen times, the same souls who sniggle about with ugly fact until it looks like fancy will turn right-about and ask you to believe that ugly fancy is fact.

I went down the road not running any more, nor thinking more about Father Horan. I thought of Eden.

Then I thought about my mother, who is going to marry Blind Hamlin the candlemaker, I'm told. She wouldn't tell me herself, the winds told me. (Toby Omstrong told me, because he doesn't like me.) Let's hope the jolly wedding isn't delayed by concern over my absence—I am not coming back, Mother. Think of me kindly while tumbling with your waxy man, or better, think of me not at all, the cord is cut, and anyhow didn't you pick me up somewhere as a changeling?

Hoy, there I was on your doorstep all red and nasty, wrapped up in a cabbage leaf! Likely story. But we can't have it thought that *you* gave birth to a monster, even one begotten by a little shoemaker whose image you did your best to destroy for me. (But I saved some pieces, I try to put them together now and then. I wish I could remember him; the memories of others are not much more help than wind under the door, for people don't understand what I want to know—small blame to them, they can't hear the questions I don't know how to ask—and I think your memories of him are mostly lies, Mother, though you may not know it.) "He was a poor sad soul, Benvenuto." Was he, Mother? "He broke my heart with his unfaithfulness, Benvenuto." But Blind Hamlin is going to stick it back together with mutton-fat, remember?

"He drank, you know, Benvenuto, that was why he could never make a decent living." Why, I will drink to you, Mother, I will drink to the wedding in Mam Miriam's best apple brandy before I leave this poor empty house where I am writing.

Don't destroy Blind Hamlin, Mother. I don't like him, he's a cross-patch bag of guts, but don't destroy him, don't whittle him down as you must have scraped my father down with the rasp of words—but I forget, I am a changeling. Poor Blind Hamlin!—there may be witchcraft in it, Mother. It troubles me that a man who can't see makes candles for those who will not. Don't destroy him. Make another monster with him. I'd like a monster for a half-brother—but there, never mind, I'm not coming back to Trempa, make all the monsters you wish. The world's already full of them.

I am not writing this for my mother. She will not be the one to find it here. Whoever does—I pray you, read this page if you like and the one before it that begins "She wouldn't tell me herself"—read and then throw away, in God's name. For I would like the truth to be somewhere in the world, maybe in your head, whoever you are, but I don't wish to slap my mother in the face with it, nor Blind Hamlin either. Blind Hamlin was never unkind to me. I am all soreness, the tenderest touch smarts on a burned skin. I will mend. I don't hate my mother—do I hate anyone?—is it a sign of my monsterhood that I don't hate anyone? —or if I do, I will *mend,* I'll cease hating wherever I am going, and even forget. Especially forget. Read those pages and throw away and then, you too, forget. But save the rest, if you will. I don't want to die altogether in your mind, whoever you are.

Down that road I came. I think I left behind me most of what had appeared certain in the world; the new uncertainties are still to find. Where did I encounter you? Who are you?—oh, merely the one supposed to find this letter. So then you are not the new person I need to find—someone not Eden, nor Andrea whom I loved, but some other. But with Andrea I understood that heaven would open whenever he looked on me.

In that road through the woods beyond Wayland's field the trees stand close on either side, oak and pine and enormous tulip trees where the white parrots like to gather and squabble with the bluejays, and thickets that swell with a passion of growth wherever an opening like that road lets through the sun. Oaks had shifted into the bronze along with the clear gold of maple trees when I passed by, yet I saw few leaves fallen. You remember some of the wise prophets in Trempa have been saying it'll be a hard winter, with snow in January for sure. The Lord must save a special kind of forgiveness for the weather prophets—other kinds of liars have some chance of learning better. As I looked along the slender channel of the road, I saw the stirring of distant treetops under the wind, but here that wind was hushed, cut to a modest breeze or to no motion at all. And suddenly the stillness was charged with the fishy loathsome reek of black wolf.

It is a poison in the air and we live with it. I remember how it has always happened in the village: days, weeks, with no hint of the evil, and when we have forgotten and grown careless, then without warning the sour stench of them comes on the air, and we hear their rasping howl in the nights—nothing like the musical uproar of the common wolves who seldom do worse than pick up a sheep now and then—and people will die, ambushed, throat-torn, stripped of flesh and bones cracked for the marrow. Some tell of seeing the Devil walk with them. He teaches them tricks that only human beings ought-to know. He leads them to the trail of late travelers, to lonely houses where a door may be unlatched, or someone seized on the way to shed or outhouse. And yet they do say that black wolf will not attack by day; if a man comes at him then, even if he is at his carrion, he may slink off; now I know this is true. At night black wolf is invincible, I suppose. The smell hung dense on that woodland road, coming from all around me, so that I could not run away from it.

I had my thin strength, and a knife; my knife is from the hands of Wise Wayland the Smith, and there is a spell on it. For look you, no harm comes to me if I am wearing it. I was not wearing it when Andrea's family moved away and took him with them—all the way to Penn, God help me. I was not wearing it when they came on me with Eden in Wayland's field and called me monster.

In fear I went ahead, not trying for quiet because no one ever surprises black wolf. I came on the beast on the far side of a boulder that jutted into the road, but before that I heard the sounds of tearing. It had ripped the liver from the body. Blood still oozed from all the wounds. Enough remained of the face so that I knew the man was old Kobler. His back-pack was not with him, nor any gear, so he had not been on his way to the village. Perhaps he had been taken with some sickness, and so the wolf dared to bring him down in broad day.

By this time Kobler will be expected in the village. They'll wonder why he doesn't come marching to the General Store with his stack of reed baskets and Mam Miriam's beautiful embroideries and such-like, and slap down his one silver coin, and fill his back-pack with the provisions for Mam Miriam and himself. True, he was never regular in the timing of his visits; another week or two might go by before anyone turns curious. People don't think much unless their convenience is joggled, and old Kobler was so silent a man, never granting anyone a word that could be held back—and Mam Miriam herself hardly more than a legend to the town folk—no, I suppose they won't stir themselves unduly. All the same I must leave, I must not be caught here by those who would stone me for their souls' benefit. Nothing keeps me in this house now except a wish to write these words for you, whoever you are. Then I will go when the night wind is blowing.

It was an old dog wolf, and foul, alone, his fangs yellowed. He held his ground hardly a moment when I walked down on him with the knife of Wayland flashing sunlight on his eyes. I did not understand immediately that Kobler was past help—then the wolf moved, I saw the liver, I knew the look on the old man's mask was no-way meant for me. Jon Kobler, a good fellow I think, Mam Miriam's servant, companion, and more. He shrank from the world as she did, nor do I see how you could hold it against either of them, for often the world stinks so that even a fool like me must hold his nose. It will not harm them now if I tell you they were lovers.

The wolf slunk off through the brush into a ravine. It must have been the power of Wayland's knife—or is it possible that black wolf is not so terrible as folk say? Well, mine is a knife that Wayland made long since, when he was young; he told me so.

He gave it to me on the morning of the best day of my life. Andrea had come to me the day before, had chosen me out of all the others in the training yard—although I seldom shone there, my arm is not heavy enough for the axe or the spear-throwing, and in archery I am only fair, undistinguished. He challenged me to wrestle, I put forth my best, almost I had his shoulders down and he laughing up at me, and then presto! somehow I am flung over on my back and my heart close to cracking with happiness because he has won. And he invited me to go on the morrow with him and some of his older friends for a stag hunt through Bindiaan Wood, and I had to say, "I have no knife, no gear."

"Oh," says Andrea, and April is no kinder, "we'll find extra gear for you at my father's house, and as for a knife of your own, maybe Wayland the Smith has one for you."

I knew that Wayland Smith did sometimes make such gifts to boys just turning men, but had never imagined he would trouble with one so slight-built as I am and supposed to be simple-minded from the hours with the books. "You do hide your light," says Andrea, whom I had already loved for a year, scarcely daring to speak to him. He laughed and pressed my shoulder. "Go to ancient Wayland, do him some little favor—there's no harm in him—and maybe he'll have a knife for you. I would give you mine, Benvenuto," he said, "only that's bad magic between friends, but come to me with a knife of your own and we'll make blood brotherhood."

So the next morning I went to Wayland the Smith with all my thoughts afire, and I found the old man about to draw a bucket of water from his well, but looking ill and drooping, and he said, "O Benvenuto, I have a crick in my arm—would you, in kindness?" So I drew the water for him, and we drank together. I saw the smithy was untidy with cobwebs, and swept it out for him, he watching me and rambling on with his tales and sayings and memories that some call wanton blasphemies—I paid little heed to them, thinking of Andrea, until he asked me, "Are you a good boy, Benvenuto?" His tone made me know he would like to hear me laugh, or anyway not mind it, indeed I could hardly help laughing at a thousand silly notions, and for the pleasure of it, and the joy of the day; and that was when he gave me this knife I always carry. I don't think I answered his question, or at least only to say, "I try to be," or some such nonsense. He gave me the knife, kissed me, told me not to be too unhappy in my life; but I don't know what one must do to follow that counsel, unless it is to live the way all others do, like baa-sheep who come and go at the will of the shepherd and his dog and must never stray from the tinkle of the wether's bell.

Oh, yes, that day I went on the hunt with Andrea, armed with the knife that was given me by Wayland Smith. We killed a stag together, he marked my forehead, with our own blood then we made brotherhood; but he is gone away.

There was nothing anyone could have done for old Kobler except pray for him. I did that—if there's anything to hear our prayers, if the prayers of a monster can be noticed. But who is God? Who is this cloud-thing that has nothing better to do than stare on human pain and now and then poke it with his finger? Is he not bored? Will he not presently wipe it all away, or go away and forget? Or has he already gone away, forgotten?

You will not have me burnt for these words because you will not find me. Besides, I must remember you are simply the unknown who will happen on this letter in Mam Miriam's house, and you may even be a friend. I must remember there are friends.

When I rose from kneeling beside the poor mess that was what remained of Kobler, I heard rustling in the brush. That wolf had no companions or they would have been with him tearing at the meat, but perhaps he was rallying from his fright, hungry for something young and fresh. I understood too that the sun was lowering, night scarcely more than an hour away. Night's arrival would be sudden in the manner of autumn, which has a cruelty in it, as if we did not know that winter is near but must be reminded with a slap and a scolding. Only then did I think of Mam Miriam, who would expect Kobler's return.

When was the last time any of you in Trempa saw Mam Miriam Coletta? I had not even known she was daughter to Roy Coletta, who was governor of Ulsta in his time. Or was this only something she dreamed for me, something to tell me when perhaps her wits were wandering? It doesn't matter: I will think her a princess if I choose.

She was twenty-five and yet unmarried, hostess of the governor's mansion at Sortees after her mother's death, and she fell in love with a common archer, one of the Governor's Guard, and ran away with him, escaping from her locked bedroom on a rope made from a torn blanket. O the dear romantic tale! I've heard none better from the gyppos—their stories are too much alike, but this was like some of the poems of Old Time, especially as she told it me, and never mind if her wits wandered; I have ceased speculating whether it was true.

You think the archer was this same man who became Poor Old Kobler, marching into town fortnightly with his back-pack and his baskets, and the embroideries by a crazy old bedridden dame who lived off in the Haunted Stone House and wouldn't give anyone the time of day?

He was not. That archer abandoned her in a brothel at Nuber. Kobler was an aging soldier, a deserter. He took her out of that place and brought her to Trempa. He knew of the old stone house in the woods so long abandoned—for he was a Trempa man in his beginnings, Jon Kobler, but you may not find any bones to bury—and he took her there. He repaired the solid old ruin; you would not believe what good work he did there, mostly with wood cut and shaped out of the forest with his own hands. He cared for her there, servant and lover; they seem not to have had much need of the world. They grew old there, like that.

Rather, he did, I suppose. When I saw her she did not seem very old.

Why, I first heard talk and speculation about them (most of it malicious) when I was six years old; I think they must have been new-come then, and that's only nine years ago. Yesterday or perhaps the day before, nine years would have seemed like a long time to me. Now I wonder if a thousand years is a long time, and I can't answer my own question. I am not clever at guessing ages, but I would think Mam Miriam was hardly past forty; and certainly she spoke like a lady, and told me of the past glories as surely no one could have done who had not known them—the governor's mansion, the dances all night long and great people coming on horseback or in fine carriages from all over the county; she made me see the sweaty faces of the musicians in the balcony, and didn't she herself go up one night (the dance at her tenth birthday party) to share a box of candy with them? She spoke of the gardens, the lilac and wisteria and many-colored roses, the like you never saw in Trempa, and there were odd musky red grapes from some incredible land far south of Penn, and from there also, limes, and oranges, and spices she could not describe for me. Telling me all this simply and truly, she did seem like a young woman, even a girl—oh, see for yourself, how should I know? There she lies, poor sweet thing, in the bed Jon Kobler must have made. I have done what I could for her, and it is not much.

I am wandering. I must tell of all this as I should, and then go. Perhaps you will never come; it may be best if you do not.

I prayed for Kobler, and then I went on down the road—despising the wolf but not forgetting him, for I wish to live—as far as its joining with the small path that I knew would take me to Mam Miriam's. There I hesitated a long while, though I think I knew from the start that I would go to her. I don't know what it is in us that (sometimes) will make us do a thing against our wishes because we know it to be good. "Conscience" is too thin a word, and "God" too misty, too spoiled by the many who mouth it constantly without any care for what they say, or as if they alone were able to inform you of God's will—and please, how came they to be so favored? But something drives, I think from within, and I must even obey it without knowing a name for it.

You see, I had never followed that path. No one does. The road like the old stone house itself is haunted. Anyone who ventures there goes in peril of destruction or bewitchment. So far, I am not destroyed.

Once on the path—why, I began to run. Maybe I ran so as to yield no room in my thought to the fear that is always, like black wolf, waiting. I ran down the path through a wilderness of peace. There were the beeches, gray and kind—I like to imagine something of peace in their nearness. I know that violence might be done in the presence, in the very shadow of the beech trees, as in any other place where the human creature goes; a little corner of my mind is a garden where I lie in the sun not believing it. In their presence on that path I ran without shortness of breath, without remembering fear, and I came to the green clearing, and the house of red-gray stone. It was growing late, the sun too low to penetrate this hidden place. In shadow therefore I came to Mam Miriam's door and pounded on the oak panel. But gossip had always said that the old woman (if she existed at all outside of Jon Kobler's head, if he didn't create those dazzling embroideries himself out of his own craziness and witchcraft) was bedridden and helpless. So my knocking was foolish. I turned the latch and pushed the heavy sluggish thing inward, closing it behind me, staring about half-blind in the gray light.

The house is trifling-small, as you will see if you dare come here. Only that big lower room with the fireplace where Jon cooked, the bench where he worked at his baskets, clogs, wooden beads, and this other room up here with the smaller hearth. There's this one chair up here where I sit now (Kobler used to sit beside his love's bed, you know) and the little table I write on, which I am sure they used drawn up beside the bed for their meals together, for the night pitcher of water she no longer needs. You will be aware now that she did exist. There's the roll of linen cloth—Kobler must have gone all the way to Maplestock to buy that—and some half-finished table mats, pillow slips, dresser covers. There's her embroidery hoop, the needles, the rolls of bright yarns, and thread—I never knew there were so many sizes and colors. And there she too is lying. She was; she lived; I closed her eyes.

I looked about me in that failing evening, and she called from upstairs, "Jon, what's wrong? Why did you make such a noise at the door? You've been long, Jon. I'm thirsty."

The tone of her voice was delicate, a music. I cannot tell you how it frightened me, that the voice of a crazy old woman should sound so mild and sweet. Desperately I wanted to run away, much more than I had wanted it when I stood out there at the beginning of the path. But the thing that I will not call Conscience or God (somewhere in the Old-Time books I think it was called Virtue, but doubtless few read them)—the thing that would never let me strike a child, or stone a criminal or a mue on the green as we are expected to do in Trempa—this mad cruel-sweet thing that may be a part of love commanded me to answer her, and I called up the stairway, "Don't be afraid. It's not Jon, but I came to help you." I followed my words, climbing the stairs slowly so that she could forbid me if she chose. She said no more until I had come to her.

The house was turning chill. I had hardly noticed it downstairs; up here the air was already cold, and I saw—preferring not to stare at her directly till she spoke to me—that she was holding the bedcovers high to her throat, and shivering. "I must build you a fire," I said, and went to the hearth. Fresh wood and kindling were laid ready, a tinderbox stood on the mantel. She watched me struggle with the clumsy tool until I won my flame and set it to the twigs and scraps of waste cloth. That ancient chimney is clean—the fire caught well without smoking into the room. I warmed my hands.

"What has happened? Where is Jon?"

"He can't come. I'm sorry." I asked her if she was hungry, and she shook her head. "I'm Benvenuto of Trempa," I told her. "I'm running away. I must get you some fresh water." I hurried out with the pitcher, obliged to retreat for that moment for my own sake, because meeting her gaze, as I had briefly done, had been a glancing through midnight windows into a country where I could never go and yet might have loved to go.

Why, even with gray-eyed Andrea this had been true, and did he not once say to me, "O Benvenuto, how I would admire to walk in the country behind your eyes!"

I know: it is always true.

(But Andrea brought me amazing gifts from his secret country, and nothing in mine was withheld from him through any wish of mine. I suppose all the folk have a word for it: we knew each other's hearts.)

I filled the pitcher at the well-pump downstairs and carried it up to her with a fresh clean cup. She drank gratefully, watching me, I think with some kind of wonder, over the rim of the cup, and she said, "You are a good boy, Benvenuto. Sit down by me now, Benvenuto." She set the cup away on the table and patted the edge of the bed, and I sat there maybe no longer afraid of her, for her plump sad little face was kind. Her soft too-white hands, the fingers short and tapered, showed me none of that threat of grasping, clinging, snatching I have many times seen in the hands of my own breed. "So tell me, where is Jon?" When I could not get words out, I felt her trembling. "Something has happened."

"He is dead, Mam Miriam." She only stared. "I found him on the road, Mam Miriam, too late for me to do anything. It was a wolf." Her hands flew up over her face. "I'm sorry—I couldn't think of any easier way to tell it." She was not weeping as I have heard a woman needs to do after such a blow.

At last her hands came down. One dropped on mine kindly, like the hand of an old friend. "Thus God intended it, perhaps," she said. "I was already thinking, I may die tonight."

"No," I said. "No."

"Why should I not, my dear?"

"Can't you walk at all?"

She looked startled, even shocked, as if that question had been laid away at the back of her mind a long time since, not to be brought forth again. "One night after we came here, Jon and I, I went downstairs— Jon had gone to Trempa and was late returning—I had a candle, but a draft caught it at the head of the stairs—oh, it was a sad night, Benve-nuto, and the night wind blowing. I stumbled, fell all the way. There was a miscarriage, but I could not move my legs. An hour later Jon got back and found me like that, all blood and misery. Since then I have not been able to walk. Nor to die, Benvenuto."

"Have you prayed?" I asked her. "Have you besought God to let you walk again? Father Horan would say that you should. Father Horan says God's grace is infinite, through the intercession of Abraham. But then—other times—he appears to deny it. Have you prayed, Mam Mir-iam?"

"Father Horan—that will be your village priest." She was consider-ing what I said, not laughing at me. "I believe he came here once some years ago, and Jon told him to go away, and he did—but no charge of witchcraft was ever brought against us." She smiled at me, a smile of strangeness, but it warmed me. "Yes, I have prayed, Benvenuto . . . You said you were running away. Why that, my dear? And from what?"

"They would stone me. I've heard it muttered behind windows when I passed. The only reason they haven't yet is that Father Horan was my friend—I thought he was, I'm sure he wanted to be, once. But I have learned he is not, he also believes me sinful."

"Sinful?" She stroked the back of my hand, and her look was won-dering. "Perhaps any sin you might have done has been atoned for by coming out of your way to help an old witch."

"You're not a witch!" I said. "Don't call yourself that!"

"Why, Benvenuto! Then you do believe in witches!"

"Oh, I don't know." For the first time in my life I was wondering whether I did, if she in all her trouble could be so amused at the thought of them. "I don't know," I said, "but you're not one. You're good, Mam Miriam. You're beautiful."

"Well, Benvenuto, when I am busy with my embroideries, I sometimes feel like a good person. And in Jon's embraces I've thought so, after the pleasure, in the time when there can be quiet and a bit of thinking. Other times I've just lain here wondering what goodness is, and whether anyone really knows. Bless you, am I beautiful? I'm too fat, from lying here doing nothing. The wrinkles spread over my puffy flesh just the same, like frost lines coming on a windowpane, only dark, dark." She closed her eyes and asked me, "What sin could you have done to make them after stoning you?"

"The one I most loved went away last spring—all the way to Penn, God help me, and I don't even know what town. I was lonely, and full of desire too, for we had been lovers, and I've learned I have a great need of that, a fire in me that flares up at a breath. In Wayland's field a few days ago, where the corn shocks are standing like golden women, I came on someone else, Eden—we had been loving friends, though not in that way. We were both lonely and hungry for loving, and so we comforted each other—and still, in spite of Father Horan, I can see no harm in it—but Eden's people found us. Eden is younger than me—was only driven home and whipped, and will suffer no worse, I hope. Me they call monster. I ran away from Eden's father and brother, but now all the village is muttering."

"But surely, surely, boy and girl playing the old sweet game in an autumn cornfield—"

"Eden is a boy, Mam Miriam. The one I love, who went away, is Andrea Benedict, the eldest son of a patrician."

She put her hand behind my neck. "Come here awhile," she said, and drew me down to her.

"Father Horan says such passion is the Eternal Corruption. He says the people of Old Time sinned in this way, so God struck them with fire and plague until their numbers were as nothing. Then he sent Abraham to redeem us, taking away the sin of the world, so—"

"Hush," she said, "hush. Nay—go on if you will, but I care nothing for your Father Horan."

"And so God placed upon us, he says, the command to be fruitful and multiply until our numbers are again the millions they were in Old Time, destroying only the mues. And those who sin as I did, he says, are no better than mues, are a *kind* of mue, and are to be stoned in a

public place and their bodies burned. After telling me that, he spoke of
God's infinite mercy, but I did not want to hear about it. I ran from
him. But I know that in the earlier days of Old Time people like me
were tied up in the marketplaces and burned alive, I know this from the
books—it was Father Horan taught me the books, the reading—isn't
that strange?"

"Yes," she said. She was stroking my hair, and I loved her. "Lying
here useless, I've thought about a thousand things, Benvenuto. Most of
them idle. But I do tell you that any manner of love is good if there's
kindness in it. Does anyone know you came here, Benvenuto?" She
made my name so loving a sound!

"No, Mam Miriam."

"Then you can safely stay the night. I'm frightened when the night
wind blows around the eaves, if I'm alone. You can keep the fright
away. It sounds like children crying, some terror pursues them or some
grief is on them and there's nothing I can do."

"Why, to me the night wind sounds like children laughing, or the
wood gods running and shouting across the top of the world."

"Are there wood gods?"

"I don't know. The forest's a living place. I never feel alone there,
even if I lose my way awhile."

"Benvenuto, I think I'm hungry now. See what you can find downstairs—there's cheese, maybe sausage, some of the little red Snow Apples, and Jon made bread—" Her face crumpled and she caught at my
hand. "Was it very bad—about Jon?"

"I think he was dead before the wolf came," I told her. "Maybe his
heart failed, or—a stroke? I've heard black wolf won't attack in broad
day. He must have died first in some quick way, without pain."

"Oh, if we all could!" That cry was forced from her because her
courage had gone, and I think it was only then that she really knew Jon
Kobler was dead. "How could he go before me? I have been dying for
ten years."

"I won't leave you, Mam Miriam."

"Why, you must. I won't allow you to stay. I saw a stoning once in
Sortees when I was a girl—or maybe that was when my girlhood ended.
You must be gone by first light. Now, find us some little supper, Benvenuto. Before you go downstairs—that ugly thing over there, the bedpan
—if you would reach it to me. God, I hate it so!—the body of this
death."

There's nothing offensive in such services, certainly not if you love the one who needs them: we're all bound to the flesh—even Father Horan said it. I wished to tell her so, and found no words; likely she read my thought.

Downstairs everything had been left in order. Jon Kobler must have been a careful, sober man. While I was busy building a fire to cook the sausage, arranging this and that on the tray Jon must have used, I felt him all around us in the work of his hands—the baskets, the beads, the furniture, the very shutters at the windows. Those were all part of a man.

In some way my own works shall live after me. This letter I am finishing is part of a man. Read it so.

When I took the tray, Mam Miriam smiled at it, and at me. She would not talk during our meal about our troubles. She spoke of her young years at Sortees, and that is when I came to learn those things I wrote down for you about the governor's mansion, the strange people she used to see who came from far off, even two or three hundred miles away; about the archer, the elopement, all that. And I learned much else that I have not written down, about the world that I shall presently go and look upon in my own time.

We had two candles at our supper table. Afterward, and the night wind was rising, she asked me to blow out one and set the other behind a screen; so all night long we had the dark, but it was not so dark we could not see each other's faces. We talked on awhile; I told her more about Andrea. She slept some hours. The night wind calling and crying through the trees and over the rooftop did not waken her, but she woke when for a moment I took my hand away from hers. I returned it, and she slept again.

And once I think she felt some pain, or maybe it was grief that made her stir and moan. The wind had hushed, speaking only of trifling illusions; no other sound except some dog barking in Trempa village, and an owl. I said, "I'll stay with you, Mam Miriam."

"You cannot."

"Then I'll take you with me."

"How could that be?"

"I'll carry you. I'll steal a horse and carriage."

"Dear fool!"

"No, I mean it. There must be a way."

"Yes," she said, "and I'll dream of it awhile." And I think she did sleep again. I did, I know; then morning was touching the silence of our windows.

The daylight was on her face, and I blew out the candle, and I told her, "Mam Miriam, I'll make you walk. I believe you can, and you know it too." She stared up at me, not answering, not angry. "You are good. I think you've made me believe in God again, and so I've been praying that God should help you walk."

"Have I not prayed?"

"Come!" I said, and took her hands and lifted her in the bed. "Come now, and I'll make you walk."

"I will do what I can," she said. "Set my feet on the floor, Benvenuto, and I will try to lift myself."

This I did. She was breathing hard. She said I was not to lift her, she must do it herself. "There's money in the drawer of that table," she said, and I was puzzled that she should speak of it now when she ought to be summoning all her forces to rise and walk. "And a few jewels brought from Sortees, we never sold them. Put them in your pocket, Benvenuto. I want to see you do that, to be sure you have them." I did as she said—never mind what I found in the drawer, since you have only my word for it that I did not rob her.

When I turned back to her, she was truly struggling to rise. I could see her legs tensing with life, and I believed we had won, even that God had answered a prayer, a thing I had never known to happen. A blood vessel was throbbing fiercely at her temple, her face had gone red, her eyes were wild with anger at her weakness.

"Now let me help," I said, and put my hands under her armpits, and with that small aid she did rise, she did stand on her own legs and smile at me with the sweat on her face.

"I thank you, Benvenuto," she said, and her face was not red any more but white, her lips bluish. She was collapsing. I got her back on the bed Jon Kobler made, and that was the end of it.

I will go into the world and find my way, I will not die by my own hand, I will regret no act of love. If it may be, I will find Andrea, and if he wishes, we may travel into new places, the greater oceans, the wilderness where the sun goes down. Wherever I go I shall be free and shameless; take heed of me. I care nothing for your envy, your anger, your fear that simulates contempt. The God you invented has nothing to say to me; but I hear my friend say that any manner of love is good if there's kindness in it. Take heed of me. I am the night wind and the quiet morning light: take heed of me.

This is one that almost got away. Fritz Leiber sent me the story late in 1974 during a period when I was between contracts for volumes of *Universe;* I told him I loved the story but I wouldn't be able to buy it till the following year, and reluctantly returned it to him. He sent it to his agent, Robert P. Mills, with a note saying I'd buy it if it was available later, and Mills wrote me that he'd try it on *Playboy* and such nongenre high-paying markets but unless one of them bought it he'd hold it for me.

The story was much too long for such magazines, so eventually I did get to buy it. I was very glad, because "A Rite of Spring" is a delightful tour de force, a love story based on a supposedly dry, outdated science. Only Leiber could have written it.

A Rite of Spring

Fritz Leiber

This is the story of the knight in shining armor and the princess imprisoned in a high tower, only with the roles reversed. True, young Matthew Fortree's cell was a fabulously luxurious, quaintly furnished suite in the vast cube of the most secret Coexistence Complex in the American Southwest, not terribly far from the U. S. Government's earlier most secret project, the nuclear one. And he was free to roam most of the rest of the cube whenever he wished. But there were weightier reasons which really did make him the knight in shining armor imprisoned in the high tower: his suite was on the top, or mathematicians', floor and the cube was very tall and he rarely wished to leave his private quarters except for needful meals and exercise, medical appointments, and his unonerous specified duties; his unspecified duties were more taxing. And while he did not have literal shining armor, he did have some very handsome red silk pajamas delicately embroidered with gold.

With the pajamas he wore soft red leather Turkish slippers, the toes of which actually turned up, and a red nightcap with a tassel, while over them and around his spare, short frame he belted tightly a fleece-lined long black dressing gown of heavier, ribbed silk also embroidered with gold, somewhat more floridly. If Matthew's social daring had equaled his flamboyant tastes, he would in public have worn small clothes and a powdered wig and swung a court sword at his side, for he was much enamored of the Age of Reason and yearned to quip wittily in a salon filled with appreciative young Frenchwomen in daringly low-cut gowns, or perhaps only one such girl. As it was, he regularly did wear gray kid gloves, but that was partly a notably unsuccessful effort to disguise his large powerful hands, which sorted oddly with his slight, almost girlish figure.

The crueler of Math's colleagues (he did not like to be called Matt) relished saying behind his back that he had constructed a most alluring love nest, but that the unknown love bird he hoped to trap never deigned to fly by. In this they hit the mark, as cruel people so often do, for young mathematicians need romantic sexual love, and pine away without it, every bit as much as young lyric poets, to whom they are closely related. In fact, on the night this story begins, Math had so wasted away emotionally and was gripped by such a suicidally extreme Byronic sense of futility and Gothic awareness of loneliness that he had to bite his teeth together harshly and desperately compress his lips to hold back sobs as he knelt against his mockingly wide bed with his shoulders and face pressed into its thick, downy, white coverlet, as if to shut out the mellow light streaming on him caressingly from the tall bedside lamps with pyramidal jet bases and fantastic shades built up of pentagons of almost paper-thin, translucent ivory joined with silver leading. This light was strangely augmented at irregular intervals.

For it was a Gothic night too, you see. A dry thunderstorm was terrorizing the desert outside with blinding flashes followed almost instantly by deafening crashes which reverberated very faintly in the outer rooms of the Complex despite the mighty walls and partitions, which were very thick, both to permit as nearly perfect soundproofing as possible (so the valuable ideas of the solitary occupants might mature without disturbance, like mushrooms in a cave) and also to allow for very complicated, detection-proof bugging. In Math's bedroom, however, for a reason which will be made clear, the thunderclaps were almost as loud as outside, though he did not start at them or otherwise show he even heard them. They were, nevertheless, increasing his Gothic mood in a geometrical progression. While the lightning flashes soaked through the ceiling, a point also to be explained later. Between flashes, the ceiling and walls were very somber, almost black, yet glimmering with countless tiny random highlights like an indoor Milky Way or the restlessly shifting points of light our eyes see in absolute darkness. The thick-piled black carpet shimmered similarly.

Suddenly Matthew Fortree started up on his knees and bent his head abruptly back. His face was a grimacing mask of self-contempt as he realized the religious significance of his kneeling posture and the disgusting religiosity of what he was about to utter, for he was a devout atheist, but the forces working within him were stronger than shame.

"Great Mathematician, hear me!" he cried hoarsely aloud, secure in his privacy and clutching at Eddington's phrase to soften a little the impact on his conscience of his hateful heresy. "Return me to the realm of my early childhood, or otherwise moderate my torments and my loneliness, or else terminate this life I can no longer bear!"

As if in answer to his prayer there came a monstrous flash-and-crash dwarfing all of the storm that had gone before. The two lamps arced out, plunging the room into darkness through which swirled a weird jagged wildfire, as if all the electricity in the wall-buried circuits, augmented by that of the great flash, had escaped to lead a brief free life of its own, like ball lightning or St. Elmo's fire.

(This event was independently confirmed beyond question or doubt. As thousands in the big cube testified, all the lights in the Coexistence Complex went out for one minute and seventeen seconds. Many heard the crash, even in rooms three or four deep below the outermost layer. Several score saw the wildfire. Dozens felt tingling electric shocks. Thirteen were convinced at the time that they had been struck by lightning. Three persons died of heart failure at the instant of the big flash, as far as can be determined. There were several minor disasters in the areas of medical monitoring and continuous experiments. Although a searching investigation went on for months, and still continues on a smaller scale, no completely satisfactory explanation has ever been found, though an odd rumor continues to crop up that the final monster flash was induced by an ultrasecret electrical experiment which ran amuck, or else succeeded too well, all of which resulted in a permanent increment in the perpetual nervousness of the masters of the cube.)

The monster stroke was the last one of the dry storm. Two dozen or
so seconds passed. Then against the jagged darkness and the ringing
silence, Math heard his door's mechanical bell chime seven times. (He'd
insisted on the bell being installed in such a way as to replace the tiny
fish-eye lens customary on all the cube's cubicles. Surely the designer
was from Manhattan!)

He struggled to his feet, half blinded, his vision still full of the wildfire (or afterimages) so like the stuff of ocular migraine. He partly
groped, partly remembered his way out of the bedroom, shutting the
door behind him, and across the living room to the outer door. He
paused there to reassure himself that his red nightcap was set properly
on his head, the tassel falling to the right, and his black robe securely
belted. Then he took a deep breath and opened the door.

Like his suite, the corridor was steeped in darkness and aswirl with
jaggedy, faint blues and yellows. Then, at the level of his eyes, he saw
two brighter, twinkling points of green light about two and a half inches
horizontally apart. A palm's length below them was another such floating emerald. At the height of his chest flashed another pair of the green
points, horizontally separated by about nine inches. At waist level was a
sixth, and a hand's length directly below that, a seventh. They moved a
bit with the rest of the swirling, first a little to the left, then to the right,
but maintained their positions relative to each other.

Without consciousness of having done any thinking, sought any answers, it occurred to him that they were what might be called the seven
crucial points of a girl: eyes, chin, nipples, umbilicus, and the center of
all wonder and mystery. He blinked his eyes hard, but the twinkling
points were still there. The migraine spirals seemed to have faded a
little, but the seven emeralds were bright as ever and still flashed the
same message in their cryptic positional Morse. He even fancied he saw
the shimmer of a clinging dress, the pale triangle of an elfin face in a
flow of black hair, and pale serpents of slender arms.

Behind and before him the lights blazed on, and there, surely enough,
stood a slim young woman in a long dark-green grandmother's skirt
and a frilly salmon blouse, sleeveless but with ruffles going up her neck
to her ears. Her left hand clutched a thick envelope purse sparkling
with silver sequins, her right dragged a coat of silver fox. While between
smooth black cascades and from under black bangs, an elfin face
squinted worriedly into his own through silver-rimmed spectacles.

Her gaze stole swiftly and apologetically up and down him, without
hint of a smile, let alone giggle, at either his nightcap and its tassel, or

the turned-up toes of his Turkish slippers, and then returned to confront him anxiously.

He found himself bowing with bent left knee, right foot advanced, right arm curved across his waist, left arm trailing behind, eyes still on hers (which *were* green), and he heard himself say, "Matthew Fortree, at your service, mademoiselle."

Somehow, she seemed French. Perhaps because of the raciness of the emeralds' twinkling message, though only the top two of them had turned out to be real.

Her accent confirmed this when she answered, " 'Sank you. I am Severeign Saxon, sir, in search of my brother. And mooch scared. 'Scuse me."

Math felt a pang of delight. Here was a girl as girls should be, slim, soft-spoken, seeking protection, calling him sir, not moved to laughter by his picturesque wardrobe, and favoring the fond, formal phrases he liked to use when he talked to himself. The sort of girl who, interestingly half undressed, danced through his head on lonely nights abed.

That was what he felt. What he did, quite characteristically, was frown at her severely and say, "I don't recall any Saxon among the mathematicians, madam, although it's barely possible there is a new one I haven't met."

"Oh, but my brother has not my name . . ." she began hurriedly, then her eyelashes fluttered, she swayed and caught herself. *"Pardonne,"* she went on faintly, gasping a little. "Oh, do not think me forward, sir, but might I not come in and catch my breath? I am frightened by ze storm, I have searched so long, and ze halls are so lonely . . ."

Inwardly cursing his gauche severity, Math instantly resumed his courtly persona and cried softly, *"Your* pardon, madam. Come in, come in by all means and rest as long as you desire." Shaping the beginning of another bow, he took her trailing coat and wafted her past him inside. His fingertips tingled at the incredibly smooth, cool, yet electric texture of her skin.

He hung up her coat, marveling that the silky fur was not so softly smooth as his fingertips' memory of her skin, and found her surveying his spacious sanctum with its myriad shelves and spindly little wallside tables.

"Oh, sir, this room is like fairyland," she said, turning to him with a smile of delight. "Tell me, are all zoze tiny elephants and ships and lacy spheres ivory?"

"They are, madam, such as are not jet," he replied quite curtly. He had been preparing a favorable, somewhat flowery, but altogether sincere comparison of her pale complexion to the hue of his ivories (and of her hair to his jets), but something, perhaps "fairyland," had upset him. "And now will you be seated, Miss Saxon, so you may rest?"

"Oh, yes, sir . . . Mr. Fortree," she replied flusteredly, and let herself be conducted to a long couch facing a TV screen set in the opposite wall. With a bob of her head she hurriedly seated herself. He had intended to sit beside her, or at least at the other end of the couch, but a sudden gust of timidity made him stride to the farthest chair, a straight-backed one, facing the couch, where he settled himself bolt upright.

"Refreshment? Some coffee perhaps?"

She gulped and nodded without lifting her eyes. He pushed a button on the remote control in the left-hand pocket of his dressing gown and felt more in command of the situation. He fixed his eyes on his guest and, to his horror, said harshly, "What is your number, madam . . . of years?" he finished in a voice less bold.

He had intended to comment on the storm and its abrupt end, or inquire about her brother's last name, or even belatedly compare her complexion to ivory and her skin to fox fur, anything but demand her age like some police interrogator. And even then not simply, "Say, would you mind telling me how old you are?" but to phrase it so stiltedly . . . Some months back, Math had gone through an acute attack of sesquipedalianism—of being unable to find the simple word for anything, or even a circumlocution, but only a long, usually Latin one. Attending his first formal reception in the Complex, he had coughed violently while eating a cookie. The hostess, a formidably poised older lady, had instantly made solicitous inquiry. He wanted to answer, "I got a crumb in my nose," but could think of nothing but "nasal cavity," and when he tried to say that, there was another and diabolic misfire in his speech centers, and what came out was, "I got a crumb in my navel."

The memory of it could still reduce him to jelly.

"Seven—" he heard her begin. Instantly his feelings did another flip-flop and he found himself thinking of how nice it would be, since he himself was only a few years into puberty, if she were younger still.

"Seventeen?" he asked eagerly.

And now it was her mood that underwent a sudden change. No longer downcast, her eyes gleamed straight at him, mischievously, and she said, "No, sir, I was about to copy your 'number of years' and say 'seven and a score.' And now I am of a mind not to answer your rude question at all." But she relented and went on with a winning smile, "No, seven and a decade, only seventeen—that's my age. But to tell the truth, sir, I thought you were asking my ruling number. And I answered you. Seven."

"Do you mean to tell me you believe in numerology?" Math demanded, his concerns doing a third instant flip-flop. Acrobatic moods are a curse of adolescence.

She shrugged prettily. "Well, sir, among the sciences—"

"Sciences, madam?" he thundered like a small Doctor Johnson. "Mathematics itself is not a science, but only a game men have invented and continue to play. The supreme game, no doubt, but still only a game. And that you should denominate as a science that . . . that farrago of puerile superstitions—! Sit still now, madam, and listen carefully while I set you straight."

She crouched a little, her eyes apprehensively on his.

"The first player of note of the game of mathematics," he launched out in lecture-hall tones, "was a Greek named Pythagoras. In fact, in a sense he probably invented the game. Yes, surely he did—twenty-five centuries ago, well before Archimedes, before Aristotle. But those were times when men's minds were still befuddled by the lies of the witch doctors and priests, and so Pythagoras (or his followers, more likely!) conceived the mystical notion"—his words dripped sarcastic contempt —"that numbers had a real existence of their own, as if—"

She interrupted rapidly. "But do they not? Like the little atoms we cannot see, but which—"

"Silence, Sovereign!"

"But Matthew—"

"Silence, I said!—as if numbers came from another realm or world, yet had power over this one—"

"That's what the little atoms have—power, especially when they explode." She spoke with breathless rapidity.

"—and as if numbers had all kinds of individual qualities, even personalities—some lucky, some unlucky, some good, some bad, et cetera —as if they were real beings, even gods! I ask you, have you ever heard of anything more ridiculous than numbers—mere pieces in a game— being alive? Yes, of course—the idea of gods being real. But with the Pythagoreans (they became a sort of secret society) such nonsense was the rule. For instance, Pythagoras was the first man to analyze the musical scale mathematically—brilliant!—but then he (his followers!)

went on to decide that some scales (the major) are stimulating and healthy and others (the minor) unhealthy and sad—"

Severeign interjected swiftly yet spontaneously. "Yes, I've noticed that, sir. Major keys make me feel 'appy, minor keys sad—no, pleasantly melancholy . . ."

"Autosuggestion! The superstitions of the Pythagoreans became endless—the transmigration of souls, metempsychosis (a psychosis, all right!), reincarnation, immortality, you name it. They even refused to eat beans—"

"They were wrong there. Beans cassolette—"

"Exactly! In the end, Plato picked up their ideas and carried them to still sillier lengths. Wanted to outlaw music in minor scales—like repealing the law of gravity! He also asserted that not only numbers, but all ideas were more real than things—"

"But excuse me, sir—I seem to recall hearing my brother talk about real numbers . . ."

"Sheer semantics, madam! Real numbers are merely the most primitive and obvious ones in the parlor game we call mathematics. Q.E.D."

And with that, he let out a deep breath and subsided, his arms folded across his chest.

She said, "You have quite overwhelmed me, sir. Henceforth I shall call seven only my favorite number . . . if I may do that?"

"Of course you may. God (excuse the word) forbid I ever try to dictate to you, madam."

With that, silence descended, but before it could become uncomfortable, Math's remote control purred discreetly in his pocket and prodded him in the thigh. He busied himself fetching the coffee on a silver tray in hemispheres of white eggshell china, whose purity of form Severeign duly admired.

They made a charming couple together, looking surprisingly alike, quite like brother and sister, the chief differences being his more prominent forehead, large strong hands, and forearms a little thick with the muscles that powered the deft fingers. All of which made him seem like a prototype of man among the animals, a slight and feeble being except for hands and brain—manipulation and thought.

He took his coffee to his distant chair. The silence returned and did become uncomfortable. But he remained tongue-tied, lost in bitter reflections. Here the girl of his dreams (why not admit it?) had turned up, and instead of charming her with courtesies and witticisms, he had merely become to a double degree his unpleasant, critical, didactic, quarrelsome, rejecting, lonely self, perversely shrinking from all chances of warm contact. Better find out her brother's last name and send her on her way. Still, he made a last effort.

"How may I entertain you, madam?" he asked lugubriously.

"Any way you wish, sir," she answered meekly.

Which made it worse, for his mind instantly became an unbearable blank. He concentrated hopelessly on the toes of his red slippers.

"There *is* something we could do," he heard her say tentatively. "We could play a game . . . if you'd care to. Not chess or go or any sort of mathematical game—there I couldn't possibly give you enough competition—but something more suited to my scatter brain, yet which would, I trust, have enough complications to amuse you. The Word Game . . ."

Once more Math was filled with wild delight, unconscious of the wear and tear inflicted on his system by these instantaneous swoops and soarings of mood. This incredibly perfect girl had just proposed they do the thing he loved to do more than anything else, and at which he invariably showed at his dazzling best. Play a game, any game!

"Word Game?" he asked cautiously, almost suspiciously. "What's that?"

"It's terribly simple. You pick a category, say Musicians with names beginning with B, and then you—"

"Bach, Beethoven, Brahms, Berlioz, Bartók, C. P. E. Bach (J.S.' son)," he rattled off.

"Exactly! Oh, I can see you'll be much too good for me. When we play, however, you can only give one answer at one time and then wait for me to give another—else you'd win before I ever got started."

"Not at all, madam. I'm mostly weak on words," he assured her, lying in his teeth.

She smiled and continued, "And when one player can't give another word or name in a reasonable time, the other wins. And now, since I suggested the Game, I insist that in honor of you, and my brother, but without making it at all mathematical really, we play a subvariety called the Numbers Game."

"Numbers Game?"

She explained, "We pick a small cardinal number, say between one and twelve, inclusive, and alternately name groups of persons or things traditionally associated with it. Suppose we picked four (we won't); then the right answers would be things like the Four Gospels, or the Four Horsemen of the Apocalypse—"

"Or of Notre Dame. How about units of time and vectors? Do they count as things?"

She nodded. "The four seasons, the four major points of the compass. Yes. And now, sir, what number shall we choose?"

He smiled fondly at her. She really was lovely—a jewel, a jewel green as her eyes. He said like a courtier, "What other, madam, than your favorite?"

"Seven. So be it. Lead off, sir."

"Very well." He had been going to insist politely that she take first turn, but already gamesmanship was vying with courtesy, and the first rule of gamesmanship is, Snatch Any Advantage You Can.

He started briskly, "The seven crucial—" and instantly stopped, clamping his lips.

"Go on, sir," she prompted. " 'Crucial' sounds interesting. You've got me guessing."

He pressed his lips still more tightly together, and blushed—at any rate, he felt his cheeks grow hot. Damn his treacherous, navel-fixated subconscious mind! Somehow it had at the last moment darted to the emerald gleams he'd fancied seeing in the hall, and he'd been within a hairsbreadth of uttering, "The seven crucial points of a girl."

"Yes . . . ?" she encouraged.

Very gingerly he parted his lips and said, his voice involuntarily going low, "The Seven Deadly Sins: Pride, Covetousness—"

"My, that's a stern beginning," she interjected. "I wonder what the crucial sins are?"

"—Envy, Sloth," he continued remorselessly.

"Those are the cold ones," she announced. "Now for the hot."

"Anger—" he began, and only then realized where he was going to end—and cursed the show-off impulse that had made him start to enumerate them. He forced himself to say, "Gluttony, and—" He shied then and was disastrously overtaken for the first time in months by his old stammer. "Lul-lul-lul-lul-lul—" he trilled like some idiot bird.

"Lust," she cooed, making the word into another sort of bird call, delicately throaty. Then she said, "The seven days of the week."

Math's mind again became a blank, through which he hurled himself like a mad rat against one featureless white wall after another, until at last he saw a single dingy star. He stammered out, "The Seven Sisters, meaning the seven antitrust laws enacted in 1913 by New Jersey while Woodrow Wilson was Governor."

"You begin, sir," she said with a delighted chuckle, "by scraping the bottom of your barrel, a remarkable feat. But I suppose that being a mathematician you get at the bottom of the barrel while it's still full by way of the fourth dimension."

"The fourth dimension is no hocus-pocus, madam, but only time," he reproved, irked by her wit and by her having helped him out when he first stuttered. "Your seven?"

"Oh. I could repeat yours, giving another meaning, but why not the Seven Seas?"

Instantly he saw a fantastic ship with a great eye at the bow sailing on them. "The seven voyages of Sinbad."

"The Seven Hills of Rome."

"The seven colors of the spectrum," he said at once, beginning to feel less fearful of going word-blind. "Though I can't imagine why Newton saw indigo and blue as different prismatic colors. Perhaps he wanted them to come out seven for some mystical reason—he had his Pythagorean weaknesses."

"The seven tones of the scale, as discovered by Pythagoras," she answered sweetly.

"Seven-card stud," he said, somewhat gruffly.

"Seven-up, very popular before poker."

"This one will give you one automatically," he said stingily. "However, a seventh son."

"And I'm to say the seventh son of a seventh son? But I cannot accept yours, sir. I said cardinal, not ordinal numbers. No sevenths, sir, if you please."

"I'll rephrase it then. Of seven sons, the last."

"Not allowed. I fear you quibble, sir." Her eyes widened, as if at her own temerity.

"Oh, very well. The Seven Against Thebes."

"The Epigoni, their sons."

"I didn't know there were seven of *them*," he objected.

"But there should be seven, for the sake of symmetry," she said wistfully.

"Allowed," he said, proud of his superior generosity in the face of a feminine whim. "The Seven Bishops."

"Dear Sancroft, Ken, and Company," she murmured. "The Seven Dials. In London. Does that make you think of time travel?"

"No, big newspaper offices. *The Seven Keys to Baldpate,* a book."

"The Seven Samurai, a Kurosawa film."

"*The Seventh Seal,* a Bergman film!" He was really snapping them out now, but—

"Oh, oh. No sevenths—remember, sir?"

"A silly rule—I should have objected at the start. The seven liberal arts, being the quadrivium (arithmetic, music, geometry, and astronomy) added to the trivium (grammar, logic, and rhetoric)."

"Delightful," she said. "The seven planets—"

"No, madam! There are nine."

"I was about to say," she ventured in a small, defenseless voice, "—of the ancients. The ones out to Saturn and then the sun and moon."

"Back to Pythagoras again!" he said with a quite unreasonable nastiness, glaring over her head. "Besides, that would make eight planets."

"The ancients didn't count the Earth as one." Her voice was even tinier.

He burst out with, "Earth not a planet, fourth dimension, time travel, indigo not blue, no ordinals allowed, the ancients—madam, your mind is a sink of superstitions!" When she did not deny it, he went on, "And now I'll give you the master answer: all groups of persons or things belong to the class of the largest successive prime among the odd numbers—your seven, madam!"

She did not speak. He heard a sound like a mouse with a bad cold, and looking at her, saw that she was dabbing a tiny handkerchief at her nose and cheeks. "I don't think I want to play the Game any more," she said indistinctly. "You're making it too mathematical."

How like a woman, he thought, banging his hand against his thigh. He felt the remote control and, on a savage impulse, jabbed another button. The TV came on. "Perhaps your mind needs a rest," he said unsympathetically. "See, we open the imbecile valve."

The TV channel was occupied by one of those murderous chases in a detective series (subvariety: military police procedural) where the automobiles became the real protagonists, dark passionate monsters with wills of their own to pursue and flee, or perhaps turn on their pursuer, while the drivers become grimacing puppets whose hands are dragged around by the steering wheels.

Math didn't know if his guest was watching the screen, and he told himself he didn't care—to suppress the bitter realization that instead of cultivating the lovely girl chance had tossed his way, he was browbeating her.

Then the chase entered a multistory garage, and he was lost in a topology problem on the order of: "Given three entrances, two exits, n two-way ramps, and so many stories, what is the longest journey a car can make without crossing its path?" When Math had been a small child—even before he had learned to speak—his consciousness had for long periods been solely a limitless field, or even volume filled with points of light, which he could endlessly count and manipulate. Rather like the random patterns we see in darkness, only he could marshal them endlessly in all sorts of fascinating arrays, and wink them into or out of existence at will. Later he learned that at such times he had gone into a sort of baby-trance, so long and deep that his parents had become worried and consulted psychologists. But then words had begun to replace fields and sets of points in his mind, his baby-trances had become infrequent and finally vanished altogether, so that he was no longer able to enter the mental realm where he was in direct contact with the stuff of mathematics. Thinking about topological problems, such as that of the multilevel garage, was the closest he could get to it now. He had come from that realm "trailing clouds of glory," but with the years they had faded. Yet it was there, he sometimes believed, that he had done all his really creative work in mathematics, the work that had enabled him to invent a new algebra at the age of eleven. And it was there he had earlier tonight prayed the Great Mathematician to return him when he had been in a mood of black despair—which, he realized with mild surprise, he could no longer clearly recall, at least in its intensity.

He had solved his garage problem and was setting up another when, "License plates, license plates!" he heard Severeign cry out in the tones of one who shouts, "Onionsauce, onionsauce!" at baffled rabbits.

Her elfin face, which Math had assumed to be still tearful, was radiant.

"What about license plates?" he asked gruffly.

She jabbed a finger at the TV, where in the solemn finale of the detective show, the camera had just cut to the hero's thoroughly wrecked vehicle while he looked on from under bandages, and while the sound track gave out with taps. "Cars have them!"

"Yes, I know, but where does that lead?"

"Almost all of them have seven digits!" she announced triumphantly. "So do phone numbers!"

"You mean, you want to go on with the Game?" Math asked with an eagerness that startled him.

Part of her radiance faded. "I don't know. The Game is really dreadful. Once started, you can't get your mind off it until you perish of exhaustion of ideas."

"But you want nevertheless to continue?"

"I'm afraid we must. Sorry I got the megrims back there. And now I've gone and wasted an answer by giving two together. The second counts for yours. Oh well, my fault."

"Not at all, madam. I will balance it out by giving two at once too. The seven fat years and the seven lean years."

"Anyone would have got the second of those once you gave the first," she observed, saucily rabbiting her nose at him. "The number of deacons chosen by the Apostles in Acts. Nicanor's my favorite. Dear Nicky," she sighed, fluttering her eyelashes.

"Empson's Seven Types of Ambiguity," Math proclaimed.

"You're not enumerating?"

He shook his head. "Might get too ambiguous."

She flashed him a smile. Then her face slowly grew blank—with thought, he thought at first, but then with eyes half closed she murmured, "Sleepy."

"You want to rest?" he asked. Then, daringly, "Why not stretch out?"

She did not seem to hear. Her head drooped down. "Dopey too," she said somewhat indistinctly.

"Should I step up the air conditioning?" he asked. A wild fear struck him. "I assure you, madam, I didn't put anything in your coffee."

"And Grumpy!" she said triumphantly, sitting up. "Snow White's seven dwarfs!"

He laughed and answered, "The Seven Hunters, which are the Flannan Islands in the Hebrides."

"The Seven Sisters, a hybrid climbing rose, related to the rambler," she said.

"The seven common spectral types of stars—B-A-F-G-K-M . . . and O," he added a touch guiltily because O wasn't really a common type, and he'd never heard of this particular Seven (or Six, for that matter). She gave him a calculating look. Must be something else she's thinking of, he assured himself. Women don't know much astronomy except maybe the ancient sort, rubbed off from astrology.

She said, "The seven rays of the spectrum: radio, high frequency, infrared, visible, ultraviolet, X, and gamma." And she looked at him so bright-eyed that he decided she'd begun to fake a little too.

"And cosmic?" he asked sweetly.

"I thought those were particles," she said innocently.

He grumphed, wishing he could take another whack at the Pythagoreans. An equally satisfying target occurred to him—and a perfectly legitimate one, so long as you realized that this was a game that could be played creatively. "The Seven Subjects of Sensational Journalism: crime, scandal, speculative science, insanity, superstitions such as numerology, monsters, and millionaires."

Fixing him with a penetrating gaze, she immediately intoned, "The Seven Sorrows of Shackleton: the crushing of the *Endurance* in the ice, the inhospitality of Elephant Island, the failure of the whaler *Southern Sky,* the failure of the Uruguayan trawler *Instituto de Pesca No. 1,* the failure on first use of the Chilean steamer *Yelcho,* the failure of the *Emma,* and the South Pole unattained!"

She continued to stare at him judicially. He realized he was starting to blush. He dropped his eyes and laughed uncomfortably. She chortled happily. He looked back at her and laughed with her. It was a very nice moment, really. He had cheated inventively and she had cheated right back at him the same way, pulling him up short without a word.

Feeling very, very good, very free, Math said, "The Seven Years War."

"The Seven Weeks War, between Prussia and Austria."

"The Seven Days War, between Israel and the Arabs."

"Surely Six?"

He grinned. "Seven. For six days the Israelis labored, and on the seventh day they rested."

She laughed delightedly, whereupon Math guffawed too.

She said, "You're witty, sir—though I can't allow that answer. I must tell my brother that one of his colleagues—" She stopped, glanced at her wrist, shot up. "I didn't realize it was so late. He'll be worried. Thanks for everything, Matthew—I've got to split." She hurried toward the door.

He got up too. "I'll get dressed and take you to his room. You don't know where it is. I'll have to find out."

She was reaching down her coat. "No time for that. And now I remember where."

He caught up with her as she was slipping her coat on. "But Sovereign, visitors aren't allowed to move around the Complex unescorted—"

"Oh pish!"

It was like trying to detain a busy breeze. He said desperately, "I won't bother to change."

She paused, grinned at him with uplifted brows, as though surprised and pleased. Then, "No, Matthew," settling her coat around her and opening the door.

He conquered his inhibitions and grabbed her by her silky shoulders —gently at the last moment. He faced her to him. They were exactly the same height.

"Hey," he asked smiling, "what about the Game?"

"Oh, we'll *have* to finish that. Tomorrow night, same time? G'bye now."

He didn't release her. It made him tremble. He started to say, "But Miss Saxon, you really can't go by yourself. After midnight all sorts of invisible eyes pick up anyone in the corridors."

He got as far as the "can't," when with a very swift movement she planted her lips precisely on his.

He froze, as if they had been paralysis darts—and he did feel an electric tingling. Even his invariable impulse to flinch was overridden, perhaps by the audacity of the contact. A self he'd never met said from a corner of his mind in the voice of Rex Harrison, "They're Anglo body-contact taboos, but not Saxon."

And then, between his parted lips and hers still planted on them, he felt an impossible third swift touch. There was a blind time—he didn't know how long—in which the universe filled with unimagined shocking possibility: tiny ondines sent anywhere by matter transmission, a live velvet ribbon from the fourth dimension, pet miniwatersnakes, a little finger with a strange silver ring on it poking out of a young witch's mouth . . . and then another sort of shocked wonder, as he realized it could only have been her tongue.

His lips, still open, were pressing empty air. He looked both ways down the corridor. It was empty too. He quietly closed the door and turned to his ivory-lined room. He closed his lips and worked them together curiously. They still tingled, and so did a spot on his tongue. He felt very calm, not at all worried about Severeign being spotted, or who her brother was, or whether she would really come back tomorrow night. Although he almost didn't see the forest for the trees, it occurred to him that he was happy.

Next morning he felt the same, but very eager to tell someone all about it. This presented a problem, for Math had no friends among his colleagues. Yet a problem easily solved, after a fashion. Right after breakfast he hunted up Elmo Hooper.

Elmo was classed and quartered with the mathematicians, though he couldn't have told you the difference between a root and a power. He was an idiot savant, able to do lightning calculations and possessing a perfect eidetic memory. He was occasionally teamed with a computer to supplement its powers, and it was understood, as it is understood that some people will die of cancer, that he would eventually be permanently cyborged to one. In his spare time, of which he had a vast amount, he mooned around the Complex, ignored except when he came silently up behind gossipers and gave them fits because of his remarkable physical resemblance to Warren Dean, Coexistence's security chief. Both looked like young Vermont storekeepers and were equally laconic, though for different reasons.

Math, who though no lightning calculator, had a nearly eidetic memory himself, found Elmo the perfect confidant. He could tell him all his most private thoughts and feelings, and retrieve any of his previous remarks, knowing that Elmo would never retrieve any of them on his own initiative and never, never make a critical comment.

This morning he found Elmo down one floor in Physics, and soon was pouring out in a happy daze every detail about last night's visit and lovely visitor and all his amazing reactions to her, with no more thought for Elmo than he would have had for a combined dictaphone and information-storage-and-retrieval unit.

He would have been considerably less at ease had he known that Warren Dean regularly drained Elmo of all conversations by "sensitive" persons he overheard in his moonings. Though Math wouldn't have had to feel that way, for the dour security man had long since written Math off as of absolutely no interest to security, being anything but "sensitive" and quite incapable of suspicious contacts, or any other sort. (How else could you class a man who talked of nothing but ivories, hurt vanities, and pure abstractions?) If Elmo began to parrot Math, Dean would simply turn off the human bug, while what the bugs in Math's walls heard was no longer even taped.

Math's happy session with Elmo lasted until lunchtime, and he approached the Mathematics, Astronomy and Theoretical Physics Commons with lively interest. Telling the human memory bank every last thing he knew about Sovereign had naturally transferred his attention to the things he didn't know about her, including the identity of her brother. He was still completely trustful that she would return at evening and answer his questions, but it would be nice to know a few things in advance.

The Commons was as gorgeous as Math's apartment, though less eccentrically so. It still gave him a pleasant thrill to think of all the pure intellect gathered here, busily chomping and chatting, though the presence of astronomers and especially theoretical physicists from the floor below added a sour note. Ah well, they weren't quite as bad as their metallurgical, hardware-mongering brothers. (These in turn were disgusted at having to eat with the chemists from the second floor below. The Complex, dedicated to nourishing all pure science, since that provably paid off better peacewise or warwise than applied science, arranged all the sciences by floors according to degree of purity and treated them according to the same standards, with the inhabitants of the top floor positively coddled. Actually, the Complex was devoted to the corruption of pure science, and realized that mathematics was at least fully as apt as any other discipline to turn up useful ideas. Who knew when a new geometry would not lead to a pattern of nuclear bombardment with less underkill? Or a novel topological concept point the way to the more efficient placement of offshore oil wells?)

So as Math industriously nibbled his new potatoes, fresh green peas, and roast lamb (the last a particularly tender mutation from the genetics and biology floors, which incidentally was a superb carrier of a certain newly developed sheep-vectored disease of the human nervous system), he studied the faces around him for ones bearing a resemblance to Severeign's—a pleasantly titillating occupation merely for its own sake. Although Math's colleagues believed the opposite, he was a sensitive student of the behavior of crowds, as any uninvolved spectator is apt to be. He had already noted that there was more and livelier conversation than usual and had determined that the increase was due to talk about last night's storm and power failure, with the physicists contributing rather more than their share, both about the storm and power failure and also about some other, though related topic which he hadn't yet identified.

While coffee was being served, Math decided on an unprecedented move: to get up and drift casually about in order to take a closer look at his candidates for Severeign's brother (or half brother, which would account elegantly for their different last names). And as invariably happens when an uninvolved spectator abandons that role and mixes in, it was at once noticed. Thinking of himself as subtly invisible as he moved about dropping nods and words here and there, he actually became a small center of attention. Whatever was that social misfit up to? (A harsh term, especially coming from members of a group with a high percentage of social misfits.) And why had he taken off his gray kid gloves? (In his new freedom he had simply forgotten to put them on.)

He saved his prime suspect until last, a wisp of a young authority on synthetic projective geometry named Angelo Spirelli, the spiral angel, whose floating hair was very black and whose face could certainly be described as girlish, though his eyes (Math noted on closer approach) were yellowish-brown, not green.

Unlike the majority, Spirelli was a rather careless, outgoing soul of somewhat racier and more voluble speech than his dreamy appearance might have led one to expect. "Hi, Fortree. Take a pew. What strange and unusual circumstance must I thank for this unexpected though pleasant encounter? The little vaudeville act Zeus and Hephaestus put on last night? One of the downstairs boys suspects collusion by the Complex."

Emboldened, Math launched into a carefully rehearsed statement. "At the big do last week I met a female who said she was related to you. A Miss Severeign Saxon."

Spirelli scowled at him, then his eyes enlarged happily. "Saxon, you say? Was she a squirmy little sexpot?"

Math's eyebrows lifted. "I suppose someone might describe her in that fashion." He didn't look as if he'd care much for such a someone.

"And you say you met her in El 'Bouk?"

"No, here at the fortnightly reception."

"That," Spirelli pronounced, scowling again, "does not add up."

"Well," Math said after a hiatus, "does it add down?"

Spirelli eyed him speculatively, then shrugged his shoulders with a little laugh. Leaning closer, he said, "Couple weeks ago I was into Albuquerque on a pass. At the Spurs 'n' Chaps this restless little saucer makes up to me. Says call her Saxon, don't know if it was supposed to be last name, first, or nick."

"Did she suggest you play a game?"

Spirelli grinned. "Games. I think so, but I never got around to finding out for sure. You see, she began asking me too many questions, like she was pumping me, and I remembered what Grandmother Dean teaches us at Sunday school about strange women, and I cooled her fast, feeling like a stupid, miserably well-behaved little choirboy. But a minute later Warren himself wanders in and I'm glad I did." His eyes swung, his voice dropped. "Speak of the devil."

Math looked. Across the Commons, Elmo Hooper—no, Warren Dean—had come in. Conversation did not die, but it did become muted —in waves going out from that point.

Math asked, "Did this girl in 'Bouk have black hair?"

Grown suddenly constrained, Spirelli hesitated, then said, "No, blond as they come. Saxon was a Saxon type."

After reaching this odd dead end, Math spent the rest of the afternoon trying to cool his own feelings about Severeign, simply because they were getting too great. He was successful except that in the mathematics library *Webster's Unabridged,* second edition, tempted him to look up the "seven" entries (there were three columns), and he was halfway through them before he realized what he was doing. He finished them and resolutely shut the big book and his mind. He didn't think of Severeign again until he finished dressing for bed, something he regularly did on returning to his room from dinner. It was a practice begun as a child to ensure he did nothing but study at night, but continued, with embellishments, when he began to think of himself as a gay young bachelor. He furiously debated changing back until he became irked at his agitation and decided to retain his "uniform of the night."

But he could no longer shut his mind on Severeign. Here he was having an assignation (a word which simultaneously delighted him and gave him cold shivers) with a young female who had conferred on him a singular favor (another word that worked both ways, while the spot on his tongue tingled reminiscently). How should he behave? How would she behave? What would she expect of him? How would she react to his costume? (He redebated changing back.) Would she even come? Did he really remember what she looked like?

In desperation he began to look up everything on seven he could, including Shakespeare and ending with the Bible. A cross-reference had led him to the Book of Revelation, which he found surprisingly rich in that digit. He was reading, "And when he had opened the seventh seal, there was silence in heaven about the space of half an hour . . ." when, once again, there came the seven chimes at his door. He was there in a rush and had it open, and there was Severeign, looking exactly like he remembered her—the three points of merry green eyes and tapered chin of flustered, triangular elf-face, silver spectacles, salmon blouse and green grandmother's skirt (with line of coral buttons going down the one, and jade ones down the other), the sense of the other four crucial points of a girl under them, slender bare arms, one clutching silver-sequined purse, the other trailing coat of silver fox—and their faces as close together again as if the electric kiss had just this instant ended.

He leaned closer still, his lips parted, and he said, "The seven metals of the ancients: iron, lead, mercury, tin, copper, silver, and gold."

She looked as startled as he felt. Then a fiendish glint came into her eyes and she said, "The seven voices of the classical Greek actor: king, queen, tyrant, hero, old man, young man, maiden—that's me."

He said, "The Island of the Seven Cities. Antilia, west of Atlantis."

She said, "The seven Portuguese bishops who escaped to that island."

He said, "The Seven Caves of Aztec legend."

She said, "The Seven Walls of Ekbatana in old Persia: white, black, scarlet, blue, orange, silver, and (innermost) golden."

He said, " 'Seven Come Eleven,' a folk cry."

She said, "The Seven Cities of Cibola. All golden."

"But which turned out to be merely the pueblos of the Zuni," he jeered.

"Do you always have to deprecate?" she demanded. "Last night the ancients, the Pythagoreans. Now some poor aborigines."

He grinned. "Since we're on Amerinds, the Seven Council Fires, meaning the Sioux, Tetons, and so forth."

She scowled at him and said, "The Seven Tribes of the Tetons, such as the Hunkpapa."

Math said darkly, "I think you studied up on seven and then conned me into picking it. *Seven Came Through,* a book by Eddie Rickenbacker."

"The Seven Champions of Christendom. Up Saint Dennis of France! To the death! No, I didn't, but you know, I sometimes feel I know everything about sevens, past, present, or future. It's strange."

They had somehow got to the couch and were sitting a little apart but facing each other, totally engrossed in the Game.

"Hmph! Up Saint David of Wales!" he said. "The Seven Churches in Asia Minor addressed in Revelation. Thyatira, *undsoweiter.*"

"Philadelphia too. The seven golden candlesticks, signifying the Seven Churches. Smyrna's really my favorite—I like figs." She clenched her fist with the tip of her thumb sticking out between index and middle fingers. Math wondered uncomfortably if she knew the sexual symbolism of the gesture. She asked, "Why are you blushing?"

"I'm not. The Seven Stars, meaning the Seven Angels of the Seven Churches."

"You were! And it got you so flustered you've given me one. The Seven Angels!"

"I'm not any more," he continued unperturbed, secure in his knowledge that he'd just read part of Revelation. "The seven trumpets blown by the Seven Angels."

"The beast with seven heads, also from Revelation. He also had the mouth of a lion and the feet of a bear *and* ten horns, but he looked like a leopard."

"The seven consulships of Gaius Marius," he said.

"The seven eyes of the Lamb," she countered.

"The Seven Spirits of God, another name for the Seven Angels, I think."

"All right. The seven sacraments."

"Does that include exorcism?" he wanted to know.

"No, but it does include order, which ought to please your mathematical mind."

"Thanks. The Seven Gifts of the Holy Ghost. Say, I know tongues, prophecy, vision, and dreams, but what are the other three?"

"Those are from Acts two—an interesting notion. But try Isaiah eleven—wisdom, understanding, counsel, might, knowledge, fear of the Lord, and righteousness."

Math said, "Whew, that's quite a load."

"Yes. On with the Game! To the death! The seven steps going up to Ezekiel's gate. Zeek forty twenty-six."

"Let's change religions," he said, beginning to feel snowed under by Christendom and the Bible. "The seven Japanese gods of luck."

"Or happiness. The seven major gods of Hinduism: Brahma, Vishnu, Siva, Varuna, Indra, Agni, and Surya. Rank male chauvinism! They didn't even include Lakshmi, the goddess of luck."

Math said sweetly, "The Seven Mothers, meaning the seven wives of the Hindu gods."

"Chauvinism, I said! Wives indeed! *Seven Daughters of the Theater,* a book by Edward Wagenknecht."

"The seven ages of man," Math announced, assuming a Shakespearean attitude. "At first the infant, mewling and puking—"

"And then the whining schoolboy—"

"And then the lover," he cut in, in turn, "sighing like furnace, with a woeful ballad made to his mistress' eyebrow."

"Have you ever sighed like furnace, Matthew?"

"No, but . . ." And raising a finger for silence, he scowled in thought.

"What are you staring at?" she asked.

"Your left eyebrow. Now listen . . .

"Slimmest crescent of delight,
Why set so dark in sky so light?

My mistress' brow is whitest far;
Her eyebrow—the black evening star!"

"But it's not woeful," she objected. "Besides, how can the moon be a star?"

"As easily as it can be a planet—your ancients, madam. In any case, I invoke poetic license."

"But my eyebrow bends the wrong way for setting," she persisted. "Its ends point at the earth instead of skyward."

"Not if you were standing on your head, madam," he countered.

"But then my skirt would set too, showing my stockings. Shocking. Sir, I refuse! The Seven Sisters, meaning the Pleiades, those little stars."

Matthew's eyes lit up. He grinned excitedly. "Before I give you my next seven I want to show you yours," he told her, standing up.

"What do you mean?"

"I'll show you. Follow me," he said mysteriously and led her into his bedroom.

While she was ooh-ahing at the strangely glimmering black floor, walls, and ceiling, the huge white-fleeced bed, the scattered ivories which included the five regular solids of Pythagoras, the jet bedside lamps with their shades that were dodecahedrons of silver-joined pentagons of translucent ivory—and all the other outward signs of the U. S. Government's coddling of Matthew—he moved toward the lamps and switched them off, so the only light was that which had followed them into the bedroom.

Then he touched another switch and with the faintest whir and rustling the ceiling slowly parted like the Red Sea and moved aside, showing the desert night crusted with stars. The Coexistence Complex really catered to their mathematicians, and when Matthew had somewhat diffidently (for him) mentioned his fancy, they had seen no difficulty in removing the entire ceiling of his bedroom and the section of flat roof above and replacing them with a slightly domed plate-glass skylight, and masking it below with an opaque fabric matching the walls, which would move out of the way sidewise and gather in little folds at the urging of an electric motor.

Severeign caught her breath.

"Stars of the winter sky," Matthew said with a sweep of his arm and then began to point. "Orion. Taurus the bull with his red-eye Aldebaran. And, almost overhead, your Pleiades, madam. While there to the north is my reply. The Big Dipper, madam, also called the Seven Sisters."

Their faces were pale in the splendid starlight and the glow seeping from the room they'd left. They were standing close. Sovereign did not speak at once. Instead she lifted her hand, forefinger and middle finger spread and extended, slowly toward his eyes. He involuntarily closed them. He heard her say, "The seven senses. Sight. And hearing." He felt the side of her hand lightly brush his neck. "Touch. No, keep your eyes closed." She laid the back of her hand against his lips. He inhaled with a little gasp. "Smell," came her voice. "That's myrrh, sir." His lips surprised him by opening and kissing her wrist. "And now you've added taste too, sir. Myrrh is bitter." It was true.

"But that's all the senses," he managed to say, "and you said seven. In common usage there are only five."

"Yes, that's what Aristotle said," she answered dryly. She pressed her warm palm against the curve of his jaw. "But there's heat too." He grasped her wrist and brought it down. She pulled her hand to free it and he automatically gripped it more tightly for a moment before letting go.

"And kinesthesia," she said. "You felt it in your muscles then. That makes seven."

He opened his eyes. Her face was close to his. He said, "Seventh heaven. No, that's an ordinal—"

"It will do, sir," she said. She knelt at his feet and looked up. In the desert starlight her face was solemn as a child's. "For my next seven I must remove your handsome Turkish slippers," she apologized.

He nodded, feeling lost in a dream, and lifted first one foot, then the other, as she did it.

As she rose, her hands went to his gold-worked black dressing gown. "And this too, sir," she said softly. "Close your eyes once more."

He obeyed, feeling still more dream-lost. He heard the slithering hrush of his robe dropping to the floor, he felt the buttons of his handsome red silk pajama tops loosened one by one from the top down, as her little fingers worked busily, and then the drawstring of the bottoms loosened.

He felt his ears lightly touched in their centers. She breathed, "The seven natural orifices of the male body, sir." The fingers touched his nostrils, brushed his mouth. "That's five, sir." Next he was briefly touched where only he had ever touched himself before. There was an electric tingling, like last night's kiss. The universe seemed to poise around him. Finally he was touched just as briefly where he'd only been touched by his doctor. His universe grew.

He opened his eyes. Her face was still child-grave. The light shining past him from the front room was enough to show the green of her skirt, the salmon of her blouse, the ivory of her skin dancing with starlight. He felt electricity running all over his body. He swallowed with difficulty, then said harshly, "For my next seven, madam, you must undress."

There was a pause. Then, "Myself?" she asked. "*You* didn't have to." She closed her eyes and blushed, first delicately under her eyes, along her cheekbones, then richly over her whole face, down to the salmon ruffles around her neck. His hands shook badly as they moved out toward the coral buttons, but by the time he had undone the third, his strong fingers were working with their customary deftness. The jade buttons of her skirt yielded as readily. Matthew, who knew from his long studious perusals of magazine advertisements that all girls wore pantyhose, was amazed and then intrigued that she had separate stockings and a garter belt. He noted for future reference in the Game that that made seven separate articles of clothing, if you counted shoes. With some difficulty he recalled his main purpose in all this. His hands edged under her long black curving hair until his middle fingers touched her burning ears.

He softly said, "The seven natural orifices of the *female* body, madam."

"What?" Her eyes blinked open wide and searched his face. Then a comic light flashed in them, though Matthew did not recognize it as such. Saying, "Oh, very well, sir. Go on," she closed them and renewed her blush. Matthew delicately touched her neat nostrils and her lips, then his right hand moved down while his eyes paused, marveling in admiration, at the two coral-tipped crucial points of a girl embellished on Severeign's chest.

"Seven," he finished triumphantly, amazed at his courage while lost in wonder at the newness of it all.

Her hands lightly clasped his shoulders, she leaned her head against his and whispered in his ear, "No, eight. You missed one." Her hand went down and her fingers instructed his. It was true! Matthew felt himself flushing furiously from intellectual shame. He'd known *that* about girls, of course, and yet he'd had a blind spot. There was a strange difference, he had to admit, between things read about in books of human physiology and things that were concretely there, so you could touch them. Severeign reminded him he still owed the Game a seven, and in his fluster he gave her the seven crucial points of a girl, which she was inclined to allow, though only by making an exception, for as she pointed out, they seemed very much Matthew's private thing, though possibly others had hit on them independently.

Still deeply mortified by his fundamental oversight, though continuing to be intensely interested in everything (the loose electricity lingered on him), Matthew would not accept the favor. "The Seven Wise Men of Greece—Solon, Thales, and so on," he said loudly and somewhat angrily, betting himself that those old boys had made a lot of slips in their time.

She nodded absently, and looking somewhat smugly down herself, said (quite fatuously, Matthew thought), "The seven seals on the Book of the Lamb."

He said more loudly, his strange anger growing, "In the Civil War, the Battle of Seven Pines, also called the Battle of Fair Oaks."

She looked at him, raised an eyebrow, and said, "The Seven Maxims of the Seven Wise Men of Greece." She looked down herself again and then down and up him. Her eyes, merry, met his. "Such as Pittacus: *Know thy opportunity.*"

Matthew said still more loudly, "The Seven Days Battles, also Civil War, June twenty-fifth to July first inclusive, 1862—Mechanicsville, et cetera!"

She winced at the noise. "You've got to the fourth age now," she told him.

"What are you talking about?" he demanded.

"You know, Shakespeare. You gave it: the Seven Ages of Man. Fourth: 'Then a soldier, full of strange oaths and bearded like the pard, jealous in honor, sudden and quick in quarrel, seeking the bubble reputation even in the cannon's mouth.' You haven't got a beard, but you're roaring like a cannon."

"I don't care. You watch out. What's your seven?"

She continued to regard herself demurely, her eyes half closed. "Seven swans a-swimming," she said liltingly and a dancing vibration seemed to move down her white body, like that which goes out from a swan across the still surface of a summer lake.

Matthew roared, "The Seven Sisters, meaning the Scotch cannon at the Battle of Flodden!"

She shrugged maddeningly and murmured, "Sweet Seventeen," again giving herself the once-over.

"That's Sixteen," he shouted. "And it's not a seven anyhow!"

She wrinkled her nose at him, turned her back, and said smiling over her shoulder, "Chilon: *Consider the end.*" And she jounced her little rump.

In his rage Matthew astonished himself by reaching her in a stride, picking her up like a feather, and dropping her in the middle of the bed, where she continued to smile self-infatuatedly as she bounced.

He stood glaring down at her and taking deep breaths preparatory to roaring, but then he realized his anger had disappeared.

"The Seven Hells," he said anticlimactically.

She noticed him, rolled over once and lay facing him on her side, chin in hand. "The seven virtues," she said. "Prudence, justice, temperance, and fortitude—those are Classical—and faith, hope and charity—those are Christian."

He lay down facing her. "The seven sins—"

"We've had those," she cut him off. "You gave them last night."

He at once remembered everything about the incident except the embarrassment.

"*Seven Footprints to Satan,* a novel by Abraham Merritt," he said, eyeing her with interest and idly throwing out an arm.

"*The Seven-Year Itch,* a film with Marilyn Monroe," she countered, doing likewise. Their fingers touched.

He rolled over toward her, saying, "*Seven Conquests,* a book by Poul Anderson," and ended up with his face above hers. He kissed her. She kissed him. In the starlight her face seemed to him that of a young goddess. And in the even, tranquil, shameless voice such a supernatural being would use, she said, "The seven stages of loving intercourse. First kissing. Then foreplay." After a while, "Penetration," and with a wicked starlit smile, "Bias: *Most men are bad.* Say a seven."

"Why?" Matthew asked, almost utterly lost in what they were doing, because it was endlessly new and heretofore utterly unimaginable to him—which was a very strange concept for a mathematician.

"So I can say one, stupid."

"Oh, very well. The seven spots to kiss: ears, eyes, cheeks, mouth," he said, suiting actions to words.

"How very specialized a seven. Try eyebrow flutters too," she suggested, demonstrating. "But it will do for an answer in the Game. The seven gaits in running the course you're into. First the walk. Slowly, slowly. No, more slowly." After a while, she said, "Now the amble, not much faster. Shakespeare made it the slowest gait of Time, when he moves at all. Leisurely, stretchingly. Yes, that's right," and after a while, "Now the pace. In a horse, which is where all this comes from, that means first the hoofs on the one side, then those on the other. Right, left, right, see?—only doubled. There's a swing to it. Things are picking up." After a while she said, "Now the trot. I'll tell you who Time trots withal. Marry, he trots hard with a maid between the contract of her marriage and the day it is solemnized. A little harder. There, that's right." After a while she said, gasping slightly, "Now the canter. Just for each seventh instant we've all hoofs off the ground. Can you feel that? Yes, there it came again. Press on." After a while she said, gasping, "And now the rack. That's six gaits. Deep penetration too. Which makes five stages. Oh, press on." Matthew felt he was being tortured on a rack, but the pain was wonderful, each frightening moment an utterly new revelation. After a while she gasped, "Now, sir, the gallop!"

Matthew said, gasping too, "Is this wise, madam? Won't we come apart? Where are you taking me? Recall Cleobulus: *Avoid Excess!*"

But she cried ringingly, her face lobster-red, "No, it's not sane, it's mad! But we must run the risk. To the heights and above! To the ends of the earth and beyond! Press on, press on, the Game is all! Epimenides: *Nothing is impossible to industry!*" After a while he redded out.

After another while he heard her say, remotely, tenderly, utterly without effort, "Last scene of all, that ends this strange, eventful history, is mere oblivion. Now Time stands still withal. After the climax— sixth stage—there is afterplay. What's your seven?"

He answered quite as dreamily, "The Seven Heavens, abodes of bliss to the Mohammedans and cabalists."

She said, "That's allowable, although you gave it once before by inference. The seven syllables of the basic hymn line, as 'Hark, the herald angels sing.' "

He echoed with, "Join the triumph of the skies."

She said, "Look at the stars." He did. She said, "Look how the floor of heaven is thick inlaid with patens of bright gold." It was.

He said, "There's not the smallest orb which thou behold'st but in his motion like an angel sings. Hark." She did.

Math felt the stars were almost in his head. He felt they were the realm in which he'd lived in infancy and that with a tiny effort he could at this very moment push across the border and live there again. What was so wrong about Pythagoreanism? Weren't numbers real, if you could live among them? And wouldn't they be alive and have personalities, if they were everything there was? Something most strange was happening.

Severeign nodded, then pointed a finger straight up. "Look, the Pleiades. I always thought they were the Little Dipper. They'd hit us in our tummies if they fell."

He said, gazing at them, "You've already used that seven."

"Of course I have," she said, still dreamily. "I was just making conversation. It's your turn, anyway."

He said, "Of course. The Philosophical Pleiad, another name for the Seven Wise Men of Greece."

She said, "The Alexandrian Pleiad—Homer the younger and six other poets."

He said, "The French Pleiad—Ronsard and his six."

She said, "The Pleiades again, meaning the seven nymphs, attendant on Diana, for whom the stars were named—Alcyone, Celaeno, Electra, Maia (she's Illusion), Taygete (she got lost), Sterope (she wed war) and Merope (she married Sisyphus). My, that got gloomy."

Matthew looked down from the stars and fondly at her, counting over her personal and private sevens.

"What's the matter?" she asked.

"Nothing," he said. Actually, he'd winced at the sudden memory of his eight-orifices error. The recollection faded back as he continued to study her.

"The Seven Children of the Days of the Week, Fair-of-Face and Full-of-Grace, and so on," he said, drawing out the syllables. "Whose are you?"

"Saturday's—"

"Then you've got far to go," he said.

She nodded, somewhat solemnly.

"And that makes another seven that belongs to you," he added. "The seventh day of the week."

"No, sixth," she said. "Sunday's the seventh day of the week."

"No, it's the first," he told her with a smile. "Look at any calendar." He felt a lazy pleasure at having caught her out, though it didn't make up for a Game error like the terrible one he'd made.

She said, " 'The Seven Ravens,' a story by the Brothers Grimm. Another gloomy one."

He said, gazing at her and speaking as if they too belonged to her, "The Seven Wonders of the World. The temple of Diana at Ephesus, et cetera. Say, what's the matter?"

She said, "You said the World when we were in the Stars. It brought me down. The world's a nasty place."

"I'm sorry, Sev," he said. "You are a goddess, did you know? I saw it when the starlight freckled you. Diana coming up twice in the Game reminded me. Goddesses are supposed to be up in the stars, like in line drawings of the constellations with stars in their knees and heads."

"The world's a nasty place," she repeated. "Its number's nine."

"I thought six sixty-six," he said. "The number of the beast. Somewhere in Revelation."

"That too," she said, "but mostly nine."

"The smallest odd number that is not a prime," he said.

"The number of the Dragon. Very nasty. Here, I'll show you just how nasty."

She dipped over the edge of the bed for her purse and put in his hands something that felt small, hard, cold and complicated. Then, kneeling upright on the bed, she reached out and switched on the lamps.

Matthew lunged past her and hit the switch for the ceiling drapes.

"Afraid someone might see us?" she asked as the drapes rustled toward each other.

He nodded mutely, catching his breath through his nose. Like her, he was now kneeling upright on the bed.

"The stars are far away," she said. "Could they see us with telescopes?"

"No, but the roof is close," he whispered back. "Though it's unlikely anyone would be up there."

Nevertheless he waited, watching the ceiling, until the drapes met and the faint whirring stopped. Then he looked at what she'd put in his hands.

He did not drop it, but he instantly shifted his fingers so that he was holding it with a minimum of contact between his skin and it, very much as a man would hold a large dark spider which for some occult reason he may not drop.

It was a figurine, in blackened bronze or else in some dense wood, of a fearfully skinny, wiry old person tautly bent over backward like a bow, knees somewhat bent, arms straining back overhead. The face was witchy, nose almost meeting pointed chin across toothlessly grinning gums pressed close together, eyes bulging with mad evil. What seemed at first some close-fitting, ragged garment was then seen to be only loathsomely diseased skin, here starting to peel, there showing pustules, open ulcers, and other tetters, all worked in the metal (or carved in even harder wood) in abominably realistic minuscule detail. Long empty dugs hanging back up the chest as far as the neck made it female, but the taut legs, somewhat spread, showed a long flaccid penis caught by the artificer in extreme swing to the left, and far back from it a long grainy scrotum holding shriveled testicles caught in similar swing to the right, and in the space between them long leprous vulva gaping.

"It's nasty, isn't it?" Sovereign said dryly of the hideous hermaphrodite. "My Aunt Helmintha bought it in Crotona, that one-time Greek colony in the instep of the Italian Boot where Pythagoras was born— bought it from a crafty old dealer in antiquities, who said it came from 'Earth's darkest center' by way of Mali and North Africa. He said it was a figure of the World, a nine-thing, *Draco homo.* He said it can't be broken, must not, in fact, for if you break it, the world will disappear or else you and those with you will forever vanish—no one knows where."

Staring at the figurine, Math muttered, "The seven days and nights the Ancient Mariner saw the curse in the dead man's eye."

She echoed, "The seven days and nights his friends sat with Job."

He said, his shoulders hunched, "The Seven Words, meaning the seven utterances of Christ on the cross."

She said, "The seven gates to the land of the dead through which Ishtar passed."

He said, his shoulders working, "The seven golden vials full of the wrath of God that the four beasts gave to the seven angels."

She said, shivering a little, "The birds known as the Seven Whistlers and considered to be a sign of some great calamity impending." Then, "Stop it, Math!"

Still staring at the figurine, he had shifted his grip on it, so that his thick forefingers hooked under its knees and elbows while his big thumbs pressed against its arched narrow belly harder and harder. But at her command his hands relaxed and he returned the thing to her purse.

"Fie on you, sir!" she said, "to try to run out on the Game, and on me, and on yourself. The seven letters in Matthew, and in Fortree. Remember Solon: *Know thyself.*"

He answered, "The fourteen letters in Sovereign Saxon, making two sevens too."

"The seven syllables in Master Matthias Fortree," she said, flicking off the lamps before taking a step toward him on her knees.

"The seven syllables in Mamsel Sovereign Saxon," he responded, putting his arms around her.

And then he was murmuring, "Oh Sovereign, my sovereign," and they were both wordlessly indicating sevens they'd named earlier, beginning with the seven crucial points of a girl ("Crucial green points," he said, and "Of a green girl," said she), and the whole crucial part of the evening was repeated, only this time it extended endlessly with infinite detail, although all he remembered of the Game from it was her saying "The Dance of the Seven Veils," and him replying "The seven figures in the Dance of Death as depicted on a hilltop by Ingmar Bergman in his film," and her responding, "The Seven Sleepers of Ephesus," and him laboriously getting out, "In the like legend in the Koran, the seven sleepers guarded by the dog Al Rakim," and her murmuring, "Good doggie, good doggie," as he slowly, slowly, sank into bottomless slumber.

Next morning Math woke to blissful dreaminess instead of acutely stabbing misery for the first time in his life since he had lost his childhood power to live wholly in the world of numbers. Strong sunlight was seeping through the ceiling. Sovereign was gone with all her things, including the purse with its disturbing figurine, but that did not bother him in the least (nor did his eight-error, the only other possible flyspeck on his paradise), for he knew with absolute certainty that he would see her again that evening. He dressed himself and went out into the corridor and wandered along it until he saw from the corner of his eye that he was strolling alongside Elmo Hooper, whereupon he poured out to that living memory bank all his joy, every detail of last night's revelations.

As he ended his long litany of love, he noticed bemusedly that Elmo had dropped back, doubtless because they were overtaking three theoretical physicists headed for the Commons. Their speech had a secretive tone, so he tuned his ears to it and was soon in possession of a brand-new top secret they did well to whisper about, and they none the wiser —a secret that just might allow him to retrieve his eight-error, he realized with a throb of superadded happiness. (In fact, he was so happy he even thought on the spur of the moment of a second string for that bow.)

So when Sovereign came that night, as he'd known she would, he was ready for her. Craftily he did not show his cards at first, but when she began with, "The Seven Sages, those male Scheherazades who night after night keep a king from putting his son wrongfully to death," he followed her lead with "The Seven Wise Masters, another name for the Seven Sages."

She said, "The Seven Questions of Timur the Lame—Tamurlane."

He said, "The Seven Eyes of Ningauble."

"Pardon?"

"Never mind. *Seven Men* (including 'Enoch Soames' and 'A. V. Laider'), a book of short stories by Max Beerbohm."

She said, *"The Seven Pillars of Wisdom,* a book by Lawrence of Arabia."

He said, *"The Seven Faces of Dr. Lao,* a fantasy film."

She said, "Just *The Seven Faces* by themselves, a film Paul Muni starred in."

He said, "The seven Gypsy jargons mentioned by Borrow in his *Bible in Spain.*"

She said, *"Seven Brides for Seven Brothers,* another film."

He said, "The dance of the seven veils—how did we miss it?"

She said, "Or miss the seven stars in the hair of the blessed damosel?"

He said, "Or the Seven Hills of San Francisco when we got Rome's?"

She said, *"Seven Keys to Baldpate,* a play by George M. Cohan."

He said, *"Seven Famous Novels,* an omnibus by H. G. Wells."

She said, *"The Seven That Were Hanged,* a novella by Andreyev."

That's my grim cue, he thought, but I'll try my second string first. "The seven elements whose official names begin with N, and their symbols," he said, and then recited rapidly, poker-faced, "N for Nitrogen, Nb for Nobelium, Nd for Neodymium, Ne for Neon, Ni for Nickel, No for Niobrium, Np for Neptunium."

She grinned fiendishly, started to speak, then caught herself. Her eyes widened at him. Her grin changed, though not much.

"Matthew, you rat!" she said. "You wanted me to correct you, say there were eight and that you'd missed Na. But then I'd have been in the wrong, for Na is for Sodium—its old and unofficial name Natrium."

Math grinned back at her, still poker-faced, though his confidence had been shaken. Nevertheless he said, "Quit stalling. What's your seven?"

She said, *"The Seven Lamps of Architecture,* a book of essays by John Ruskin."

He said, baiting his trap, "The seven letters in the name of the radioactive element Pluton—I mean Uranium."

She said, "That's feeble, sir. All words with seven letters would last almost forever. But you've made me think of a very good one, entirely legitimate. The seven isotopes of Plutonium and Uranium, sum of their Pleiades."

"Huh! I got you, madam," he said, stabbing a finger at her.

Her face betrayed exasperation of a petty sort, but then an entirely different sort of consternation, almost panic fear.

"You're wrong, madam," he said triumphantly. "There are, as I learned only today—"

"Stop!" she cried. "Don't say it! You'll be sorry! Remember Thales: *Suretyship is the precursor of ruin.*"

He hesitated a moment. He thought, that means don't cosign checks. Could that be stretched to mean don't share dangerous secrets? No, too far-fetched.

"You won't escape being shown up that easily," he said gleefully. "There are *eight* isotopes now, as I learned only this morning. Confess yourself at fault."

He stared at her eagerly, triumphantly, but only saw her face growing pale. Not ashamed, not exasperated, not contumacious even, but fearful. Dreadfully fearful.

There were three rapid, very loud knocks on the door.

They both started violently.

The knocks were repeated, followed by a bellow that penetrated all soundproofing. "Open up in there!" it boomed hollowly. "Come on out, Fortree! *And* the girl."

Matthew goggled. Severeign suddenly dug in her purse and tossed him something. It was the figurine.

"Break it!" she commanded. "It's our only chance of escape."

He stared at it stupidly.

There was a ponderous pounding on the door, which groaned and crackled.

"Break it!" she cried. "Night before last you prayed. I brought the answer to your prayer. You have it in your hands. It takes us to your lost world that you loved. Break it, I say!"

A kind of comprehension came to Math's face. He hooked his fingers round the figure's evil ends, pressed on the arching loathsome midst.

"Who is your brother, Severeign?" he asked.

"You are my brother, in the other realm," she said. "Press, press!— and break the thing!"

The door began visibly to give under the strokes, now thunderous. The cords in Math's neck stood out, and the veins in his forehead; his knuckles grew white.

"Break it for me," she cried. "For Severeign! *For Seven!*"

The sound of the door bursting open masked a lesser though sharper crack. Warren Dean and his party plunged into the room to find it empty, and no one in the bedroom or bathroom either.

It had been he, of course, whom Matthew, utterly bemused, had mistaken for Elmo Hooper that morning. Dean had immediately reactivated the bugs in Matthew's apartment. It is from their record that this account of Matthew's and Severeign's last night is reconstructed. All the rest of the story derives from the material overheard by Dean (who quite obviously, from this narrative, has his own Achilles' heel) or retrieved from Elmo Hooper.

The case is still very open, of course. That fact alone has made the Coexistence Complex an even more uneasy place than before—something that most connoisseurs of its intrigues had deemed impossible. The theory of security is the dread one that Matthew Fortree was successfully spirited away to one of the hostiles by the diabolical spy Severeign Saxon. By what device remains unknown, although the walls of the Coexistence Complex have been systematically burrowed through in search of secret passageways more thoroughly than even termites could have achieved, without discovering anything except several lost bugging systems.

A group of daring thinkers believes that Matthew, on the basis of his satanic mathematical cunning and his knowledge of the eighth isotope of the uranium-plutonium pair, and probably with technological know-how from behind some iron curtain supplied by Severeign, devised an innocent-looking mechanism, which was in fact a matter transmitter, by means of which they escaped to the country of Severeign's employers. All sorts of random setups were made of Matthew's ivories. Their investigation became a sort of hobby-in-itself for some and led to several games and quasi-religious cults, and to two suicides.

Others believe Severeign's employers were extraterrestrial. But a rare few quietly entertain the thought and perhaps the hope that hers was a farther country than that even, that she came from the Pythagorean universe where Matthew spent much of his infancy and early childhood, the universe where numbers are real and one can truly fall in love with Seven, briefly incarnate as a Miss S. S.

Whatever the case, Matthew Fortree and Severeign Saxon are indeed gone, vanished without a trace or clue except for a remarkably nasty figurine showing a fresh, poisonously green surface where it was snapped in two, which is the only even number that is a prime.

John Varley's fiction almost got away from *Universe,* too. He sent me a story early in 1974 that I liked almost enough to buy . . . but it seemed more Damon Knight's kind of thing than mine, so I suggested he send it to *Orbit.* (He did, and Damon bought it.) I also asked him to send me more stories, but that was the year Varley began to sell his stories as quickly as he could write them—he was an overnight success in science fiction—and it wasn't till five years later that my pleas to both him and his agent coaxed another manuscript into my mailbox.

In a way this worked to my benefit, for by that time Varley had been writing about his self-consistent future of cloning and simple sex-change operations long enough to have worked his way to the crucial story in the series, the one in which he would tell how people initially reacted to such drastic changes in body- and gender-roles. The result was a fascinating tale of speculation about people and their emotions.

Options

John Varley

Cleo hated breakfast.

Her energy level was lowest in the morning, but not so the children's. There was always some school crisis, something that had to be located at the last minute, some argument that had to be settled.

This morning it was a bowl of cereal spilled in Lilli's lap. Cleo hadn't seen it happen; her attention had been diverted momentarily by Feather, her youngest.

And of course it had to happen *after* Lilli was dressed.

"Mom, this was the *last* outfit I *had.*"

"Well, if you wouldn't use them so hard they might last more than three days, and if you didn't . . ." She stopped before she lost her temper. "Just take it off and go as you are."

"But Mom, nobody goes to school naked. *No*body. Give me some money and I'll stop at the store on—"

Cleo raised her voice, something she tried never to do. "Child, I know there are kids in your class whose parents can't afford to buy clothes at all."

"All right, so the poor kids don't—"

"That's enough. You're late already. Get going."

Lilli stalked from the room. Cleo heard the door slam.

Through it all Jules was an island of calm at the other end of the table, his nose in his newspad, sipping his second cup of coffee. Cleo glanced at her own bacon and eggs cooling on the plate, poured herself a first cup of coffee, then had to get up and help Paul find his other shoe.

By then Feather was wet again, so she put her on the table and peeled off the sopping diaper.

"Hey, listen to this," Jules said. " 'The City Council today passed without objection an ordinance requiring—' "

"Jules, aren't you a little behind schedule?"

He glanced at his thumbnail. "You're right. Thanks." He finished his coffee, folded his newspad and tucked it under his arm, bent over to kiss her, then frowned.

"You really ought to eat more, honey," he said, indicating the untouched eggs. "Eating for two, you know. 'By, now."

"Good-by," Cleo said, through clenched teeth. "And if I hear that 'eating for two' business again, I'll . . ." But he was gone.

She had time to scorch her lip on the coffee, then was out the door, hurrying to catch the train.

There were seats on the sun car, but of course Feather was with her and the UV wasn't good for her tender skin. After a longing look at the passengers reclining with the dark cups strapped over their eyes—and a rueful glance down at her own pale skin—Cleo boarded the next car and found a seat by a large man wearing a hardhat. She settled down in the cushions, adjusted the straps on the carrier slung in front of her, and let Feather have a nipple. She unfolded her newspad and spread it out in her lap.

"Cute," the man said. "How old is he?"

"She," Cleo said, without looking up. "Eleven days." And five hours and thirty-six minutes. . . .

She shifted in the seat, pointedly turning her shoulder to him, and made a show of activating her newspad and scanning the day's contents. She did not glance up as the train left the underground tunnel and emerged on the gently rolling, airless plain of Mendeleev. There was little enough out there to interest her, considering she made the forty-minute commute run to Hartman crater twice a day. They had discussed moving to Hartman, but Jules liked living in King City near his work, and of course the kids would have missed all their school friends.

There wasn't much in the news storage that morning. She queried when the red light flashed for an update. The pad printed some routine city business. Three sentences into the story she punched the reject key.

There was an Invasion Centennial parade listed for 1900 hours that evening. Parades bored her, and so did the Centennial. If you've heard one speech about how liberation of Earth is just around the corner if we all pull together, you've heard them all. Semantic content zero, nonsense quotient high.

She glanced wistfully at sports, noting that the J Sector jumpball team was doing poorly in the intracity tournament without her. Cleo's small stature and powerful legs had served her well as a starting sprintwing in her playing days, but it just didn't seem possible to make practices any more.

As a last resort, she called up the articles, digests, and analysis listings, the newspad's *Sunday Supplement* and Op-Ed department. A title caught her eye, and she punched it up.

Changing: The Revolution in Sex Roles
(Or, Who's on Top?)

Twenty years ago, when cheap and easy sex changes first became available to the general public, it was seen as the beginning of a revolution that would change the shape of human society in ways impossible to foresèe. Sexual equality is one thing, the sociologists pointed out, but certain residual inequities—based on biological imperatives or on upbringing, depending on your politics—have proved impossible to weed out. Changing was going to end all that. Men and women would be able to see what it was like from the other side of the barrier that divides humanity. How could sex roles survive that?

Ten years later the answer was obvious. Changing had appealed to only a tiny minority. It was soon seen as a harmless aberration, practiced by only 1 per cent of the population. Everyone promptly forgot about the tumbling of barriers.

But in the intervening ten years a quieter revolution has been building. Almost unnoticed on the broad scale because it is an invisible phenomenon (how do you know the next woman you meet was not a man last week?), changing has been gaining growing, matter-of-fact acceptance among the children of the generation that rejected it. The chances are now better than even that you know someone who has had at least one sex change. The chances are better than one out of fifteen that you yourself have changed; if you are under twenty, the chance is one in three.

The article went on to describe the underground society which was springing up around changing. Changers tended to band together, frequenting their own taprooms, staging their own social events, remaining aloof from the larger society which many of them saw as outmoded and irrelevant. Changers tended to marry other changers. They divided the childbearing equally, each preferring to mother only one child. The author viewed this tendency with alarm, since it went against the socially approved custom of large families. Changers retorted that the time for that was past, pointing out that Luna had been tamed long ago. They quoted statistics proving that at present rates of expansion, Luna's population would be in the billions in an amazingly short time.

There were interviews with changers, and psychological profiles. Cleo read that the males had originally been the heaviest users of the new technology, stating sexual reasons for their decision, and the change had often been permanent. Today, the changer was slightly more likely to have been born female, and to give social reasons, the most common of which was pressure to bear children. But the modern changer committed him/herself to neither role. The average time between changes in an individual was two years, and declining.

Cleo read the whole article, then thought about using some of the reading references at the end. Not that much of it was really new to her. She had been aware of changing, without thinking about it much. The idea had never attracted her, and Jules was against it. But for some reason it had struck a chord this morning.

Feather had gone to sleep. Cleo carefully pulled the blanket down around the child's face, then wiped milk from her nipple. She folded her newspad and stowed it in her purse, then rested her chin on her palm and looked out the window for the rest of the trip.

Cleo was chief on-site architect for the new Food Systems, Inc., plantation that was going down in Hartman. As such, she was in charge of three junior architects, five construction bosses, and an army of drafters and workers. It was a big project, the biggest Cleo had ever handled.

She liked her work, but the best part had always been being there on the site when things were happening, actually supervising construction instead of running a desk. That had been difficult in the last months of carrying Feather, but at least there were maternity pressure suits. It was even harder now.

She had been through it all before, with Lilli and Paul. Everybody works. That had been the rule for a century, since the Invasion. There was no labor to spare for baby-sitters, so having children meant the mother or father must do the same job they had been doing before, but do it while taking care of the child. In practice, it was usually the mother, since she had the milk.

Cleo had tried leaving Feather with one of the women in the office, but each had her own work to do, and not unreasonably felt Cleo should bear the burden of her own offspring. And Feather never seemed to respond well to another person. Cleo would return from her visit to the site to find the child had been crying the whole time, disrupting everyone's work. She had taken Feather in a crawler a few times, but it wasn't the same.

That morning was taken up with a meeting. Cleo and the other section chiefs sat around the big table for three hours, discussing ways of dealing with the cost overrun, then broke for lunch only to return to the problem in the afternoon. Cleo's back was aching and she had a headache she couldn't shake, so Feather chose that day to be cranky. After ten minutes of increasingly hostile looks, Cleo had to retire to the booth with Leah Farnham, the accountant, and her three-year-old son, Eddie. The two of them followed the proceedings through earphones while trying to cope with their children and make their remarks through throat mikes. Half the people at the conference table either had to turn around when she spoke, or ignore her, and Cleo was hesitant to force them to that choice. As a result, she chose her remarks with extreme care. More often, she said nothing.

There was something at the core of the world of business that refused to adjust to children in the board room, while appearing to make every effort to accommodate the working mother. Cleo brooded about it, not for the first time.

But what did she want? Honestly, she could not see what else could be done. It certainly wasn't fair to disrupt the entire meeting with a crying baby. She wished she knew the answer. Those were her friends out there, yet her feeling of alienation was intense, staring through the glass wall that Eddie was smudging with his dirty fingers.

Luckily, Feather was a perfect angel on the trip home. She gurgled and smiled toothlessly at a woman who had stopped to admire her, and Cleo warmed to the infant for the first time that day. She spent the trip playing hand games with her, surrounded by the approving smiles of other passengers.

"Jules, I read the most interesting article on the pad this morning." There, it was out, anyway. She had decided the direct approach would be best.

"Hmm?"

"It was about changing. It's getting more and more popular."

"Is that so?" He did not look up from his book.

Jules and Cleo were in the habit of sitting up in bed for a few hours after the children were asleep. They spurned the video programs that were designed to lull workers after a hard day, preferring to use the time to catch up on reading, or to talk if either of them had anything to say. Over the last few years, they had read more and talked less.

Cleo reached over Feather's crib and got a packet of dopesticks. She flicked one to light with her thumbnail, drew on it, and exhaled a cloud of lavender smoke. She drew her legs up under her and leaned back against the wall.

"I just thought we might talk about it. That's all."

Jules put his book down. "All right. But what's to talk about? We're not into that."

She shrugged and picked at a cuticle. "I know. We did talk about it, way back. I just wondered if you still felt the same, I guess." She offered him the stick and he took a drag.

"As far as I know, I do," he said easily. "It's not something I spend a great deal of thought on. What's the matter?" He looked at her suspiciously. "You weren't having any thoughts in that direction, were you?"

"Well, no, not exactly. No. But you really ought to read the article. More people are doing it. I just thought we ought to be aware of it."

"Yeah, I've heard that," Jules conceded. He laced his hands behind his head. "No way to tell unless you've worked with them and suddenly one day they've got a new set of equipment." He laughed. "First time it was sort of hard for me to get used to. Now I hardly think about it."

"Me, either."

"They don't cause any problem," Jules said with an air of finality. "Live and let live."

"Yeah." Cleo smoked in silence for a time and let Jules get back to his reading, but she still felt uncomfortable. "Jules?"

"What is it now?"

"Don't you ever wonder what it would be like?"

He sighed and closed his book, then turned to face her.

"I don't quite understand you tonight," he said.

"Well, maybe I don't, either, but we could talk—"

"Listen. Have you thought about what it would do to the kids? I mean, even if I was willing to seriously consider it, which I'm not."

"I talked to Lilli about that. Just theoretically, you understand. She said she has two teachers who change, and one of her best friends used to be a boy. There's quite a few kids at school who've changed. She takes it in stride."

"Yes, but she's older. What about Paul? What would it do to his concept of himself as a young man? I'll tell you, Cleo, in the back of my mind I keep thinking this business is a little sick. I feel it would have a bad effect on the children."

"Not according to—"

"Cleo, Cleo. Let's not get into an argument. Number one, I have no intention of getting a change, now or in the future. Two, if only one of us was changed, it would sure play hell with our sex life, wouldn't it? And three, I like you too much as you are." He leaned over and began to kiss her.

She was more than a little annoyed, but said nothing as his kisses became more intense. It was a damnably effective way of shutting off debate. And she could not stay angry: she was responding in spite of herself, easily, naturally.

It was as good as it always was with Jules. The ceiling, so familiar, once again became a calming blankness that absorbed her thoughts.

No, she had no complaints about being female, no sexual dissatisfactions. It was nothing as simple as that.

Afterward she lay on her side with her legs drawn up, her knees together. She faced Jules, who absently stroked her leg with one hand.

Her eyes were closed, but she was not sleepy. She was savoring the warmth she cherished so much after sex; the slipperiness between her legs, holding his semen inside.

She felt the bed move as he shifted his weight.

"You did make it, didn't you?"

She opened one eye enough to squint at him.

"Of course I did. I always do. You know I never have any trouble in that direction."

He relaxed back onto the pillow. "I'm sorry for . . . well, for springing on you like that."

"It's okay. It was nice."

"I had just thought you might have been . . . faking it. I'm not sure why I would think that."

She opened the other eye and patted him gently on the cheek.

"Jules, I'd never be that protective of your poor ego. If you don't satisfy me, I promise you'll be the second to know."

He chuckled, then turned on his side to kiss her.

"Good night, babe."

"G'night."

She loved him. He loved her. Their sex life was good—with the slight mental reservation that he always seemed to initiate it—and she was happy with her body.

So why was she still awake three hours later?

Shopping took a few hours on the vidphone Saturday morning. Cleo bought the household necessities for delivery that afternoon, then left the house to do the shopping she fancied: going from store to store, looking at things she didn't really need.

Feather was with Jules on Saturdays. She savored a quiet lunch alone at a table in the park plaza, then found herself walking down Brazil Avenue in the heart of the medical district. On impulse, she stepped into the New Heredity Body Salon.

It was only after she was inside that she admitted to herself she had spent most of the morning arranging for the impulse.

She was on edge as she was taken down a hallway to a consulting room, and had to force a smile for the handsome young man behind the desk. She sat, put her packages on the floor, and folded her hands in her lap. He asked what he could do for her.

"I'm not actually here for any work," she said. "I wanted to look into the costs, and maybe learn a little more about the procedures involved in changing."

He nodded understandingly, and got up.

"There's no charge for the initial consultation," he said. "We're happy to answer your questions. By the way, I'm Marion, spelled with an 'O' this month." He smiled at her and motioned for her to follow him. He stood her in front of a full-length mirror mounted on the wall.

"I know it's hard to make that first step. It was hard for me, and I do it for a living. So we've arranged this demonstration that won't cost you anything, either in money or worry. It's a nonthreatening way to see some of what it's all about, but it might startle you a little, so be prepared." He touched a button in the wall beside the mirror, and Cleo saw her clothes fade away. She realized it was not really a mirror, but a holographic screen linked to a computer.

The computer introduced changes in the image. In thirty seconds she faced a male stranger. There was no doubt the face was her own, but it was more angular, perhaps a little larger in its underlying bony structure. The skin on the stranger's jaw was rough, as if it needed shaving.

The rest of the body was as she might expect, though overly muscled for her tastes. She did little more than glance at the penis; somehow that didn't seem to matter so much. She spent more time studying the hair on the chest, the tiny nipples, and the ridges that had appeared on the hands and feet. The image mimicked her every movement.

"Why all the brawn?" she asked Marion. "If you're trying to sell me on this, you've taken the wrong approach."

Marion punched some more buttons. "I didn't choose this image," he explained. "The computer takes what it sees, and extrapolates. You're more muscular than the average woman. You probably exercise. This is what a comparable amount of training would have produced with male hormones to fix nitrogen in the muscles. But we're not bound by that."

The image lost about eight kilos of mass, mostly in the shoulders and thighs. Cleo felt a little more comfortable, but still missed the smoothness she was accustomed to seeing in her mirror.

She turned from the display and went back to her chair. Marion sat across from her and folded his hands on the desk.

"Basically, what we do is produce a cloned body from one of your own cells. Through a process called Y-Recombinant Viral Substitution we remove one of your X chromosomes and replace it with a Y.

"The clone is forced to maturity in the usual way, which takes about six months. After that, it's just a simple non-rejection-hazard brain transplant. You walk in as a woman, and leave an hour later as a man. Easy as that."

Cleo said nothing, wondering again what she was doing here.

"From there we can modify the body. We can make you taller or shorter, rearrange your face, virtually anything you like." He raised his eyebrows, then smiled ruefully and spread his hands.

"All right, Ms. King," he said. "I'm not trying to pressure you. You'll need to think about it. In the meantime, there's a process that would cost you very little, and might be just the thing to let you test the waters. Am I right in thinking your husband opposes this?"

She nodded, and he looked sympathetic.

"Not uncommon, not uncommon at all," he assured her. "It brings out castration fears in men who didn't even suspect they had them. Of course, we do nothing of the sort. His male body would be kept in a tank, ready for him to move back whenever he wanted to."

Cleo shifted in her chair. "What was this process you were talking about?"

"Just a bit of minor surgery. It can be done in ten minutes, and corrected in the same time before you even leave the office if you find you don't care for it. It's a good way to get husbands thinking about changing; sort of a signal you can send him. You've heard of the androgynous look. It's in all the fashion tapes. Many women, especially if they have large breasts like you do, find it an interesting change."

"You say it's cheap? And reversible?"

"All our processes are reversible. Changing the size or shape of breasts is our most common body operation."

Cleo sat on the examining table while the attendant gave her a quick physical.

"I don't know if Marion realized you're nursing," the woman said. "Are you sure this is what you want?"

How the hell should I know? Cleo thought. She wished the feeling of confusion and uncertainty would pass.

"Just do it."

Jules hated it.

He didn't yell or slam doors or storm out of the house; that had never been his style. He voiced his objections coldly and quietly at the dinner table, after saying practically nothing since she walked in the door.

"I just would like to know why you thought you should do this without even talking to me about it. I don't demand that you *ask* me, just discuss it with me."

Cleo felt miserable, but was determined not to let it show. She held Feather in her arm, the bottle in her other hand, and ignored the food cooling on her plate. She was hungry but at least she was not eating for two.

"Jules, I'd ask you before I rearranged the furniture. We both own this apartment. I'd ask you before I put Lilli or Paul in another school. We share the responsibility for their upbringing. But I don't ask you when I put on lipstick or cut my hair. It's my body."

"I like it, Mom," Lilli said. "You look like me."

Cleo smiled at her, reached over and tousled her hair.

"What do you like?" Paul asked, around a mouthful of food.

"See?" said Cleo. "It's not that important."

"I don't see how you can say that. And I said you didn't have to ask me. I just would . . . you should have . . . I should have *known.*"

"It was an impulse, Jules."

"An impulse. An *impulse.*" For the first time, he raised his voice, and Cleo knew how upset he really was. Lilli and Paul fell silent, and even Feather squirmed.

But Cleo liked it. Oh, not forever and ever: as an interesting change. It gave her a feeling of freedom to be that much in control of her body, to be able to decide how large she wished her breasts to be. Did it have anything to do with changing? She really didn't think so. She didn't feel the least bit like a man.

And what was a breast, anyway? It was anything from a nipple sitting flush with the rib cage to a mammoth hunk of fat and milk gland. Cleo realized Jules was suffering from the more-is-better syndrome, thinking of Cleo's action as the removal of her breasts, as if they had to be large to exist at all. What she had actually done was reduce their size.

No more was said at the table, but Cleo knew it was for the children's sake. As soon as they got into bed, she could feel the tension again.

"I can't understand why you did it *now.* What about Feather?"

"What about her?"

"Well, do you expect me to nurse her?"

Cleo finally got angry. "Damn it, that's *exactly* what I expect you to do. Don't tell me you don't know what I'm talking about. You think it's all fun and games, having to carry a child around all day because she needs the milk in your breasts?"

"You never complained before."

"I . . ." She stopped. He was right, of course. It amazed even Cleo that this had all come up so suddenly, but here it was, and she had to deal with it. *They* had to deal with it.

"That's because it isn't an awful thing. It's great to nourish another human being at your breast. I loved every minute of it with Lilli. Sometimes it was a headache, having her there all the time, but it was worth it. The same with Paul." She sighed. "The same with Feather, too, most of the time. You hardly think about it."

"Then why the revolt now? With no warning?"

"It's not a revolt, honey. Do you see it as that? I just . . . I'd like you to try it. Take Feather for a few months. Take her to work like I do. Then you'd . . . you'd see a little of what I go through." She rolled on her side and playfully punched his arm, trying to lighten it in some way. "You might even like it. It feels real good."

He snorted. "I'd feel silly."

She jumped from the bed and paced toward the living room, then turned, more angry than ever. "Silly? Nursing is silly? Breasts are silly? Then why the hell do you wonder why I did what I did?"

"Being a *man* is what makes it silly," he retorted. "It doesn't look right. I almost laugh every time I see a man with breasts. The hormones mess up your system, I heard, and—"

"That's *not true!* Not any more. You can lactate—"

"—and besides, it's my body, as you pointed out. I'll do with it what pleases me."

She sat on the edge of the bed with her back to him. He reached out and stroked her, but she moved away.

"All right," she said. "I was just suggesting it. I thought you might like to try it. *I'm* not going to nurse her. She goes on the bottle from now on."

"If that's the way it has to be."

"It is. I want you to start taking Feather to work with you. Since she's going to be a bottle baby, it hardly matters which of us cares for her. I think you owe it to me, since I carried the burden alone with Lilli and Paul."

"All right."

She got into bed and pulled the covers up around her, her back to him. She didn't want him to see how close she was to tears.

But the feeling passed. The tension drained from her, and she felt good. She thought she had won a victory, and it was worth the cost. Jules would not stay angry at her.

She fell asleep easily, but woke up several times during the night as Jules tossed and turned.

He did adjust to it. It was impossible for him to say so all at once, but after a week without love-making he admitted grudgingly that she looked good. He began to touch her in the mornings and when they kissed after getting home from work. Jules had always admired her slim muscularity, her athlete's arms and legs. The slim chest looked so natural on her, it fit the rest of her so well that he began to wonder what all the fuss had been about.

One night while they were clearing the dinner dishes, Jules touched her nipples for the first time in a week. He asked her if it felt any different.

"There is very little feeling anywhere but the nipples," she pointed out, "no matter how big a woman is. You know that."

"Yeah, I guess I do."

She knew they would make love that night and determined it would be on her terms.

She spent a long time in the bathroom, letting him get settled with his book, then came out and took it away. She got on top of him and pressed close, kissing and tickling his nipples with her fingers.

She was aggressive and insistent. At first he seemed reluctant, but soon he was responding as she pressed her lips hard against his, forcing his head back into the pillow.

"I love you," he said, and raised his head to kiss her nose. "Are you ready?"

"I'm ready." He put his arms around her and held her close, then rolled over and hovered above her.

"Jules. *Jules.* Stop it." She squirmed onto her side, her legs held firmly together.

"What's wrong?"

"I want to be on top tonight."

"Oh. All right." He turned over again and reclined passively as she repositioned herself. Her heart was pounding. There had been no reason to think he would object—they had made love in any and all positions, but basically the exotic ones were a change of pace from the "natural" one with her on her back. Tonight she had wanted to feel in control.

"Open your legs, darling," she said, with a smile. He did, but didn't return the smile. She raised herself on her hands and knees and prepared for the tricky insertion.

"Cleo."

"What is it? This will take a little effort, but I think I can make it worth your while, so if you'd just—"

"Cleo, what the hell is the purpose of this?"

She stopped dead and let her head sag between her shoulders.

"What's the matter? Are you feeling silly with your feet in the air?"

"Maybe. Is that what you wanted?"

"Jules, humiliating you was the farthest thing from my mind."

"Then what *was* on your mind? It's not like we've never done it this way before. It's—"

"Only when *you* chose to do so. It's always your decision."

"It's not degrading to be on the bottom."

"Then why were you feeling silly?"

He didn't answer, and she wearily lifted herself away from him, sitting on her knees at his feet. She waited, but he didn't seem to want to talk about it.

"I've never complained about that position," she ventured. "I don't *have* any complaints about it. It works pretty well." Still he said nothing. "All right. I wanted to see what it looked like from up there. I was tired of looking at the ceiling. I was curious."

"And *that's* why I felt *silly*. I never minded you being on top before, have I? But before . . . well, it's never been in the context of the last couple weeks. I *know* what's on your mind."

"And you feel threatened by it. By the fact that I'm curious about changing, that I want to know what it's like to take charge. You know I can't—and wouldn't if I could—force a change on you."

"But your curiosity is wrecking our marriage."

She felt like crying again, but didn't let it show except for a trembling of her lower lip. She didn't want him to try and soothe her; that was all too likely to work, and she would find herself on her back with her legs in the air. She looked down at the bed and nodded slowly, then got up. She went to the mirror and took the brush, began running it through her hair.

"What are you doing now? Can't we talk about this?"

"I don't feel much like talking right now." She leaned forward and examined her face as she brushed, then dabbed at the corners of her eyes with a tissue. "I'm going out. I'm still curious."

He said nothing as she started for the door.
"I may be a little late."

The place was called Oophyte. The capital "O" had a plus sign hanging from it, and an arrow in the upper right side. The sign was built so that the symbols revolved; one moment the plus was inside and the arrow out, the next moment the reverse.

Cleo moved in a pleasant haze across the crowded dance floor, pausing now and then to draw on her dopestick. The air in the room was thick with lavender smoke, illuminated by flashing blue lights. She danced when the mood took her. The music was so loud that she didn't have to think about it; the noise gripped her bones and animated her arms and legs. She glided through a forest of naked skin, feeling the occasional roughness of a paper suit and, rarely, expensive cotton clothing. It was like moving underwater, like wading through molasses.

She saw him across the floor and began moving in his direction. He took no notice of her for some time, though she danced right in front of him. Few of the dancers had partners in more than the transitory sense. Some were celebrating life, others were displaying themselves, but all were looking for partners, so eventually he realized she had been there an unusual length of time. He was easily as stoned as she was.

She told him what she wanted.

"Sure. Where do you want to go? Your place?"

She took him down the hall in back and touched her credit bracelet to the lock on one of the doors. The room was simple, but clean.

He looked a lot like her phantom twin in the mirror, she noted with one part of her mind. It was probably why she had chosen him. She embraced him and lowered him gently to the bed.

"Do you want to exchange names?" he asked. The grin on his face kept getting sillier as she toyed with him.

"I don't care. Mostly I think I want to use you."

"Use away. My name's Saffron."

"I'm Cleopatra. Would you get on your back, please?"

He did, and they did. It was hot in the little room, but neither of them minded it. It was healthy exertion, the physical sensations were great, and when Cleo was through she had learned nothing. She collapsed on top of him. He did not seem surprised when tears began falling on his shoulder.

"I'm sorry," she said, sitting up and getting ready to leave.

"Don't go," he said, putting his hand on her shoulder. "Now that you've got that out of your system, maybe we can make love."

She didn't want to smile, but she had to, then she was crying harder, putting her face to his chest and feeling the warmth of his arms around her and the hair tickling her nose. She realized what she was doing, and tried to pull away.

"For God's sake, don't be ashamed that you need someone to cry on."

"It's weak. I . . . I just didn't want to be weak."

"We're all weak."

She gave up struggling and nestled there until the tears stopped. She sniffed, wiped her nose, and faced him.

"What's it like? Can you tell me?" She was about to explain what she meant, but he seemed to understand.

"It's like . . . nothing special."

"You were born female, weren't you? I mean, you . . . I thought I might be able to tell."

"It's no longer important how I was born. I've been both. It's still me, on the inside. You understand?"

"I'm not sure I do."

They were quiet for a long time. Cleo thought of a thousand things to say, questions to ask, but could do nothing.

"You've been coming to a decision, haven't you?" he said, at last. "Are you any closer after tonight?"

"I'm not sure."

"It's not going to solve any problems, you know. It might even create some."

She pulled away from him and got up. She shook her hair and wished for a comb.

"Thank you, Cleopatra," he said.

"Oh. Uh, thank you . . ." She had forgotten his name. She smiled again to cover her embarrassment, and shut the door behind her.

"Hello?"

"Yes. This is Cleopatra King. I had a consultation with one of your staff. I believe it was ten days ago."

"Yes, Ms. King. I have your file. What can I do for you?"

She took a deep breath. "I want you to start the clone. I left a tissue sample."

"Very well, Ms. King. Did you have any instructions concerning the chromosome donor?"

"Do you need consent?"

"Not as long as there's a sample in the bank."

"Use my husband, Jules La Rhin. Security number 4454390."

"Very good. We'll be in contact with you."

Cleo hung up the phone and rested her forehead against the cool metal. She should never get this stoned, she realized. What had she done?

But it was not final. It would be six months before she had to decide if she would ever use the clone. Damn Jules. Why did he have to make such a big thing of it?

Jules did *not* make a big thing of it when she told him what she had done. He took it quietly and calmly, as if he had been expecting it.

"You know I won't follow you in this?"

"I know you feel that way. I'm interested to see if you change your mind."

"Don't count on it. I want to see if you change yours."

"I haven't *made up* my mind. But I'm giving myself the option."

"All I ask is that you bear in mind what this could do to our relationship. I love you, Cleo. I don't think that will ever change. But if you walk into this house as a man, I don't think I'll be able to see you as the person I've always loved."

"You could if you were a woman."

"But I won't be."

"And I'll be the same person I always was." But would she be? What the hell was *wrong*? What had Jules ever done that he should deserve this? She made up her mind never to go through with it, and they made love that night and it was very, very good.

But somehow she never got around to calling the vivarium and telling them to abort the clone. She made the decision not to go through with it a dozen times over the next six months, and never had the clone destroyed.

Their relationship in bed became uneasy as time passed. At first, it was good. Jules made no objections when she initiated sex, and was willing to do it any way she preferred. Once that was accomplished she no longer cared whether she was on top or underneath. The important thing had been having the option of making love when she wanted to, the way she wanted to.

"That's what this is all about," she told him one night, in a moment of clarity when everything seemed to make sense except his refusal to see things from her side. "It's the option I want. I'm not unhappy being female. I don't like the feeling that there's *anything* I *can't* be. I want to know how much of me is hormones, how much is genetics, how much is upbringing. I want to know if I feel more secure being aggressive as a man, because I sure don't, most of the time, as a woman. Or do men feel the same insecurities I feel? Would Cleo the man feel free to cry? I don't know any of those things."

"But you said it yourself. You'll still be the same person."

They began to drift apart in small ways. A few weeks after her outing to the Oophyte she returned home one Sunday afternoon to find him in bed with a woman. It was not like him to do it like that; their custom had been to bring lovers home and introduce them, to keep it friendly and open. Cleo was amused, because she saw it as his way of getting back at her for her trip to the encounter bar.

So she was the perfect hostess, joining them in bed, which seemed to disconcert Jules. The woman's name was Harriet, and Cleo found herself liking her. She was a changer—something Jules had not known or he certainly would not have chosen her to make Cleo feel bad. Harriet was uncomfortable when she realized why she was there. Cleo managed to put her at ease by making love to her, something that surprised Cleo a little and Jules considerably, since she had never done it before.

Cleo enjoyed it; she found Harriet's smooth body to be a whole new world. And she felt she had neatly turned the tables on Jules, making him confront once more the idea of his wife in the man's role.

The worst part was the children. They had discussed the possible impending change with Lilli and Paul.

Lilli could not see what all the fuss was about; it was a part of her life, something that was all around her which she took for granted as something she herself would do when she was old enough. But when she began picking up the concern from her father, she drew subtly closer to her mother. Cleo was tremendously relieved. She didn't think she could have held to it in the face of Lilli's displeasure. Lilli was her first born, and though she hated to admit it and did her best not to play favorites, her darling. She had taken a year's leave from her job at appalling expense to the household budget so she could devote all her time to her infant daughter. She often wished she could somehow return to those simpler days, when motherhood had been her whole life.

Feather, of course, was not consulted. Jules had assumed the responsibility for her nurture without complaint, and seemed to be enjoying it. It was fine with Cleo, though it maddened her that he was so willing about taking over the mothering role without being willing to try it as a female. Cleo loved Feather as much as the other two, but sometimes had trouble recalling why they had decided to have her. She felt she had gotten the procreation impulse out of her system with Paul, and yet there Feather was.

Paul was the problem.

Things could get tense when Paul expressed doubts about how he would feel if his mother were to become a man. Jules's face would darken, and he might not speak for days. When he did speak, often in the middle of the night when neither of them could sleep, it would be in a verbal explosion that was as close to violence as she had ever seen him.

It frightened her, because she was by no means sure of herself when it came to Paul. Would it hurt him? Jules spoke of gender identity crises, of the need for stable role models, and finally, in naked honesty, of the fear that his son would grow up to be somehow less than a man.

Cleo didn't know, but cried herself to sleep over it many nights. They had read articles about it and found that psychologists were divided. Traditionalists made much of the importance of sex roles, while changers felt sex roles were important only to those who were trapped in them; with the breaking of the sexual barrier, the concept of roles vanished.

The day finally came when the clone body was ready. Cleo still did not know what she should do.

"Are you feeling comfortable now? Just nod if you can't talk."

"Wha . . ."

"Relax. It's all over. You'll be feeling like walking in a few minutes. We'll have someone take you home. You may feel drunk for a while, but there's no drugs in your system."

"Wha' . . . happen?"

"It's over. Just relax."

Cleo did, curling up in a ball. Eventually he began to laugh.

Drunk was not the word for it. He sprawled on the bed, trying on pronouns for size. It was all so funny. *He* was on *his* back with *his* hands in *his* lap. He giggled and rolled back and forth, over and over, fell on the floor in hysterics.

He raised his head.

"Is that you, Jules?"

"Yes, it's me." He helped Cleo back onto the bed, then sat on the edge, not too near, but not unreachably far away. "How do you feel?"

He snorted. "Drunker 'n a skunk." He narrowed his eyes, forced them to focus on Jules. "You must call me Leo now. Cleo is a woman's name. You shouldn't have called me Cleo then."

"All right. I didn't call you Cleo, though."

"You didn't? Are you *sure?*"

"I'm very sure it's something I wouldn't have said."

"Oh. Okay." He lifted his head and looked confused for a moment. "You know what? I'm gonna be sick."

Leo felt much better an hour later. He sat in the living room with Jules, both of them on the big pillows that were the only furniture.

They spoke of inconsequential matters for a time, punctuated by long silences. Leo was no more used to the sound of his new voice than Jules was.

"Well," Jules said, finally, slapping his hands on his knees and standing up. "I really don't know what your plans are from here. Did you want to go out tonight? Find a woman, see what it's like?"

Leo shook his head. "I tried that out as soon as I got home," he said. "The male orgasm, I mean."

"What was it like?"

He laughed. "Certainly you know that by now."

"No, I meant, after being a woman—"

"I know what you mean." He shrugged. "The erection is interesting. So much larger than what I'm used to. Otherwise . . ." He frowned for a moment. "A lot the same. Some different. More localized. Messier."

"Um." Jules looked away, studying the electric fireplace as if seeing it for the first time. "Had you planned to move out? It isn't necessary, you know. We could move people around. I can go in with Paul, or we could move him in with me in . . . in our old room. You could have his." He turned away from Leo, and put his hand to his face.

Leo ached to get up and comfort him, but felt it would be exactly the wrong thing to do. He let Jules get himself under control.

"If you'll have me, I'd like to continue sleeping with you."

Jules said nothing, and didn't turn around.

"Jules, I'm perfectly willing to do whatever will make you most comfortable. There doesn't have to be any sex. Or I'd be happy to do what I used to do when I was in late pregnancy. You wouldn't have to do anything at all."

"No sex," he said.

"Fine, fine. Jules, I'm getting awfully tired. Are you ready to sleep?"

There was a long pause, then he turned and nodded.

They lay quietly, side by side, not touching. The lights were out; Leo could barely see the outline of Jules's body.

After a long time, Jules turned on his side.

"Cleo, are you in there? Do you still love me?"

"I'm here," she said. "I love you. I always will."

Jules jumped when Leo touched him, but made no objection. He began to cry, and Leo held him close. They fell asleep in each other's arms.

The Oophyte was as full and noisy as ever. It gave Leo a headache.

He did not like the place any more than Cleo had, but it was the only place he knew to find sex partners quickly and easily, with no emotional entanglements and no long process of seduction. Everyone there was available; all one needed to do was ask. They used each other for sexual calisthenics just one step removed from masturbation, cheerfully admitted the fact, and took the position that if you didn't approve, what were you doing there? There were plenty of other places for romance and relationships.

Leo didn't normally approve of it—not for himself, though he cared not at all what other people did for amusement. He preferred to know someone he bedded.

But he was here tonight to learn. He felt he needed the practice. He did not buy the argument that he would know just what to do because he had been a woman and knew what they liked. He needed to know how people reacted to him as a male.

Things went well. He approached three women and was accepted each time. The first was a mess—so *that's* what they meant by too soon! —and she was rather indignant about it until he explained his situation. After that she was helpful and supportive.

He was about to leave when he was propositioned by a woman who said her name was Lynx. He was tired, but decided to go with her.

Ten frustrating minutes later she sat up and moved away from him.

"What are you here for, if that's all the interest you can muster? And don't tell me it's my fault."

"I'm sorry," he said. "I forgot. I thought I could . . . well, I didn't realize I had to be really interested before I could perform."

"Perform? That's a funny way to put it."

"I'm sorry." He told her what the problem was, how many times he had made love in the last two hours. She sat on the edge of the bed and ran her hands through her hair, frustrated and irritable.

"Well, it's not the end of the world. There's plenty more out there. But you could give a girl a warning. You didn't have to say yes back there."

"I know. It's my fault. I'll have to learn to judge my capacity, I guess. It's just that I'm used to being *able* to, even if I'm not particularly—"

Lynx laughed. "What am I saying? Listen to me. Honey, I used to have the same problem myself. *Weeks* of not getting it up. And I know it hurts."

"Well," Leo said, "I know what you're feeling like, too. It's no fun."

Lynx shrugged. "In other circumstances, yeah. But like I said, the woods are full of 'em tonight. I won't have any problem." She put her hand on his cheek and pouted at him. "Hey, I didn't hurt your poor male ego, did I?"

Leo thought about it, probed around for bruises, and found none. "No."

She laughed. "I didn't think so. Because you don't have one. Enjoy it, Leo. A male ego is something that has to be grown carefully, when you're young. People have to keep pointing out what you have to do to be a man, so you can recognize failure when you can't 'perform.' How come you used that word?"

"I don't know. I guess I was just thinking of it that way."

"Trying to be a quote *man* unquote. Leo, you don't have enough emotional investment in it. And you're *lucky*. It took me over a year to shake mine. Don't be a man. Be a male human, instead. The switch-over's a lot easier that way."

"I'm not sure what you mean."

She patted his knee. "Trust me. Do you see me getting all upset because I wasn't sexy enough to turn you on, or some such garbage? No. I wasn't brought up to worry that way. But reverse it. If I'd done to you what you just did to me, wouldn't something like that have occurred to you?"

"I think it would. Though I've always been pretty secure in that area."

"The most secure of us are whimpering children beneath it, at least some of the time. You understand that I got upset because you said yes when you weren't ready? And that's *all* I was upset about? It was impolite, Leo. A male human shouldn't do that to a female human. With a man and a woman, it's different. The poor fellow's got a lot of junk in his head, and so does the woman, so they shouldn't be held responsible for the tricks their egos play on them."

Leo laughed. "I don't know if you're making sense at all. But I like the sound of it. 'Male human.' Maybe I'll see the difference one day."

Some of the expected problems never developed.

Paul barely noticed the change. Leo had prepared himself for a traumatic struggle with his son, and it never came. If it changed Paul's life at all, it was in the fact that he could now refer to his maternal parent as Leo instead of Mother.

Strangely enough, it was Lilli who had the most trouble at first. Leo was hurt by it, tried not to show it, and did everything he could to let her adjust gradually. Finally she came to him one day about a week after the change. She said she had been silly, and wanted to know if she could get a change, too, since one of her best friends was getting one. Leo talked her into remaining female until after the onset of puberty. He told her he thought she might enjoy it.

Leo and Jules circled each other like two tigers in a cage, unsure if a fight was necessary but ready to start clawing out eyes if it came to it. Leo didn't like the analogy; if he had still been a female tiger, he would have felt sure of the outcome. But he had no wish to engage in a dominance struggle with Jules.

They shared an apartment, a family, and a bed. They were elaborately polite, but touched each other only rarely, and Leo always felt he should apologize when they did. Jules would not meet his eyes; their gazes would touch, then rebound like two cork balls with identical static charges.

But eventually Jules accepted Leo. He was "that guy who's always around" in Jules's mind. Leo didn't care for that, but saw it as progress. In a few more days Jules began to discover that he liked Leo. They began to share things, to talk more. The subject of their previous relationship was taboo for a while. It was as if Jules wanted to know Leo from scratch, not acknowledging there had ever been a Cleo who had once been his wife.

It wasn't that simple; Leo would not let it be. Jules sometimes sounded like he was mourning the passing of a loved one when he hesitantly began talking about the hurt inside him. He was able to talk freely to Leo, and it was in a slightly different manner from the way he had talked to Cleo. He poured out his soul. It was astonishing to Leo that there were so many bruises on it, so many defenses and insecurities. There was buried hostility which Jules had never felt free to tell a woman.

Leo let him go on, but when Jules started a sentence with, "I could never tell this to Cleo," or, "Now that she's gone," Leo would go to him, take his hand, and force him to look.

"I'm Cleo," he would say. "I'm right here, and I love you."

They started doing things together. Jules took him to places Cleo had never been. They went out drinking together and had a wonderful time getting sloshed. Before, it had always been dinner with a few drinks or dopesticks, then a show or concert. Now they might come home at 0200, harmonizing loud enough to get thrown in jail. Jules admitted he hadn't had so much fun since his college days.

Socializing was a problem. Few of their old friends were changers, and neither of them wanted to face the complications of going to a party as a couple. They couldn't make friends among changers, because Jules correctly saw he would be seen as an outsider.

So they saw a lot of men. Leo had thought he knew all of Jules's close friends, but found he had been wrong. He saw a side of Jules he had never seen before: more relaxed in ways, some of his guardedness gone, but with other defenses in place. Leo sometimes felt like a spy, looking in on a stratum of society he had always known was there, but had never been able to penetrate. If Cleo had walked into the group its structure would have changed subtly; she would have created a new milieu by her presence, like light destroying the atom it was meant to observe.

After his initial outing to the Oophyte, Leo remained celibate for a long time. He did not want to have sex casually; he wanted to love Jules. As far as he knew, Jules was abstaining, too.

But they found an acceptable alternative in double-dating. They shopped around together for a while, taking out different women and having a lot of fun without getting into sex, until each settled on a woman he could have a relationship with. Jules was with Diane, a woman he had known at work for many years. Leo went out with Harriet.

The four of them had great times together. Leo loved being a pal to Jules, but would not let it remain simply that. He took to reminding Jules that he could do this with Cleo, too. What Leo wanted to emphasize was that he could be a companion, a buddy, a confidant no matter which sex he was. He wanted to combine the best of being a woman and being a man, be both things for Jules, fulfill all his needs. But it hurt to think that Jules would not do the same for him.

"Well, hello, Leo. I didn't expect to see you today."

"Can I come in, Harriet?"

She held the door open for him.

"Can I get you anything? Oh, yeah, before you go any further, that 'Harriet' business is finished. I changed my name today. It's Joule from now on. That's spelled j-o-u-l-e."

"Okay, Joule. Nothing for me, thanks." He sat on her couch.

Leo was not surprised at the new name. Changers had a tendency to get away from "name" names. Some did as Cleo had done by choosing a gender equivalent or a similar sound. Others ignored gender connotations and used the one they had always used. But most eventually chose a neutral word, according to personal preference.

"Jules, Julia," he muttered.

"What was that?" Joule's brow wrinkled slightly. "Did you come here for mothering? Things going badly?"

Leo slumped down and contemplated his folded hands.

"I don't know. I guess I'm depressed. How long has it been now? Five months? I've learned a lot, but I'm not sure just what it is. I feel like I've grown. I see the world . . . well, I see things differently, yes. But I'm still basically the same person."

"In the sense that you're the same person at thirty-three as you were at ten?"

Leo squirmed. "Okay. Yeah, I've changed. But it's not any kind of reversal. Nothing turned topsy-turvy. It's an expansion. It's not a new viewpoint. It's like filling something up, moving out into unused spaces. Becoming . . ." His hands groped in the air, then fell back into his lap. "It's like a completion."

Joule smiled. "And you're disappointed? What more could you ask?"

Leo didn't want to get into that just yet. "Listen to this, and see if you agree. I always saw male and female—whatever that is, and I don't know if the two *really* exist other than physically and don't think it's important anyway. . . . I saw those qualities as separate. Later, I thought of them like Siamese twins in everybody's head. But the twins were usually fighting, trying to cut each other off. One would beat the other down, maim it, throw it in a cell, and never feed it, but they were always connected and the beaten-down one would make the winner pay for the victory.

"So I wanted to try and patch things up between them. I thought I'd just introduce them to each other and try to referee, but they got along a lot better than I expected. In fact, they turned into one whole person, and found they could be very happy together. I can't tell them apart any more. Does that make any sense?"

Joule moved over to sit beside him.

"It's a good analogy, in its way. I feel something like that, but I don't think about it any more. So what's the problem? You just told me you feel whole now."

Leo's face contorted. "Yes. I do. And if I am, what does that make Jules?" He began to cry, and Joule let him get it out, just holding his hand. She thought he'd better face it alone, this time. When he had calmed down, she began to speak quietly.

"Leo, Jules is happy as he is. I think he could be much happier, but there's no way for us to show him that without having him do something that he fears so much. It's possible that he will do it someday, after more time to get used to it. And it's possible that he'll hate it and run screaming back to his manhood. Sometimes the maimed twin can't be rehabilitated."

She sighed heavily, and got up to pace the room.

"There's going to be a lot of this in the coming years," she said. "A lot of broken hearts. We're not really very much like them, you know. We get along better. We're not angels, but we may be the most civilized, considerate group the race has yet produced. There are fools and bastards among us, just like the one-sexers, but I think we tend to be a little less foolish, and a little less cruel. I think changing is here to stay.

"And what you've got to realize is that you're lucky. And so is Jules. It could have been much worse. I know of several broken homes just among my own friends. There's going to be many more before society has assimilated this. But your love for Jules and his for you has held you together. He's made a tremendous adjustment, maybe as big as the one you made. He *likes* you. In either sex. Okay, so you don't make love to him as Leo. You may never reach that point."

"We did. Last night." Leo shifted on the couch. "I . . . I got mad. I told him if he wanted to see Cleo, he had to learn to relate to me, because I'm *me*, dammit."

"I think that might have been a mistake."

Leo looked away from her. "I'm starting to think so, too."

"But I think the two of you can patch it up, if there's any damage. You've come through a lot together."

"I didn't mean to force anything on him, I just got mad."

"And maybe you *should* have. It might have been just the thing. You'll have to wait and see."

Leo wiped his eyes and stood up.

"Thanks, Harr . . . sorry. Joule. You've helped me. I . . . uh, I may not be seeing you as often for a while."

"I understand. Let's stay friends, okay?" She kissed him, and he hurried away.

She was sitting on a pillow facing the door when he came home from work, her legs crossed, elbow resting on her knee with a dopestick in her hand. She smiled at him.

"Well, you're home early. What happened?"

"I stayed home from work." She nearly choked, trying not to laugh. He threw his coat to the closet and hurried into the kitchen. She heard something being stirred, then the sound of glass shattering. He burst through the doorway.

"Cleo!"

"Darling, you look so handsome with your mouth hanging open."

He shut it, but still seemed unable to move. She went to him, feeling tingling excitement in her loins like the return of an old friend. She put her arms around him, and he nearly crushed her. She loved it.

He drew back slightly and couldn't seem to get enough of her face, his eyes roaming every detail.

"How long will you stay this way?" he asked. "Do you have any idea?"

"I don't know. Why?"

He smiled, a little sheepishly. "I hope you won't take this wrong. I'm so *happy* to see you. Maybe I shouldn't say it . . . but no, I think I'd better. I like Leo. I think I'll miss him, a little."

She nodded. "I'm not hurt. How could I be?" She drew away and led him to a pillow. "Sit down, Jules. We have to have a talk." His knees gave way under him and he sat, looking up expectantly.

"Leo isn't gone, and don't you ever think that for a minute. He's right here." She thumped her chest and looked at him defiantly. "He'll always be here. He'll never go away."

"I'm sorry, Cleo, I—"

"No, don't talk yet. It was my own fault, but I didn't know any better. I never should have called myself Leo. It gave you an easy out. You didn't have to face Cleo being a male. I'm changing all that. My name is Nile. N-i-l-e. I won't answer to anything else."

"All right. It's a nice name."

"I thought of calling myself Lion. For Leo the lion. But I decided to be who I always was, the queen of the Nile, Cleopatra. For old time's sake."

He said nothing, but his eyes showed his appreciation.

"What you have to understand is that they're both gone, in a sense. You'll never be with Cleo again. I look like her now. I resemble her inside, too, like an adult resembles the child. I have a tremendous amount in common with what she was. But I'm not her."

He nodded. She sat beside him and took his hand.

"Jules, this isn't going to be easy. There are things I want to do, people I want to meet. We're not going to be able to share the same friends. We could drift apart because of it. I'm going to have to fight resentment because you'll be holding me back. You won't let me explore your female side like I want to. You're going to resent me because I'll be trying to force you into something you think is wrong for you. But I want to try and make it work."

He let out his breath. "God, Cl . . . Nile. I've never been so scared in my life. I thought you were leading up to leaving me."

She squeezed his hand. "Not if I can help it. I want each of us to try and accept the other as they are. For me, that includes being male whenever I feel like it. It's all the same to me, but I know it's going to be hard for *you.*"

They embraced, and Jules wiped his tears on her shoulder, then faced her again.

"I'll do anything and everything in my power, up to—"

She put her finger to her lips. "I know. I accept you that way. But I'll keep trying to convince you."

This story has an almost Byzantine history. Waldrop sent it to me at a time when I was just closing *Universe 10,* having selected all the stories that would fit in the book. I loved "The Ugly Chickens" a lot, but didn't see any way to buy it that year, so I passed it over to Marta Randall, who had just taken over the editorship of *New Dimensions.* She liked it as much as I did, and made arrangements with Waldrop to buy it.

But suddenly I found that one of the stories I'd expected to buy wasn't available (it had been sold to a publisher in England and the news hadn't reached the agent involved till then). I'd returned all the submissions I had on hand, thinking my book was full, so I found myself one story short with a deadline staring me in the face. In desperation I called Marta and explained my plight. "Would you kill me if I asked you to return 'The Ugly Chickens'?"

On her behalf I must state that she ground her teeth quietly. "Well . . . he did send it to you first. Ask him how he feels."

So I called Waldrop in Texas. He said, "I'd love to appear in *New Dimensions,* but I wrote that story specifically for you. Okay. Tell Marta I'll write another story for her."

So I did buy the story, and Waldrop did write another for *New Dimensions.* "The Ugly Chickens" went on to win the Nebula Award.

The Ugly Chickens

Howard Waldrop

My car was broken, and I had a class to teach at eleven. So I took the city bus, something I rarely do.

I spent last summer crawling through the Big Thicket with cameras and tape recorder, photographing and taping two of the last ivory-billed woodpeckers on the earth. You can see the films at your local Audubon Society showroom.

This year I wanted something just as flashy but a little less taxing. Perhaps a population study on the Bermuda cahow, or the New Zealand takahe. A month or so in the warm (not hot) sun would do me a world of good. To say nothing of the advancement of science.

I was idly leafing through Greenway's *Extinct and Vanishing Birds of the World.* The city bus was winding its way through the ritzy neighborhoods of Austin, stopping to let off the chicanas, black women, and Vietnamese who tended the kitchens and gardens of the rich.

"I haven't seen any of those ugly chickens in a long time," said a voice close by.

A gray-haired lady was leaning across the aisle toward me.

I looked at her, then around. Maybe she was a shopping-bag lady. Maybe she was just talking. I looked straight at her. No doubt about it, she was talking to me. She was waiting for an answer.

"I used to live near some folks who raised them when I was a girl," she said. She pointed.

I looked down at the page my book was open to.

What I should have said was: That is quite impossible, madam. This is a drawing of an extinct bird of the island of Mauritius. It is perhaps the most famous dead bird in the world. Maybe you are mistaking this drawing for that of some rare Asiatic turkey, peafowl, or pheasant. I am sorry, but you *are* mistaken.

I should have said all that.

What she said was, "Oops, this is my stop." And got up to go.

My name is Paul Lindberl. I am twenty-six years old, a graduate student in ornithology at the University of Texas, a teaching assistant. My name is not unknown in the field. I have several vices and follies, but I don't think foolishness is one of them.

The stupid thing for me to do would have been to follow her.

She stepped off the bus.

I followed her.

I came into the departmental office, trailing scattered papers in the whirlwind behind me. "Martha! Martha!" I yelled.

She was doing something in the supply cabinet.

"Jesus, Paul! What do you want?"

"Where's Courtney?"

"At the conference in Houston. You know that. You missed your class. What's the matter?"

"Petty cash. Let me at it!"

"Payday was only a week ago. If you can't—"

"It's business! It's fame and adventure and the chance of a lifetime! It's a long sea voyage that leaves . . . a plane ticket. To either Jackson, Mississippi, or Memphis. Make it Jackson, it's closer. I'll get receipts! I'll be famous. Courtney will be famous. *You'll* even be famous! This university will make even *more* money! I'll pay you back. Give me some paper. I gotta write Courtney a note. When's the next plane out? Could you get Marie and Chuck to take over my classes Tuesday and Wednesday? I'll try to be back Thursday unless something happens. Courtney'll be back tomorrow, right? I'll call him from, well, wherever. Do you have some coffee?"

And so on and so forth. Martha looked at me like I was crazy. But she filled out the requisition anyway.

"What do I tell Kemejian when I ask him to sign these?"

"Martha, babe, sweetheart. Tell him I'll get his picture in *Scientific American.*"

"He doen't read it."

"*Nature,* then!"

"I'll see what I can do," she said.

The lady I had followed off the bus was named Jolyn (Smith) Jimson. The story she told me was so weird that it had to be true. She knew things only an expert, or someone with firsthand experience, could know. I got names from her, and addresses, and directions, and tidbits of information. Plus a year: 1927.

And a place. Northern Mississippi.

I gave her my copy of the Greenway book. I told her I'd call her as soon as I got back into town. I left her standing on the corner near the house of the lady she cleaned up for twice a week. Jolyn Jimson was in her sixties.

Think of the dodo as a baby harp seal with feathers. I know that's not even close, but it saves time.

In 1507 the Portuguese, on their way to India, found the (then unnamed) Mascarene Islands in the Indian Ocean—three of them a few hundred miles apart, all east of Madagascar.

It wasn't until 1598, when that old Dutch sea captain Cornelius van Neck bumped into them, that the islands received their names—names that changed several times through the centuries as the Dutch, French, and English changed them every war or so. They are now known as Rodriguez, Réunion, and Mauritius.

The major feature of these islands was large, flightless, stupid, ugly, bad-tasting birds. Van Neck and his men named them *dod-aarsen,* "stupid asses," or *dodars,* "silly birds," or solitaires.

There were three species: the dodo of Mauritius, the real gray-brown, hooked-beak, clumsy thing that weighed twenty kilos or more; the white, somewhat slimmer, dodo of Réunion; and the solitaires of Rodriguez and Réunion, which looked like very fat, very dumb light-colored geese.

The dodos all had thick legs, big squat bodies twice as large as a turkey's, naked faces, and big long downcurved beaks ending in a hook like a hollow linoleum knife. Long ago they had lost the ability to fly, and their wings had degenerated to flaps the size of a human hand with only three or four feathers in them. Their tails were curly and fluffy, like a child's afterthought at decoration. They had absolutely no natural enemies. They nested on the open ground. They probably hatched their eggs wherever they happened to lay them.

No natural enemies until Van Neck and his kind showed up. The Dutch, French, and Portuguese sailors who stopped at the Mascarenes to replenish stores found that, besides looking stupid, dodos *were* stupid. The men walked right up to the dodos and hit them on the head with clubs. Better yet, dodos could be herded around like sheep. Ships' logs are full of things like: "Party of ten men ashore. Drove half a hundred of the big turkey-like birds into the boat. Brought to ship, where they are given the run of the decks. Three will feed a crew of 150."

Even so, most of the dodo, except for the breast, tasted bad. One of the Dutch words for them was *walghvogel,* "disgusting bird." But on a ship three months out on a return from Goa to Lisbon, well, food was where you found it. It was said, even so, that prolonged boiling did not improve the flavor.

Even so, the dodos might have lasted, except that the Dutch, and later the French, colonized the Mascarenes. The islands became plantations and dumping places for religious refugees. Sugarcane and other exotic crops were raised there.

With the colonists came cats, dogs, hogs, and the cunning *Rattus norvegicus* and the Rhesus monkey from Ceylon. What dodos the hungry sailors left were chased down (they were dumb and stupid, but they could run when they felt like it) by dogs in the open. They were killed by cats as they sat on their nests. Their eggs were stolen and eaten by monkeys, rats, and hogs. And they competed with the pigs for all the low-growing goodies of the islands.

The last Mauritius dodo was seen in 1681, less than a hundred years after humans first saw them. The last white dodo walked off the history books around 1720. The solitaires of Rodriguez and Réunion, last of the genus as well as the species, may have lasted until 1790. Nobody knows.

Scientists suddenly looked around and found no more of the Didine birds alive, anywhere.

This part of the country was degenerate before the first Snopes ever saw it. This road hadn't been paved until the late fifties, and it was a main road between two county seats. That didn't mean it went through civilized country. I'd traveled for miles and seen nothing but dirt banks red as Billy Carter's neck and an occasional church. I expected to see Burma Shave signs, but realized this road had probably never had them.

I almost missed the turnoff onto the dirt and gravel road the man back at the service station had marked. It led onto the highway from nowhere, a lane out of a field. I turned down it, and a rock the size of a golf ball flew up over the hood and put a crack three inches long in the windshield of the rental car I'd gotten in Grenada.

It was a hot, muggy day for this early. The view was obscured in a cloud of dust every time the gravel thinned. About a mile down the road, the gravel gave out completely. The roadway turned into a rutted dirt pathway, just wider than the car, hemmed in on both sides by a sagging three-strand barbed-wire fence.

In some places the fence posts were missing for a few meters. The wire lay on the ground and in some places disappeared under it for long stretches.

The only life I saw was a mockingbird raising hell with something under a thornbush the barbed wire had been nailed to in place of a post. To one side now was a grassy field that had gone wild, the way everywhere will look after we blow ourselves off the face of the planet. The other was fast becoming woods—pine, oak, some black gum and wild plum, fruit not out this time of the year.

I began to ask myself what I was doing here. What if Ms. Jimson were some imaginative old crank who—but no. Wrong, maybe, but even the wrong was worth checking. But I knew she hadn't lied to me. She had seemed incapable of lies—a good ol' girl, backbone of the South, of the earth. Not a mendacious gland in her being.

I couldn't doubt her, or my judgment either. Here I was, creeping and bouncing down a dirt path in Mississippi, after no sleep for a day, out on the thin ragged edge of a dream. I *had* to take it on faith.

The back of the car sometimes slid where the dirt had loosened and gave way to sand. The back tire stuck once, but I rocked out of it. Getting back out again would be another matter. Didn't anyone ever use this road?

The woods closed in on both sides like the forest primeval, and the fence had long since disappeared. My odometer said ten kilometers, and it had been twenty minutes since I'd turned off the highway. In the rearview mirror, I saw beads of sweat and dirt in the wrinkles of my neck. A fine patina of dust covered everything inside the car. Clots of it came through the windows.

The woods reached out and swallowed the road. Branches scraped against the windows and the top. It was like falling down a long dark leafy tunnel. It was dark and green in there. I fought back an atavistic urge to turn on the headlights. The roadbed must be made of a few centuries of leaf mulch. I kept constant pressure on the accelerator and bulled my way through.

Half a log caught and banged and clanged against the car bottom. I saw light ahead. Fearing for the oil pan, I punched the pedal and sped out.

I almost ran through a house.

It was maybe ten meters from the trees. The road ended under one of the windows. I saw somebody waving from the corner of my eye.

I slammed on the brakes.

A whole family was on the porch, looking like a Walker Evans Depression photograph, or a fever dream from the mind of a "Hee Haw" producer. The house was old. Strips of peeling paint a meter long tapped against the eaves.

"Damned good thing you stopped," said a voice. I looked up. The biggest man I had ever seen in my life leaned down into the driver-side window.

"If we'd have heard you sooner, I'd've sent one of the kids down to the end of the driveway to warn you," he said.

Driveway?

His mouth was stained brown at the corners. I figured he chewed tobacco until I saw the sweet-gum snuff brush sticking from the pencil pocket in the bib of his coveralls. His hands were the size of catchers' mitts. They looked like they'd never held anything smaller than an ax handle.

"How y'all?" he said, by way of introduction.

"Just fine," I said. I got out of the car.

"My name's Lindberl," I said, extending my hand. He took it. For an instant, I thought of bear traps, sharks' mouths, closing elevator doors. The thought went back to wherever it is they stay.

"This the Gudger place?" I asked.

He looked at me blankly with his gray eyes. He wore a diesel truck cap and had on a checked lumberjack shirt beneath the coveralls. His rubber boots were the size of the ones Karloff wore in *Frankenstein.*

"Naw. I'm Jim Bob Krait. That's my wife, Jenny, and there's Luke and Skeeno and Shirl." He pointed to the porch.

The people on the porch nodded.

"Lessee. Gudger? No Gudgers round here I know of. I'm sorta new here." I took that to mean he hadn't lived here for more than twenty years or so.

"Jennifer!" he yelled. "You know of anybody named Gudger?" To me he said, "My wife's lived around heres all her life."

His wife came down onto the second step of the porch landing. "I think they used to be the ones what lived on the Spradlin place before the Spradlins. But the Spradlins left around the Korean War. I didn't know any of the Gudgers myself. That's while we was living over to Water Valley."

"You an insurance man?" asked Mr. Krait.

"Uh . . . no," I said. I imagined the people on the porch leaning toward me, all ears. "I'm a . . . I teach college."

"Oxford?" asked Krait.

"Uh, no. University of Texas."

"Well, that's a damn long way off. You say you're looking for the Gudgers?"

"Just their house. The area. As your wife said, I understand they left. During the Depression, I believe."

"Well, they musta had money," said the gigantic Mr. Krait. "Nobody around here was rich enough to *leave* during the Depression."

"Luke!" he yelled. The oldest boy on the porch sauntered down. He looked anemic and wore a shirt in vogue with the Twist. He stood with his hands in his pockets.

"Luke, show Mr. Lindbergh—"

"Lindberl."

". . . Mr. Lindberl here the way up to the old Spradlin place. Take him as far as the old log bridge, he might get lost before then."

"Log bridge broke down, Daddy."

"When?"

"October, Daddy."

"Well, hell, somethin' else to fix! Anyway, to the creek."

He turned to me. "You want him to go along on up there, see you don't get snakebit?"

"No, I'm sure I'll be fine."

"Mind if I ask what you're going up there for?" he asked. He was looking away from me. I could see having to come right out and ask was bothering him. Such things usually came up in the course of conversation.

"I'm a—uh, bird scientist. I study birds. We had a sighting—someone told us the old Gudger place—the area around here—I'm looking for a rare bird. It's hard to explain."

I noticed I was sweating. It was hot.

"You mean like a good God? I saw a good God about twenty-five years ago, over next to Bruce," he said.

"Well, no." (A good God was one of the names for an ivory-billed woodpecker, one of the rarest in the world. Any other time I would have dropped my jaw. Because they were thought to have died out in Mississippi by the teens, and by the fact that Krait knew they *were* rare.)

I went to lock my car up, then thought of the protocol of the situation. "My car be in your way?" I asked.

"Naw. It'll be just fine," said Jim Bob Krait. "We'll look for you back by sundown, that be all right?"

For a minute, I didn't know whether that was a command or an expression of concern.

"Just in case I get snakebit," I said. "I'll try to be careful up there."

"Good luck on findin' them rare birds," he said. He walked up to the porch with his family.

"Les go," said Luke.

Behind the Krait house were a hen house and pigsty where hogs lay after their morning slop like islands in a muddy bay, or some Zen pork sculpture. Next we passed broken farm machinery gone to rust, though there was nothing but uncultivated land as far as the eye could see. How the family made a living I don't know. I'm told you can find places just like this throughout the South.

We walked through woods and across fields, following a sort of path. I tried to memorize the turns I would have to take on my way back. Luke didn't say a word the whole twenty minutes he accompanied me, except to curse once when he stepped into a bull nettle with his tennis shoes.

We came to a creek that skirted the edge of a woodsy hill. There was a rotted log forming a small dam. Above it the water was nearly a meter deep; below it, half that much.

"See that path?" he asked.

"Yes."

"Follow it up around the hill, then across the next field. Then you cross the creek again on the rocks, and over the hill. Take the left-hand path. What's left of the house is about three-quarters the way up the next hill. If you come to a big bare rock cliff, you've gone too far. You got that?"

I nodded.

He turned and left.

The house had once been a dog-run cabin, as Ms. Jimson had said. Now it was fallen in on one side, what they called sigoglin. (Or was it anti-sigoglin?) I once heard a hymn on the radio called "The Land Where No Cabins Fall." This was the country songs like that were written in.

Weeds grew everywhere. There were signs of fences, a flattened pile of wood that had once been a barn. Farther behind the house were the outhouse remains. Half a rusted pump stood in the backyard. A flatter spot showed where the vegetable garden had been; in it a single wild tomato, pecked by birds, lay rotting. I passed it. There was lumber from three outbuildings, mostly rotten and green with algae and moss. One had been a smokehouse and woodshed combination. Two had been chicken roosts. One was larger than the other. It was there I started to poke around and dig.

Where? Where? I wish I'd been on more archaeological digs, knew the places to look. Refuse piles, midden heaps, kitchen scrap piles, compost boxes. Why hadn't I been born on a farm so I'd know instinctively where to search?

I prodded around the grounds. I moved back and forth like a setter casting for the scent of quail. I wanted more, more. I still wasn't satisfied.

Dusk. Dark, in fact. I trudged into the Kraits' front yard. The tote sack I carried was full to bulging. I was hot, tired, streaked with fifty years of chicken shit. The Kraits were on their porch. Jim Bob lumbered down like a friendly mountain.

I asked him a few questions, gave them a Xerox of one of the dodo pictures, left them addresses and phone numbers where they could reach me.

Then into the rental car. Off to Water Valley, acting on information Jennifer Krait gave me. I went to the postmaster's house at Water Valley. She was getting ready for bed. I asked questions. She got on the phone. I bothered people until one in the morning. Then back into the trusty rental car.

On to Memphis as the moon came up on my right. Interstate 55 was a glass ribbon before me. WLS from Chicago was on the radio.

I hummed along with it, I sang at the top of my voice.

The sack full of dodo bones, beaks, feet, and eggshell fragments kept me company on the front seat.

Did you know a museum once traded an entire blue whale skeleton for one of a dodo?

Driving, driving.

The Dance of the Dodos

I used to have a vision sometimes—I had it long before this madness came up. I can close my eyes and see it by thinking hard. But it comes to me most often, most vividly, when I am reading and listening to classical music, especially Pachelbel's *Canon in D*.

It is near dusk in The Hague, and the light is that of Frans Hals, of Rembrandt. The Dutch royal family and their guests eat and talk quietly in the great dining hall. Guards with halberds and pikes stand in the corners of the room. The family is arranged around the table: the King, Queen, some princesses, a prince, a couple of other children, an invited noble or two. Servants come out with plates and cups, but they do not intrude.

On a raised platform at one end of the room an orchestra plays dinner music—a harpsichord, viola, cello, three violins, and woodwinds. One of the royal dwarfs sits on the edge of the platform, his foot slowly rubbing the back of one of the dogs sleeping near him.

As the music of Pachelbel's *Canon in D* swells and rolls through the hall, one of the dodos walks in clumsily, stops, tilts its head, its eyes bright as a pool of tar. It sways a little, lifts its foot tentatively, one, then another, rocks back and forth in time to the cello.

The violins swirl. The dodo begins to dance, its great ungainly body now graceful. It is joined by the other two dodos who come into the hall, all three turning in a sort of circle.

The harpsichord begins its counterpoint. The fourth dodo, the white one from Réunion, comes from its place under the table and joins the circle with the others.

It is most graceful of all, making complete turns where the others only sway and dip on the edge of the circle they have formed.

The music rises in volume; the first violinist sees the dodos and nods to the King. But he and the others at the table have already seen. They are silent, transfixed—even the servants stand still, bowls, pots, and kettles in their hands, forgotten.

Around the dodos dance with bobs and weaves of their ugly heads. The white dodo dips, takes a half step, pirouettes on one foot, circles again.

Without a word the King of Holland takes the hand of the Queen, and they come around the table, children before the spectacle. They join in the dance, waltzing (anachronism) among the dodos while the family, the guests, the soldiers watch and nod in time with the music.

Then the vision fades, and the afterimage of a flickering fireplace and a dodo remains.

The dodo and its kindred came by ships to the ports of Europe. The first we have record of is that of Captain van Neck, who brought back two in 1599—one for the ruler of Holland, and one that found its way through Cologne to the menagerie of Emperor Rudolf II.

This royal aviary was at Schloss Negebau, near Vienna. It was here that the first paintings of the dumb old birds were done by Georg and his son Jacob Hoefnagel, between 1602 and 1610. They painted it among more than ninety species of birds that kept the Emperor amused.

Another Dutch artist named Roelandt Savery, as someone said, "made a career out of the dodo." He drew and painted the birds many times, and was no doubt personally fascinated by them. Obsessed, even. Early on, the paintings are consistent; the later ones have inaccuracies.

This implies he worked from life first, then from memory as his model went to that place soon to be reserved for all its species. One of his drawings has two of the Raphidae scrambling for some goody on the ground. His works are not without charm.

Another Dutch artist (they seemed to sprout up like mushrooms after a spring rain) named Peter Withoos also stuck dodos in his paintings, sometimes in odd and exciting places—wandering around during their owner's music lessons, or stuck with Adam and Eve in some Edenic idyll.

The most accurate representation, we are assured, comes from half a world away from the religious and political turmoil of the seafaring Europeans. There is an Indian miniature painting of the dodo that now rests in a museum in Russia. The dodo could have been brought by the Dutch or Portuguese in their travels to Goa and the coasts of the Indian subcontinent. Or it could have been brought centuries before by the Arabs who plied the Indian Ocean in their triangular-sailed craft, and who may have discovered the Mascarenes before the Europeans cranked themselves up for the First Crusade.

At one time early in my bird-fascination days (after I stopped killing them with BB guns but before I began to work for a scholarship) I once sat down and figured out where all the dodos had been.

Two with Van Neck in 1599, one to Holland, one to Austria. Another was in Count Solms's park in 1600. An account speaks of "one in Italy, one in Germany, several to England, eight or nine to Holland." William Boentekoe van Hoorn knew of "one shipped to Europe in 1640, another in 1685," which he said was "also painted by Dutch artists." Two were mentioned as "being kept in Surrat House in India as pets," perhaps one of which is the one in the painting. Being charitable, and considering "several" to mean at least three, that means twenty dodos in all.

There had to be more, when boatloads had been gathered at the time. What do we know of the Didine birds? A few ships' logs, some accounts left by travelers and colonists. The English were fascinated by them. Sir Hamon Lestrange, a contemporary of Pepys, saw exhibited "a Dodar from the Island of Mauritius . . . it is not able to flie, being so bigge." One was stuffed when it died, and was put in the Museum Tradescantum in South Lambeth. It eventually found its way into the Ashmolean Museum. It grew ratty and was burned, all but a leg and the head, in 1755. By then there were no more dodos, but nobody had realized that yet.

Francis Willughby got to describe it before its incineration. Earlier, old Carolus Clusius in Holland studied the one in Count Solms's park. He collected everything known about the Raphidae, describing a dodo leg Pieter Pauw kept in his natural-history cabinet, in *Exoticarium libri decem* in 1605, seven years after their discovery.

François Leguat, a Huguenot who lived on Réunion for some years, published an account of his travels in which he mentioned the dodos. It was published in 1690 (after the Mauritius dodo was extinct) and included the information that "some of the males weigh forty-five pound. . . . One egg, much bigger than that of a goos is laid by the female, and takes seven weeks hatching time."

The Abbé Pingré visited the Mascarenes in 1761. He saw the last of the Rodriguez solitaires and collected what information he could about the dead Mauritius and Réunion members of the genus.

After that, only memories of the colonists, and some scientific debate as to *where* the Raphidae belonged in the great taxonomic scheme of things—some said pigeons, some said rails—were left. Even this nit-picking ended. The dodo was forgotten.

When Lewis Carroll wrote *Alice in Wonderland* in 1865, most people thought he had invented the dodo.

The service station I called from in Memphis was busier than a one-legged man in an ass-kicking contest. Between bings and dings of the bell, I finally realized the call had gone through.

The guy who answered was named Selvedge. I got nowhere with him. He mistook me for a real estate agent, then a lawyer. Now he was beginning to think I was some sort of a con man. I wasn't doing too well, either. I hadn't slept in two days. I must have sounded like a speed freak. My only progress was that I found that Ms. Annie Mae Gudger (childhood playmate of Jolyn Jimson) was now, and had been, the respected Ms. Annie Mae Radwin. This guy Selvedge must have been a secretary or toady or something.

We were having a conversation comparable to that between a shrieking macaw and a pile of mammoth bones. Then there was another click on the line.

"Young man?" said the other voice, an old woman's voice, southern, very refined but with a hint of the hills in it.

"Yes? Hello! Hello!"

"Young man, you say you talked to a Jolyn somebody? Do you mean Jolyn Smith?"

"Hello! Yes! Ms. Radwin, Ms. Annie Mae Radwin who used to be Gudger? She lives in Austin now. Texas. She used to live near Water Valley, Mississippi. Austin's where I'm from. I—"

"Young man," asked the voice again, "are you sure you haven't been put up to this by my hateful sister Alma?"

"Who? No, ma'am. I met a woman named Jolyn—"

"I'd like to talk to you, young man," said the voice. Then, offhandedly, "Give him directions to get here, Selvedge."

Click.

I cleaned out my mouth as best as I could in the service station rest room, tried to shave with an old clogged Gillette disposable in my knapsack, and succeeded in gapping up my jawline. I changed into a clean pair of jeans and the only other shirt I had with me, and combed my hair. I stood in front of the mirror.

I still looked like the dog's lunch.

The house reminded me of Presley's mansion, which was somewhere in the neighborhood. From a shack on the side of a Mississippi hill to this, in forty years. There are all sorts of ways of making it. I wondered what Annie Mae Gudger's had been. Luck? Predation? Divine intervention? Hard work? Trover and replevin?

Selvedge led me toward the sun room. I felt like Philip Marlowe going to meet a rich client. The house was filled with that furniture built sometime between the turn of the century and the 1950s—the ageless kind. It never looks great, it never looks ratty, and every chair is comfortable.

I think I was expecting some formidable woman with sleeve blotters and a green eyeshade hunched over a rolltop desk with piles of paper whose acceptance or rejection meant life or death for thousands.

Who I met was a charming lady in a green pantsuit. She was in her sixties, her hair still a straw-wheat color. It didn't look dyed. Her eyes were blue as my first-grade teacher's had been. She was wiry and looked as if the word *fat* was not in her vocabulary.

"Good morning, Mr. Lindberl." She shook my hand. "Would you like some coffee? You look as if you could use it."

"Yes, thank you."

"Please sit down." She indicated a white wicker chair at a glass table.

A serving tray with coffeepot, cups, tea bags, croissants, napkins, and plates lay on the tabletop.

After I swallowed half a cup of coffee at a gulp, she said, "What you wanted to see me about must be important."

"Sorry about my manners," I said. "I know I don't look it, but I'm a biology assistant at the University of Texas. An ornithologist. Working on my master's. I met Ms. Jolyn Jimson two days ago—"

"How is Jolyn? I haven't seen her in, oh, Lord, it must be on to fifty years. The time gets away."

"She seemed to be fine. I only talked to her half an hour or so. That was—"

"And you've come to see me about . . . ?"

"Uh. The . . . about some of the poultry your family used to raise, when they lived near Water Valley."

She looked at me a moment. Then she began to smile.

"Oh, you mean the ugly chickens?" she said.

I smiled. I almost laughed. I knew what Oedipus must have gone through.

It is now four-thirty in the afternoon. I am sitting in the downtown Motel 6 in Memphis. I have to make a phone call and get some sleep and catch a plane.

Annie Mae Gudger Radwin talked for four hours, answering my questions, setting me straight on family history, having Selvedge hold all her calls.

The main problem was that Annie Mae ran off in 1928, the year *before* her father got his big break. She went to Yazoo City, and by degrees and stages worked her way northward to Memphis and her destiny as the widow of a rich mercantile broker.

But I get ahead of myself.

Grandfather Gudger used to be the overseer for Colonel Crisby on the main plantation near McComb, Mississippi. There was a long story behind that. Bear with me.

Colonel Crisby himself was the scion of a seafaring family with interests in both the cedars of Lebanon (almost all cut down for masts for His Majesty's and others' navies) and Egyptian cotton. Also teas, spices, and any other salable commodity that came its way.

When Colonel Crisby's grandfather reached his majority in 1802, he waved good-bye to the Atlantic Ocean at Charleston, S.C., and stepped westward into the forest. When he stopped, he was in the middle of the

Chickasaw Nation, where he opened a trading post and introduced slaves to the Indians.

And he prospered, and begat Colonel Crisby's father, who sent back to South Carolina for everything his father owned. Everything—slaves, wagons, horses, cattle, guinea fowl, peacocks, and dodos, which everybody thought of as atrociously ugly poultry of some kind, one of the seafaring uncles having bought them off a French merchant in 1721. (I surmised these were white dodos from Réunion, unless they had been from even earlier stock. The dodo of Mauritius was already extinct by then.)

All this stuff was herded out west to the trading post in the midst of the Chickasaw Nation. (The tribes around there were of the confederation of the Dancing Rabbits.)

And Colonel Crisby's father prospered, and so did the guinea fowl and the dodos. Then Andrew Jackson came along and marched the Dancing Rabbits off up the Trail of Tears to the heaven of Oklahoma. And Colonel Crisby's father begat Colonel Crisby, and put the trading post in the hands of others, and moved his plantation westward still to McComb.

Everything prospered but Colonel Crisby's father, who died. And the dodos, with occasional losses to the avengin' weasel and the egg-sucking dog, reproduced themselves also.

Then along came Granddaddy Gudger, a Simon Legree role model, who took care of the plantation while Colonel Crisby raised ten companies of men and marched off to fight the War for Southern Independence.

Colonel Crisby came back to the McComb plantation earlier than most, he having stopped much of the same volley of Minié balls that caught his commander, General Beauregard Hanlon, on a promontory bluff during the Siege of Vicksburg.

He wasn't dead, but death hung around the place like a gentlemanly bill collector for a month. The Colonel languished, went slapdab crazy, and freed all his slaves the week before he died (the war lasted another two years after that). Not now having any slaves, he didn't need an overseer.

Then comes the Faulkner part of the tale, straight out of *As I Lay Dying,* with the Gudger family returning to the area of Water Valley (before there was a Water Valley), moving through the demoralized and tattered displaced persons of the South, driving their dodos before them. For Colonel Crisby had given them to his former overseer for his faithful service. Also followed the story of the bloody murder of Grand-daddy Gudger at the hands of the Freedman's militia during the rising of the first Klan, and of the trials and tribulations of Daddy Gudger in the years between 1880 and 1910, when he was between the ages of four and thirty-four.

Alma and Annie Mae were the second and fifth of Daddy Gudger's brood, born three years apart. They seem to have hated each other from the very first time Alma looked into little Annie Mae's crib. They were kids by Daddy Gudger's second wife (his desperation had killed the first) and their father was already on his sixth career. He had been a lumberman, a stump preacher, a plowman-for-hire (until his mules broke out in farcy buds and died of the glanders), a freight hauler (until his horses died of overwork and the hardware store repossessed the wagon), a politician's roadie (until the politician lost the election). When Alma and Annie Mae were born, he was failing as a sharecropper. Somehow Gudger had made it through the Depression of 1898 as a boy, and was too poor after that to notice more about economics than the price of Beech-Nut tobacco at the store.

Alma and Annie Mae fought, and it helped none at all that Alma, being the oldest daughter, was both her mother's and her father's darling. Annie Mae's life was the usual unwanted-poor-white-trash-child's hell. She vowed early to run away, and recognized her ambition at thirteen.

All this I learned this morning. Jolyn (Smith) Jimson was Annie Mae's only friend in those days—from a family even poorer than the Gudgers. But somehow there was food, and an occasional odd job. And the dodos.

"My father hated those old birds," said the cultured Annie Mae Radwin, née Gudger, in the solarium. "He always swore he was going to get rid of them someday, but just never seemed to get around to it. I think there was more to it than that. But they were so much *trouble*. We always had to keep them penned up at night, and go check for their eggs. They wandered off to lay them, and forgot where they were. Sometimes no new ones were born at all in a year.

"And they got so *ugly*. Once a year. I mean, terrible-looking, like they were going to die. All their feathers fell off, and they looked like they had mange or something. Then the whole front of their beaks fell off, or worse, hung halfway on for a week or two. They looked like big old naked pigeons. After that they'd lose weight, down to twenty or thirty pounds, before their new feathers grew back.

"We were always having to kill foxes that got after them in the turkey house. That's what we called their roost, the turkey house. And we found their eggs all sucked out by cats and dogs. They were so stupid we had to drive them into their roost at night. I don't think they could have found it standing ten feet from it."

She looked at me.

"I think much as my father hated them, they meant something to him. As long as he hung on to them, he knew he was as good as Granddaddy Gudger. You may not know it, but there was a certain amount of family pride about Granddaddy Gudger. At least in my father's eyes. His rapid fall in the world had a sort of grandeur to it. He'd gone from a relatively high position in the old order, and maintained some grace and stature after the Emancipation. And though he lost everything, he managed to keep those ugly old chickens the Colonel had given him as sort of a symbol.

"And as long as he had them, too, my daddy thought himself as good as his father. He kept his dignity, even when he didn't have anything else."

I asked what happened to them. She didn't know, but told me who did and where I could find her.

That's why I'm going to make a phone call.

"Hello. Dr. Courtney. Dr. Courtney? This is Paul. Memphis. Tennessee. It's too long to go into. No, of course not, not yet. But I've got evidence. What? Okay, how do trochanters, coracoids, tarsometatarsi and beak sheaths sound? From their hen house, where else? Where would you keep *your* dodos, then?

"Sorry. I haven't slept in a couple of days. I need some help. Yes, yes. Money. Lots of money.

"Cash. Three hundred dollars, maybe. Western Union, Memphis, Tennessee. Whichever one's closest to the airport. Airport. I need the department to set up reservations to Mauritius for me . . .

"No. No. Not wild-goose chase, wild-*dodo* chase. Tame-dodo chase. I *know* there aren't any dodos on Mauritius! I know that. I could explain. I know it'll mean a couple of grand—if—but—

"Look, Dr. Courtney. Do you want *your* picture in *Scientific American,* or don't you?"

I am sitting in the airport café in Port Louis, Mauritius. It is now three days later, five days since that fateful morning my car wouldn't start. God bless the Sears Diehard people. I have slept sitting up in a plane seat, on and off, different planes, different seats, for twenty-four hours, Kennedy to Paris, Paris to Cairo, Cairo to Madagascar. I felt like a brand-new man when I got here.

Now I feel like an infinitely sadder and wiser brand-new man. I have just returned from the hateful sister Alma's house in the exclusive section of Port Louis, where all the French and British officials used to live.

Courtney will get his picture in *Scientific American,* all right. Me too. There'll be newspaper stories and talk shows for a few weeks for me, and I'm sure Annie Mae Gudger Radwin on one side of the world and Alma Chandler Gudger Molière on the other will come in for their share of glory.

I am putting away cup after cup of coffee. The plane back to Tananarive leaves in an hour. I plan to sleep all the way back to Cairo, to Paris, to New York, pick up my bag of bones, sleep back to Austin.

Before me on the table is a packet of documents, clippings, and photographs. I have come across half the world for this. I gaze from the package, out the window across Port Louis to the bulk of Mont Pieter Both, which overshadows the city and its famous racecourse.

Perhaps I should do something symbolic. Cancel my flight. Climb the mountain and look down on man and all his handiworks. Take a pitcher of martinis with me. Sit in the bright semitropical sunlight (it's early dry winter here). Drink the martinis slowly, toasting Snuffo, God of Extinction. Here's one for the great auk. This is for the Carolina parakeet. Mud in your eye, passenger pigeon. This one's for the heath hen. Most important, here's one each for the Mauritius dodo, the white dodo of Réunion, the Réunion solitaire, the Rodriguez solitaire. Here's to the Raphidae, great Didine birds that you were.

Maybe I'll do something just as productive, like climbing Mont Pieter Both and pissing into the wind.

How symbolic. The story of the dodo ends where it began, on this very island. Life imitates cheap art. Like the Xerox of the Xerox of a bad novel. I never expected to find dodos still alive here (this is the one place they would have been noticed). I still can't believe Alma Chandler Gudger Molière could have lived here twenty-five years and not *know* about the dodo, never set foot inside the Port Louis Museum, where they have skeletons and a stuffed replica the size of your little brother.

After Annie Mae ran off, the Gudger family found itself prospering in a time the rest of the country was going to hell. It was 1929. Gudger delved into politics again and backed a man who knew a man who worked for Theodore "Sure Two-Handed Sword of God" Bilbo, who had connections everywhere. Who introduced him to Huey "Kingfish" Long just after that gentleman lost the Louisiana governor's election one of the times. Gudger stumped around Mississippi, getting up steam for Long's Share the Wealth plan, even before it had a name.

The upshot was that the Long machine in Louisiana knew a rabble-rouser when it saw one, and invited Gudger to move to the Sportsman's Paradise, with his family, all expenses paid, and start working for the Kingfish at the unbelievable salary of $62.50 a week. Which prospect was like turning a hog loose under a persimmon tree, and before you could say Backwoods Messiah, the Gudger clan was on its way to the land of pelicans, graft, and Mardi Gras.

Almost. But I'll get to that.

Daddy Gudger prospered all out of proportion to his abilities, but many men did that during the Depression. First a little, thence to more, he rose in bureaucratic (and political) circles of the state, dying rich and well hated with his fingers in *all* the pies.

Alma Chandler Gudger became a debutante (she says Robert Penn Warren put her in his book) and met and married Jean Carl Molière, only heir to rice, indigo, and sugarcane growers. They had a happy wedded life, moving first to the West Indies, later to Mauritius, where the family sugarcane holdings were among the largest on the island. Jean Carl died in 1959. Alma was his only survivor.

So local family makes good. Poor sharecropping Mississippi people turn out to have a father dying with a smile on his face, and two daughters who between them own a large portion of the planet.

I open the envelope before me. Ms. Alma Molière had listened politely to my story (the university had called ahead and arranged an introduction through the director of the Port Louis Museum, who knew Ms. Molière socially) and told me what she could remember. Then she sent a servant out to one of the storehouses (large as a duplex) and he and two others came back with boxes of clippings, scrapbooks, and family photos.

"I haven't looked at any of this since we left St. Thomas," she said. "Let's go through it together."

Most of it was about the rise of Citizen Gudger.

"There's not many pictures of us before we came to Louisiana. We were so frightfully poor then, hardly anyone we knew had a camera.

Oh, look. Here's one of Annie Mae. I thought I threw all those out after Momma died."

This is the photograph. It must have been taken about 1927. Annie Mae is wearing some unrecognizable piece of clothing that approximates a dress. She leans on a hoe, smiling a snaggle-toothed smile. She looks to be ten or eleven. Her eyes are half-hidden by the shadow of the brim of a gapped straw hat she wears. The earth she is standing in barefoot has been newly turned. Behind her is one corner of the house, and the barn beyond has its upper hay windows open. Out-of-focus people are at work there.

A few feet behind her, a huge male dodo is pecking at something on the ground. The front two thirds of it shows, back to the stupid wings and the edge of the upcurved tail feathers. One foot is in the photo, having just scratched at something, possibly an earthworm, in the new-plowed clods. Judging by its darkness, it is the gray, or Mauritius, dodo.

The photograph is not very good, one of those 3½ × 5 jobs box cameras used to take. Already I can see this one, and the blowup of the dodo, taking up a double-page spread in *S.A.* Alma told me that around then they were down to six or seven of the ugly chickens, two whites, the rest gray-brown.

Besides this photo, two clippings are in the package, one from the Bruce *Banner-Times,* the other from the Oxford newspaper; both are columns by the same woman dealing with "Doings in Water Valley." Both mention the Gudger family's moving from the area to seek its fortune in the swampy state to the west, and tell how they will be missed. Then there's a yellowed clipping from the front page of the Oxford paper with a small story about the Gudger Family Farewell Party in Water Valley the Sunday before (dated October 19, 1929).

There's a handbill in the package, advertising the Gudger Family Farewell Party, Sunday Oct. 15, 1929 Come One Come All. The people in Louisiana who sent expense money to move Daddy Gudger must have overestimated the costs by an exponential factor. I said as much.

"No," Alma Molière said. "There was a lot, but it wouldn't have made any difference. Daddy Gudger was like Thomas Wolfe and knew a shining golden opportunity when he saw one. Win, lose, or draw, he was never coming back *there* again. He would have thrown some kind of soiree whether there had been money for it or not. Besides, people were much more sociable then, you mustn't forget."

I asked her how many people came.

"Four or five hundred," she said. "There's some pictures here somewhere." We searched awhile, then we found them.

Another thirty minutes to my flight. I'm not worried sitting here. I'm the only passenger, and the pilot is sitting at the table next to mine talking to an RAF man. Life is much slower and nicer on these colonial islands. You mustn't forget.

I look at the other two photos in the package. One is of some men playing horseshoes and washer toss, while kids, dogs, and women look on. It was evidently taken from the east end of the house looking west. Everyone must have had to walk the last mile to the old Gudger place. Other groups of people stand talking. Some men, in shirt sleeves and suspenders, stand with their heads thrown back, a snappy story, no doubt, just told. One girl looks directly at the camera from close up, shyly, her finger in her mouth. She's about five. It looks like any snapshot of a family reunion which could have been taken anywhere, anytime. Only the clothing marks it as backwoods 1920s.

Courtney will get his money's worth. I'll write the article, make phone calls, plan the talk show tour to coincide with publication. Then I'll get some rest. I'll be a normal person again—get a degree, spend my time wading through jungles after animals that will all be dead in another twenty years, anyway.

Who cares? The whole thing will be just another media event, just this year's Big Deal. It'll be nice getting normal again. I can read books, see movies, wash my clothes at the laundromat, listen to Johnathan Richman on the stereo. I can study and become an authority on some minor matter or other.

I can go to museums and see all the wonderful dead things there.

"That's the memory picture," said Alma. "They always took them at big things like this, back in those days. Everybody who was there would line up and pose for the camera. Only we couldn't fit everybody in. So we had two made. This is the one with us in it."

The house is dwarfed by people. All sizes, shapes, dress, and age. Kids and dogs in front, women next, then men at the back. The only exceptions are the bearded patriarchs seated toward the front with the children—men whose eyes face the camera but whose heads are still ringing with something Nathan Bedford Forrest said to them one time on a smoke-filled field. This photograph is from another age. You can recognize Daddy and Mrs. Gudger if you've seen their photographs before. Alma pointed herself out to me.

But the reason I took the photograph is in the foreground. Tables have been built out of sawhorses, with doors and boards nailed across them. They extend the entire width of the photograph. They are covered with food, more food than you can imagine.

"We started cooking three days before. So did the neighbors. Everybody brought something," said Alma.

It's like an entire Safeway had been cooked and set out to cool. Hams, quarters of beef, chickens by the tubful, quail in mounds, rabbit, butter beans by the bushel, yams, Irish potatoes, an acre of corn, eggplants, peas, turnip greens, butter in five-pound molds, cornbread and biscuits, gallon cans of molasses, red-eye gravy by the pot.

And five huge birds—twice as big as turkeys, legs capped as for Thanksgiving, drumsticks the size of Schwarzenegger's biceps, whole-roasted, lying on their backs on platters large as cocktail tables.

The people in the crowd sure look hungry.

"We ate for days," said Alma.

I already have the title for the *Scientific American* article. It's going to be called "The Dodo Is *Still* Dead."

AN INDEX TO *UNIVERSE*

Volumes 1–10

Terry Carr recently received the Milford Award for lifetime achievements in science fiction editing. In addition to the *Universe* series, he edits *The Best Science Fiction of the Year*. His own writing includes the novel *Cirque* and a short story collection, *The Light at the End of the Universe*.